FATAL
TRUST

FATAL TRUST

TODD M. JOHNSON

BETHANYHOUSE

a division of Baker Publishing Group
Minneapolis, Minnesota

JOHNSON,T.

© 2017 by Todd M. Johnson

Published by Bethany House Publishers
11400 Hampshire Avenue South
Bloomington, Minnesota 55438
www.bethanyhouse.com

Bethany House Publishers is a division of
Baker Publishing Group, Grand Rapids, Michigan

Printed in the United States of America

Library of Congress Cataloging-in-Publication Data
Names: Johnson, Todd M. (Todd Maurice), author.
Title: Fatal trust / Todd M. Johnson.
Description: Minneapolis, Minnesota : Bethany House, a division of Baker
    Publishing Group, [2017]
Identifiers: LCCN 2016059754 | ISBN 9780764230448 (cloth) | ISBN
    9780764212352 (trade paper)
Subjects: | GSAFD: Legal stories. | Mystery fiction.
Classification: LCC PS3610.O38363 F38 2017 | DDC 813/.6—dc23
LC record available at https://lccn.loc.gov/2016059754

Cover design by Paul Higdon
Cover photograph of Minneapolis Stone Arch Bridge by Riddhish Chakraborty/Getty
Images

17 18 19 20 21 22 23   7 6 5 4 3 2 1

For my Ian

Prologue

JUNE 2018
MINNEAPOLIS

In the still night air, Ian stood with his back to the Mississippi River on the Guthrie Theater's outdoor patio, his fingertips tingling and the strong beat of his heart filling his chest.

He'd stood here on other nights—during intermission or after a play had ended inside the theater. But no drama he'd ever witnessed could have conjured a scene like this. Three men stood behind him, two with dark guns in their fists. Another sat on a step beside him, calmly typing bank account information into a laptop. A young woman stood at his elbow, holding a stolen painting rolled under one arm.

Ian did a slow blink. It was as though the theater's evening play had been transplanted from an indoor stage to this small space under a waning moon for the entertainment of an invisible crowd. And now it was winding its way to an ending that hadn't yet been written.

"Seems like a family reunion," one of the men holding a gun had mocked minutes before in an Irish tone. "Everyone here?"

If Ian had answered yes, he would have been wrong. Because just now another figure was pushing through the door above them. It was a woman. She stepped onto the patio and began walking slowly, ethereally, down the stairs toward them.

It took seconds for Ian to register the identity of the new arrival. It took a moment longer to realize she also held a gun in her hand.

He stiffened, crying out, *"What are you doing here? Drop the gun!"*

She didn't answer or obey.

Even if this final scene was still a work in process, Ian had come with a plan. Hastily devised, maybe, but a plan. And it didn't involve a cross fire of bullets on this tiny space near the river's edge.

Except now, over the rising thunder in his chest, Ian knew his plan for this moment had been discarded. And when the Act was shortly over, people Ian cared for were very likely to be dead.

1

Tight as a tendon, the boxer stood under a dark sky on a carpet of closely cropped grass leading to a coffin. With his black umbrella overhead, he shuffled his feet and stewed.

The casket, dark and shiny, was propped over an open hole lined by a knot of people on the far side. Flower wreaths decorated one end of the hole. Palm branches twisted overhead in a warm breeze, loosing raindrops from the recent shower. The refreshed air smelled of orange blossoms and grass clippings and carried the low words of the priest and a mockingbird's call from a distant tree.

It wasn't an unpleasant view, the boxer thought—Christina would have appreciated it. But it still was rotten. Rotten that his boss had lost his wife to cancer. Rotten how few people were here to pay their respects to Christina, who'd always been good to him and as much a second mother as the boss had been a second father. Even ten years ago, the boxer mused, this place would've been packed and the flowers could've filled a moving van.

He shook his head and rolled his shoulders to loosen muscles tight from his punching-bag workout that morning. But that's how life worked, didn't it? People remembered you so long as you had something they needed. When that ended, they moved on without so much as a glance over their shoulder. It was all wrong. Wrong and rotten.

The boxer looked past the coffin. A young man in a well-tailored suit held an umbrella over his prim, equally well-dressed wife. A boy in a suit and a little girl in a black dress—twelve years old, he guessed—were fidgeting restlessly at the wife's side.

At least *they'd* shown up, the boxer thought. He didn't think they would. That was something anyway.

The boxer sensed nervous movement at his side as a voice muttered sadly, "Where'd he get the cash for that Rolex?"

The boxer glanced to where his boss stood under the protection of his umbrella. A fedora was pulled low on the smaller man's head; his lips were pursed tight, his eyes locked on the same young family the boxer had been watching.

"How about those diamonds hanging from the wife's ears?" his boss went on bitterly. "Or the clothes that make the kids look like English royalty?" He thrust his chin toward the parking lot, his voice deepening with disgust. "And how'd he pay for that Mercedes they drove all the way down from Minnesota?"

The boxer raised a hand to signal his boss to quiet.

The gesture was ignored. "I told him we'd give it time to cool," the older man said. "Go back to *real* work. The inheritance will come. Don't do anything to bring attention to you." He paused, shook his head. "Now look at 'em. We're supposed to say goodbye to our Christina today, and I've got to worry about what my own son's doing to earn that kinda cash."

The dresses of women mourners rustled in a gust of breeze. The priest raised his right hand to make the sign of the cross. Like a conductor ending a symphony, the motion released everyone to trickle away from the grave toward the parking lot.

But his boss didn't move, so the boxer didn't either. Car doors were shutting and engines coming to life when the boss removed his hat and walked to the coffin to place a hand on its sleek surface, dotted with droplets like a black Cadillac in the rain.

"If he gets caught doing something illegal, it'll all lead back to us," the boss said. "We'll all pay the price. *But what can I do?*"

The boxer winced at the open confession. He swiveled his head to see if anyone was near enough to have heard.

The grass on either side of the grave was empty. From the corner of his eye, he caught a shape on the hill at his back.

A small boy stood there—nine or ten maybe. Near enough to fall under the umbrella's shadow as the sun left the clouds. The boxer fixed his attention on the boy, who looked back with a bright stare.

I know that boy, the boxer thought, startled. *What is he doing here?*

Fury fired his muscles, replacing the anger at his boss's son and his graveside show of money. This boy shouldn't be here, on this day of all days, and he shouldn't have heard every careless word his boss had spoken.

Lowering the umbrella, the boxer bowed and reached out for the boy's shoulder.

"What do we think we heard, little Master?" the boxer asked, tightening to a firm grip.

The boy stayed mute. The boxer leaned further down. Fear appeared in the bright eyes.

"*What do we think we heard?*" he asked more insistently.

The fear went deeper. "Just what the man with the hat said," the boy responded, his voice trembling.

The boxer nodded his head. "Aye. And what exactly does the little Master think he understands?"

2

Ian Wells's eyes opened wide. The sheets wound a tight grip around his legs. The pillow was lost somewhere in the darkness.

He'd had the nightmare again. It had been a couple of years since the last time. The dream always seemed to surface around this time of year—his birthday dream, he called it—though he could seldom recall the details once awake. A funeral. Rain. Palm trees. A large man calling him "little Master." Vivid images that quickly slid out of memory, although not all were leaving so quickly this morning. The outline of a casket with men at its side lingered in his mind like shadows against closed eyelids.

Rolling to his stomach, he waited for the last vestiges of distress the dream always brought to disappear.

Slowly it slipped away.

He turned to the bedside clock—and groaned. Nine-fifteen.

13

He was due at the bank in half an hour, which meant no time for a shower or shave. Which also meant he'd be working at the law office less than his best, then showing up at Mom's house for his early birthday dinner the same way.

He sat up, suddenly angry. Adrianne should be here for the coming bank meeting to face the music with him. Mom's money woes weren't only his responsibility. Maybe his younger sister had moved to Seattle before Mom got sick, but after graduation she could have come back to help, couldn't she?

Ian looked around his shadowed apartment bedroom, decorated with only a single bookshelf and his bike propped against the wall. His gaze shifted to the shuttered window. Half a mile away was the Minnesota State Fairgrounds, still a ghost town for a few more months. If he wasn't dealing with this problem, he could blow out his frustration with a run past the empty vendor sheds and pavilions and silent arcades. Or take the bike west to the Mississippi and down the bluffs near the Stone Arch Bridge. An hour or two just for himself. Was that too much to ask?

None of that was happening today.

Another surge of self-pity arrived as he pushed to his feet. This one he held off. *"Wallowing is for pigs,"* his best friend, Brook, used to say when Ian would show up for class in law school complaining about the workload. Today was coming at him whether he liked it or not, whether his sister was here or not, and whether he got any exercise or not.

He rose from bed, straightened his shoulders, and in defiance of his mood started whistling the first tune that came to mind as he grabbed his clothes and trundled toward the bathroom.

PINNACLE BANK
SOUTH MINNEAPOLIS

"What I'm telling you, Mr. Wells, is that there's not enough equity left in your mother's house to support an extension of the loan. I'm very sorry."

Ian nodded, even though the twentysomething banker didn't sound particularly sorry. He thought of asking whether that sorrow extended to reaching into his own wallet for a personal loan, but the sarcasm would have been lost on a guy who was only delivering his underwriter's verdict anyway.

"What about my application for an unsecured loan?" Ian asked. "My law-practice income has gone up every year of the past five since I took on my dad's practice. Could be faster, I admit, but like I explained on the forms, I've been transitioning out of his trusts-and-estates work into criminal defense."

Ian would have gone on but stopped as he gauged the banker's expression. He'd argued before enough judges to know when not a word he could utter would affect a decision already reached.

"Again, I'm very sorry, Mr. Wells," the banker said, his pained smile unwavering, like it had been stapled there. "But Pinnacle Bank doesn't make personal loans based on service businesses without a longer track record. I'm afraid things have changed since the Great Recession."

Which you experienced while in elementary school, Ian wanted to say. Except that remark would have sounded hollow to a banker only five or six years younger than Ian himself.

"Thanks," Ian muttered, standing to leave. Third strike. Three banks in a row. He shook the banker's outstretched hand.

In the parking lot, his mood hadn't lightened. Once he started the engine, the speakers kicked in with a loud ring via the car's

Bluetooth. Ian turned down the volume, then tapped a button on the steering wheel to answer the call. "Yeah," he said.

"Getting a late start, hon?" It was Katie from the office, her church-choir voice resonating with annoying morning energy.

"Had a personal appointment," Ian grumbled at the sarcasm. "If this is a wake-up call, I'd prefer a text. I'm sure you've heard of that technology."

"Heard of it," his legal assistant said, still relentlessly cheerful. "Rejected it. I know how to use an alarm clock, though. Be happy to train you in that technology sometime."

He was too low to win the exchange. "What's the crisis?"

"Well, first, don't forget you've got Willy Dryer scheduled for later this morning."

"I know," he replied, seeing his unshaven face in the rearview mirror again. "I'm on my way in now."

"Great. Next, I sent you an email on Sunday about a new client who left a voicemail Saturday night. Needs to see you right away—as in today."

Ian recalled the email and perked up. "I saw that. That's good news. What's the name again?"

"Callahan. Sean Callahan."

It sounded familiar. "What's he been charged with?"

"It's not a criminal case. He's got a crisis with some kind of family trust."

Ian rubbed his eyes, trying to recall where he'd heard the name. It'd been over a year since the last estate work he'd done cleaning up his dad's practice. "You sure this guy asked for me and not Dennis?"

"Yep. Could be he doesn't know you're a criminal defense lawyer now, or maybe he's mixing you up with your dad. My theory is he heard you may be representing Willy Dryer again and thought you could use a client who actually pays his bills."

Ian shook his head. When she got on a roll, Katie was unstoppable. "Nice. Hope you've set up Willy's new file. Same billable rate as last time."

"Got it. Zero."

He ignored her this round. "Did this Callahan actually say it was a *crisis*?"

"His word was 'critical,'" Katie responded. "I caught it exactly, because in all the years working with your dad, I never heard *anybody* use that word in the same sentence as 'family trust.' So, you want Dennis to call him back?"

The banker's meeting he'd just left came to mind. "No. I need the cash flow, and you know Dennis is hardly coming in now—especially on Mondays. If I see it's too complicated, I'll get his advice. When did Callahan say he wanted to talk to me?"

"I haven't called him back yet."

"Alright. Set him up for a phone meeting later this morning. After I meet with Willy."

3

Rory Doyle walked up the sidewalk to the sputtering *Larry's Bar* neon sign and gave it a blow with the heel of his hand. It settled into solid blue fluorescence—before instantly sliding back into a stutter. With a shake of his head, Rory reached into his pocket.

No cigarettes. He'd forgotten: he'd quit this morning and had tossed every trace of tobacco he knew of. What was part of a fresh start at eight was bad timing at eleven, but there was nothing he could do now. Feeling shaky, he pulled open the glass door and went in.

For a late Monday morning, the place was hopping by Larry's Bar standards. Two guys in booths. A woman at the bar. Two more guys at the pool table. One of those gave Rory a nod, and he returned it.

His usual booth was open. He tossed his jacket there, then stepped up to the bar. "Larry, I'm expecting a call. That a problem?"

The big-shouldered bartender shrugged. "Nope. Things are slow enough."

"Good. I'll be at my booth."

He slid onto the bench and looked around. Hard to believe this day was finally arriving. He'd thought about it for so long it was like hitting a lottery ticket he'd always known would make things right someday.

That thought made his throat burn for a cigarette again. He twisted the ring on his index finger to take his mind off it, glancing around the bar to see if he could bum one from another patron.

"Rory," a voice called. Larry was gesturing from the bar with a phone in one hand. "It's for you."

He kept twisting the ring until he'd taken the phone and pulled it down to the empty end of the bar. Clearing his throat, he put it to his ear.

"Yeah," he said.

"Rory. So did ya think about what I suggested?"

Rory cleared his throat again. "The answer's no."

A pause, followed by, "That's not good thinkin'."

"I've done what the trust said. I deserve my share."

The caller made a clucking sound. "Well, you'd better hope so. 'Cause if the lawyer finds otherwise, you're done. You know that, right?"

"The trust rules apply to you and Ed, same as me."

"Aye, you're right, Rory. The trust rules apply to all three of us. It's just that neither Ed nor me has done a thing to be worried about. We'll get our share."

"I'm entitled to my share too."

"Entitled. Okay. So you're not interested in a deal. Well, I'm still going to offer one, and you'd be stupid not to take it. If you back away—admit you don't qualify for the trust cash—I'll still give ya three hundred thousand from my own share. A hundred to you, and a hundred for each of your kids. It's a one-time deal, and it goes away once I meet with the lawyer."

"That's not my share." Rory gripped the phone like a knife. "And what's this about *you* offering *me* a deal? I'm Jimmy Doyle's son, not you."

"I wouldn't go down that road, boyo. It's *me* your dad put in charge of the trust; it's *me* who's executor of his estate. But I hear ya. I'm settin' up a meetin' with the lawyer later today."

Rory felt his heart pounding. "Good. Let's get this done."

"Sure, Rory. Let's get this done."

The line went dead. Rory reached over the bar and set the phone back on its cradle, his hand wet with sweat. He wiped it on his jeans.

"You okay?" It was Larry, filling a mug from the tap.

"Yeah. . . . Thanks for the phone."

Rory retrieved his jacket and headed toward the exit. As he passed one of the men he'd been eyeing for a cigarette, he realized the hunger for one was gone. At least for now.

So it was really happening. A little more than a week and this would be over. The trust was finally getting passed out. The long wait was ending.

It was about time. And when it was over—when he and his kids had what they deserved—then it really would be a whole new start. For all of them. He was sure of it.

4

Ian put his Camry into park in the dark underground garage. From a distance, he saw the elevator sign that read *Out of Order*.

Perfect start for the workday, he thought, renewing his defiant whistling as he grabbed his briefcase and walked to the stairwell for the slog to the fifth floor.

Willy Dryer was slouched in front of the cedar door stenciled with *Wells & Hoy Law Office*. He looked up with relief as Ian approached. Afraid to go in and face Katie's stare alone, are you? Ian thought. He gave the client a nod and led him through the door.

Katie glanced up from behind the reception desk. Ian gave her a wide smile and a nod as they passed, headed for the library. He was confident Willy was avoiding her eyes entirely.

Neither spoke until they were seated at the library table. Ian set his case on the floor, stretched, and looked across at Wet Willy, thinking how little the man had changed in the five years

21

since walking into this office as Ian's first criminal-law client out of law school. Amazing, he thought. A few lines beginning to rim his puppy-dog eyes maybe, but so little else had changed.

"Now tell me, Willy," Ian began, "why I get the pleasure of your company again this morning."

Willy ran a hand through a flopping mass of uncombed red hair. "Sorry, man. But I *didn't* do it. I swear. They arrested me a couple of weeks ago, but I had not a thing to do with it. And they really put me through it. I barely made *bail*, man."

Ian nodded, surprised. "Why'd you wait so long to come in? And what exactly *didn't* you do?"

Willy shook his head again, his lips set firm. "I didn't want to bother you with this one. See, there's just nothing to it. 'Cause I didn't break into that house on Madison in Columbia Heights. I heard some guy from the north side's trying to fence the swag. They oughta be looking for *him*."

"You tell the police who the real thief is?"

Willy looked like he'd been slapped. "What do you *think*, man?"

No tears yet. From experience, Ian was ready to retrieve his legal assistant's box of tissues—though Willy usually reserved the water for trial. Cloudbursts on the stand while describing a life of misery were part of Willy's trademark. That and always insisting his case be tried *and* declining Ian's advice not to testify.

But then who could argue with success? Willy had never been convicted, although the acquittals likely had less to do with the performances than late alibi witnesses they'd managed to find for each of the last two trials. Katie, who'd coined the nickname Wet Willy, insisted the client enjoyed testifying even more than the State enjoyed prosecuting him, someone who saw trials as just another chance to put on a show. *"You're such a sentimentalist,"* Katie had scolded Ian when he tore up Wet Willy's last bill a year before. *"You just can't turn away the first guy who showed up at your office door and called you 'counselor.'"*

"Got an alibi this time?" Ian asked.

"I surely do," Willy said firmly. "But the police don't believe her."

Ian nodded sympathetically, wondering how many hours of free work this representation would take.

"Alright, Willy." He pulled a yellow legal pad and a pen from his briefcase and slid them across the table. "You write down the details of what you didn't do and how I can prove you didn't do it and where I can reach you. I'll also need your charging papers. You know the drill."

Willy nodded gratefully, winked, and smiled. "I surely do. You know I keep getting in trouble just to see you again, don't you? You're a *good man*. And hey, I'm gonna get you paid this time too. I am. I've started working. Get this: I've got an *acting* gig."

"Um-hm," Ian said, not for a moment believing that representing Willy made him a good man. He was, however, certain he wouldn't see a dime in attorney's fees and only mildly surprised Willy had taken up acting. The bigger surprise was for easygoing Willy to be excited about a solid job of any kind. "I'll be in my office when you're done," Ian finished.

He headed into the hall toward his office. Katie looked up, peering over her glasses, the disapproving look making her appear older than her forty-six years.

"Another day, another free client," she said, smiling sweetly. "I thought you already did enough pro bono work at the homeless shelter."

"Sarcasm's not on the menu," Ian answered. "For at least a month."

"Like that's gonna happen," Katie said with an ironic shrug. "Now, don't forget your birthday dinner tonight at your mom's. Livia called to remind me again."

"Got it."

"Oh," Katie added, "I've got the phone number and more information on the new case. Mr. Callahan gave me a few details when I called to tell him you'd contact him this morning."

Ian stopped to listen as Katie extended her notes to arm's length. "Like I said before," she said, squinting, "the man's name is Sean Callahan. He lives in St. Paul on Summit Avenue. It's got something to do with managing the distribution of assets in a family trust. Some investigation that's needed, which he claims is urgent. I've set up a file on your desk."

An investigation? Ian shrugged as he took the notes from her hand. "Okay. What's the rest of my week look like?"

His legal assistant tilted her head in thought. "The Bradley sentencing next week, Friday. An evidentiary hearing in Schumacher a week from Thursday. Nothing much this week. Oh, and Talk Show called, says he's got a referral. More good news, right?"

Ian nodded. Harry "Talk Show" Christensen was turning into his most consistent criminal-referral source. "Sure. I'll call him before I get ahold of this Callahan."

He strode to his office as Katie called out, "Oh, I forgot. While you were in with Willy . . ."

Ian had already slipped through his door.

A pair of black high-heeled shoes were crossed on his desktop from the occupant of his desk chair. Short, blond hair was visible over a brief held in one hand.

Surprised, Ian stopped for an instant before dropping into his client chair. "Brook Daniels!" he declared. "Did the U.S. Attorney's Office heed my report on your legal skill and fire you?"

Brook lowered the brief, groaning her disapproval. "Ian Wells, you have *no* credibility with the prosecutor's office. In fact, if anybody at my office thought about you at all—which they don't—it would be to ponder if you're aspiring to be a hotshot criminal-defense lawyer or a pipe-smoking trusts-and-estates guy. Given that Katie said you'll be representing Willy again, I suggest you stick to estate planning. But if I took a polygraph, I'd admit I'm really here to wish you a happy birthday."

Ian raised his eyebrows. "First, I don't do estate work any-more—as a rule. Second, my birthday's actually Friday. And third, I'm amazed you remembered."

"You bet I remembered," Brook said. "I remember a lot of things—including stuff you probably wish you'd never told me. That scar on your elbow from the bike accident at Theodore Wirth Park. The crush you had on Sandy Kelso in high school. And that crazy dream you get every year around birthday time. Something about a rainy funeral with palm trees and a lot of strange characters."

Ian could hardly believe he'd actually told Brook about that—or the rest of it for that matter. Or that she'd remembered it all. "Yeah. My 'ghost of birthdays past.'"

She smiled. "Or a clear sign of encroaching mental illness. I've got enough on you to retire comfortably on the blackmail—if only you'd actually earn some money. Speaking of which, how's the practice these days?"

Ian shrugged to hide his discomfort at the question. "Not bad. I've taken on a few new clients lately. All felons. Coincidentally, all claim to have dated you, Brook."

"Ouch." Brook grimaced, dropping her shoes to the floor. "Well, clearly you're feeling better than you look. Most lawyers shave for the office, by the way."

Ian nodded, pleased with the deflection. "So, tell me how things are on the ragged edge at the U.S. Attorney's Office since we had lunch last. What was it, a month ago?"

Brook thought for a moment. "Six weeks. But busy, as usual. Our new chief prosecutor's ambitious. Rumor has it he's gunning to make a career mark by reopening a cold case based on evidence that surfaced late last week. He hasn't involved me yet, but it's only Monday, right? Anyway, enough about me. Let me take you out for dinner to celebrate your birthday. Six weeks is too long."

"Let's do it," he said. Then he asked casually, "How's Zach?"

The question hung in the air a long moment. "He's fine," she finally answered, surveying the room. "You sure didn't change much when you took over your dad's office, did you?"

"I guess not, no." Who was doing the deflecting now?

She pointed at the large black combination safe in the corner near the window. "I was always impressed by that. Paperweight, or do you actually use it?"

"Use it, a little. Dad used it more, to store his clients' wills. I keep his remaining wills and a few of my own things in there now."

Brook's eyes shifted to a blown-up photograph on the wall beside the office door. "I love that too. Glad you kept it up when you moved in."

Ian followed her gaze. The poster-sized photo showed Ian's parents leaving a church dressed in their wedding clothes. His mother's face shone. His father's eyes were firm, though his lips bent upward in the nearest to a breakout smile Ian ever recalled in a photo. "The wall would look blank with anything else."

"Yeah," Brook said. "Your mom looks so strong and independent. Even in that moment. Know what I mean?"

Brook always saw to the heart of people, like his mom. "She is. Or was. She was only twenty-one when they married in 1987, but she's always had a mind of her own. Mom told me at Dad's funeral she came within an inch of keeping her maiden name when they married—Martha Brennan. Except it would have broken Dad's heart."

Brook lingered on the photo a moment more before saying, "Well, since I have an actual job to get back to, let's return to your birthday dinner. I'm buying. What day works?"

"Thursday. J. D. Hoyt's, six o'clock. But you don't have to buy."

"Wow, aren't we decisive today. J. D. Hoyt's is fine. And I insist on buying." Brook stood and came around his desk, pointing to the slim number of files stacked there. "You know, criminal-defense work can actually be profitable, if you take on clients who pay. Or I could swing a job offer at my office for a former classmate with some rumored skill in the courtroom."

"Thanks for the underwhelming compliment," Ian said—then realized she was unexpectedly serious. "Thanks, Brook," he added without the sarcasm. "But no. I'm doing okay."

She returned his look, then walked to the door, squeezing his shoulder as she passed. "See you Thursday, Hoyt's at six. I'll walk over from my office, and we can make our appearance together."

The door closed behind her.

She still wore the same perfume. Light. Only detectable when she was very close. In law school he'd taken the time to learn its name, though he couldn't recall it now.

Why had Brook hesitated at his question about Zach?

He shook his head. What did it matter? They were confirmed friends now. Anything more was a ship that sailed years ago.

Rising, he took back his desk chair, still warm after Brook's departure. After her comment about the files, he performed a quick, defensive inventory. His active ones, stacked in the left corner, compared poorly to the bills stacked in the right corner—including ones Katie had been hounding him for weeks to review and prioritize.

Not the greatest balance. But he wouldn't let it get him down with two potential new clients a phone call away.

He picked up the note from Harry Christensen and punched in his number.

"Talk Show here," Harry answered the phone in his booming voice. "That you, Wells?"

"It's me," Ian said. "How's the radio show going?"

"Surely you know," the lawyer's voice boomed again. "You listen every Saturday noon, right? Don't tell me you're the only lawyer or prospective client in the Twin Cities who misses my weekly gems of legal advice."

"Never miss it," Ian lied dutifully.

"Good. In that case, I've got a referral for you. Actually it's representing a *victim* who wants her hand held through an assault case. Boyfriend problem."

Ian slid over a notepad and pen. "Ready," he said.

Harry described the client briefly, ending with "This wise young lady says she listens to my show every week. I told her if she was really that good of a listener, she'd have already known I take the third week of June off every year for a fishing trip—which happens to be the very week she needs the help. After that, she asked me about other criminal lawyers I'd recommend, and when I mentioned you—first on the list, of course—she said she'd go with that. So, you want it?"

Ian knew Harry wasn't kidding. He'd gone so far as to mention his name on the radio program more than once, something he was grateful for. "Sure. Give me the number."

He did so. "She left me a cash retainer," the attorney added, "and asked if I'd get it to you. I'll messenger it over."

Ian thanked Harry and hung up. Then he picked up Katie's note and punched in the number for Sean Callahan.

"Mr. Callahan?" Ian asked when the line connected.

"Yeah," replied a voice flirting with an Irish accent.

"Mr. Callahan, this is Ian Wells. I'm the lawyer you called on Saturday with a family-trust question."

"Uh-huh. It's a critical matter."

There it was. Critical. "In the interest of full disclosure, Mr. Callahan, I limit my handling of complex trust matters. I have a partner, though, with more experience in that area. He's retiring soon, but could probably still help you."

"I said *critical*, not complicated. And I'm not interested in your partner. Also, I want to speak in person. At my home. Tonight."

Ian's shoulders stiffened at the tone. "Well, I don't usually travel to a client's home, unless you can't travel. And I have a family dinner engagement tonight—"

"Mr. Wells," Callahan interrupted, "this is a very significant matter. You'll find it's extremely good pay for limited work. And time sensitive. I have a ten-thousand-dollar retainer prepared to hand you."

Ian went silent. Did he say *ten thousand* . . . ?

His pride evaporated. "I can make it, but no earlier than nine." He quickly calculated when his mother would need to retire to bed. "If that works, give me your address."

Seconds later, Ian hung up the phone.

Ten thousand dollars. That was a big boost, and for estate work no less. He'd done little of that the past few years, even though wisdom—no, common sense—said he really should switch back to estate planning full time. Use the skills he'd been forced to learn right out of law school, winding down his dad's practice after the heart attack. Steady, predictable work. Steady, predictable pay. More than his criminal-defense practice, that was for sure.

He shook his head. Even the thought of doing trusts-and-estates work full time nearly resurrected his depression.

There was a knock on the door. Willy opened it and peeked in, his eyes wide. "Counselor," he said, "I got it all down here."

Moments later, he'd read Willy's scribbled notes. It was a defensible charge, much like the ones Willy had brought to him before. No eyewitnesses. Two people claimed Willy admitted to the crime, but an alibi witness placed him near a playhouse in the Warehouse District, miles away.

Ian glanced up at his client, who looked positively excited. Tears were nearly bursting out of him.

"This should work," Ian said, warming to the thought of being back in the courtroom—even if only to represent his serial client again. "Yeah, Willy," he finished with conviction. "Let's go teach the prosecutors another lesson."

5

The cul-de-sac in his parents' old neighborhood was quiet, re-minding Ian of spring days growing up. No lawn mowers. Not a break in the blue sky. Only a lone tree trimmer buzzing in the distance.

The image buoyed Ian, whose mood had slipped again in anticipation of this visit. The mother of those years seldom waited for him inside the home where he grew up; that Martha Wells emerged unpredictably, like sunlight through a bank of clouds. He walked to the front door, knocked twice, and was pulling out his key when his cellphone rang.

Katie again. "What's up?" Ian asked. "I thought you were heading home."

"I was. Hon, I don't like being the dark messenger, but we've got a problem."

He took a breath. "What now?"

"A former client of your dad's—one of the estate-planning

31

ones on a will your dad prepared. A couple of the heirs are suing the office for malpractice. We just got served."

Ian's stomach slid. "Which estate is it?"

"Claire Holtzberg's. Apparently Claire died a month ago. Two of her kids in the will claim your dad helped the other kids strong-arm Claire into giving them less. You know it's hogwash, Ian. Your daddy was straight up the most honest lawyer this town's ever going to see."

He didn't need that assurance, after reviewing every page of his dad's files after he died. Not only was the work pristine, the man never once even chased a client who failed to pay a bill.

"Which law firm is representing the heirs?"

"Treacher and Gunney."

Bottom-feeding lawyers for bottom-feeding clients. Perfect symmetry. And they said *dogs* came to resemble their masters.

"Alright." Ian sighed. "Let the malpractice insurer know."

"Uh, Ian," Katie began again softly, "we let that go, hon. With Dennis retiring this year and money so tight, you told me to hold the check back."

Ian closed his eyes as his heart accelerated. "I thought I told you to hold back on the malpractice insurance check *for a while*."

"You did. But since then, your half of the money to cover the premium hasn't come in. I put the notice of cancellation on your desk two weeks ago and told you about it. I just checked again. The policy lapsed last Monday." Her voice grew defensive. "I've been trying to get your attention, hon. You've been so distracted. And I thought maybe you'd decided to drop the insurance."

The pile in the right corner of his desk. Perfect. And yeah, he'd been distracted. With his mom's illness and the costs piling up, he'd put money out of his head as often as possible.

"Does Dennis know?" he asked.

"I called you first."

"I'll tell him," he said, then ended the call.

The world around him became an abstraction. How could he have forgotten about the policy payment? Now the firm had a lawsuit without insurance coverage. Even if the claim was bogus, he and his partner were personally on the hook for the attorneys' fees to defend it. Just as Dennis was preparing to retire.

He tasted blood in his mouth, realized he was clutching his tongue in his teeth. He spit into the rosebushes beside the stoop, closed his eyes, and leaned down with his hands on his knees. Stood again.

The Holtzberg estate, he remembered it now. It ran over a million dollars. Even if they won the case, the firm could be out a hundred thousand for defense costs before it was through.

The sky looked darker now, yet there wasn't a cloud in sight. He couldn't let Dennis carry this one. He'd have to figure out how to pay the costs of defense for both of them. And deal with any judgment that might come along.

In a jagged haze, he stepped inside the house.

The living room, usually so neat, was cluttered with dozens of stacked boxes. Like a storage shed, he thought grimly.

"Happy birthday, Ian!"

Livia Santara stood in the hallway to the bedrooms, wrapped in a blue apron. The tiny woman smiled widely as she approached, her arms out.

Though he didn't have it in him, Ian obliged with a hug. "What's with all this?" he asked. "And where's Mom?"

"Martha's out in the backyard. I insisted *tu madre* take a break from the boxes." Livia raised her hands to the ceiling. "'Go out back and work in the vegetable garden,' I told her. You know it's her favorite place in the world."

Ian looked over the living room again. "Okay. But what's the project?"

The part-time care assistant shook her head helplessly. "Your mother, she came in Saturday afternoon from the front flower garden when I was cleaning. She was *wild-eyed*. She said we had to empty the attic *ahora mismo*. I tried to change her mind, but there was nothing on earth that would keep us from cleaning out the attic."

Even dulled by Katie's news, Ian felt renewed alarm shoot through him.

Livia smiled calmingly. "It's okay. It's okay. This happens sometimes with Alzheimer's. I've seen it before. People like your mother, they get bursts of energy or take on mystery projects. Don't let it trouble you, dear. This is why you hired me. I've got it under control."

"If you say so," he replied skeptically.

Livia put a hand on his arm. "I do. This behavior is new for Martha, but it's still under control. And now I have to tell you I must have some time off."

"I know," he said, still surveying the mess. "You already told me you need Thursday off. That's why we're having the early birthday party."

"No, Ian. More than that. *Mi madre* took a fall last night. Hurt her hip. I need more time. Ten days, I think. Starting Tuesday—tomorrow."

Ian shook his head at this newest buffet. "What am I going

to do?" he muttered vaguely—before realizing how cold the words must sound to Livia.

"I'm sorry, Ian. I think maybe you could manage things yourself by staying over the nights. I can stock the refrigerator in the morning. I think it will be okay so long as someone is here at night to check on her and make sure she's eating and getting to bed."

"Look, Livia," Ian apologized, "I'm sorry about your mother. I'm just a little . . . out of it right now. Your mother going to be okay?"

"She will be fine. But you can stay, right?"

Ian tried to gather himself. "I've got an appointment later tonight. But I'll swing by my apartment after that to pack some clothes and be back here this evening."

"Good," Livia said. "Good. Just ten days. That's settled."

Still off-center, Ian noticed an old photo album propped on the couch, open to a leaf of color pictures. He pointed. "Mom looking through that?"

Livia smiled. "We came across it in the attic. I made Martha sit and look through it this morning. Anything that takes her back a few years seems to root her. Settle her down, you know."

He made a mental note.

"Ian?"

His mother stood in the hall to the kitchen in jeans and a dirt-stained gardening shirt. "Ian, what are you doing here?"

"Why," Livia said, "we're celebrating your boy's birthday a little early, Martha. Remember? We made the cake this morning. And that's pork roast you smell."

"Oh," Martha said, smiling slowly. "Of course." She crossed the room and gave Ian a hug. "You two be patient. I'll take a quick shower and change."

Ian waved at Livia as she drove away. With much effort he'd made it through his birthday dinner. Now he had to get his mom settled for the night before heading to his appointment.

In the kitchen stacked with plates, Ian saw his mother shuffling to the counter to turn on the coffeemaker. Ian opened the sliding glass door to the backyard deck and walked outside.

This was the deck his dad was one day going to convert into a three-season room, Ian recalled while looking out into the fading light. He'd talked about it every summer for years—one of many home projects left unfinished.

His mom appeared, holding two steaming cups. They sat down together on porch chairs.

Martha was more herself tonight, a bright spot ending a bleak day. As they sipped coffee, she began the ritual of reciting local news: family friends, neighbors, church activities, the garden. Especially the garden. Ian listened as best he could. Most of it he'd already heard—a symptom of her fading memory. He was beginning a dutiful question when Martha stopped speaking and leaned forward, locking onto Ian with serious eyes.

"*Connor*," she began in a conspirator's whisper, "we need to talk about something important. I didn't want to bring it up while Ian was here. If you're tired, maybe you could come home from the office at lunchtime. But it's urgent we talk."

Ian held his mother's gaze for a moment. He set down his cup. "Mom," he said gently, "I'm Ian, not Dad. It's just me at the office now. Me and Katie and Dad's old partner, Dennis Hoy."

Martha leaned back in her chair, stabbed with confusion.

Ian took a deep breath. "Remember how I took over for Dad at the office when he died five years ago? Right out of law school?"

He pointed toward the living room. "That stuff from the attic, probably a lot of it is Dad's old things from the office. Think, Mom. Do you remember?"

Her eyelids shut. She took several breaths, then reopened them over a light smile. "Oh, *of course*, Ian. I don't know what I was saying. You look *so much* like your father these days."

Ian smiled back. Her excuse was absurd, her smile certainly a cover. Still, he retrieved his coffee and let her slide into silence. He had no stomach for more chatting anyway.

He clenched his cup tightly. His dad should be here now to take care of Mother. He had no business dying in his fifties with a mortgage on a house needing work, leaving behind a wife destined for early Alzheimer's. It shouldn't be Ian swimming in debt trying to keep the only house Mom had ever known.

"You always gave Dad too little credit." It was Adrianne's voice, and the accusation she'd slung at Ian at the funeral home the day they'd buried him.

Really? All those years of steady, slogging legal work and so little to show for it, and it was Ian giving Dad too little credit?

"Yes," she'd followed when he shook his head. *"And you did it because you've always been too protective of Mom."*

Exactly the caliber of analysis and tact he'd expect from a psych student still three years from her PhD, delivering a diagnosis the day they were burying their dad. He'd barely accepted Adrianne's apologetic look moments later when she'd taken his hand and gone mercifully silent.

What a crazy notion it had been. Martha Wells had always been the "people person" of the family, never forgetting names or faces or the emotional baggage attached to them. She was the one who smoothed bruised egos, diverting social train wrecks before others even saw the engines converging on the same track. She could make more friends in a single afternoon than quiet Connor had in a lifetime. She didn't need any protection from her son. Not then anyway.

A breeze blowing across the deck recalled Ian to the present. He looked up to Martha smiling at him. He took her hands, callused and rough. At least worrying about her tonight had stopped him from lingering on his own problems.

"Now," Ian said lightly, "tell me why you decided to get all the boxes down from the attic."

His mother paused before shaking her head. "Oh, I just wanted to clean things out."

The vague answer didn't reassure. Before Ian could ask more, she perked up.

"I've got your birthday gifts," she declared. Martha stood and hurried from the porch, returning moments later with two wrapped packages.

Ian made a show of shaking the first, by shape and weight a book. He tore off his mother's signature perfect wrapping. A Pat Conroy novel, his favorite author. And the same one she'd given him the year before. "Thanks so much, Mom," he said. "This is terrific."

The second was larger, a shoe box. He weighed it in his hands. "Much heavier. What is it?"

She thought for a moment. "Something of your father's I found in the attic," she replied.

He tore off the purple wrapping. The box had a red X in masking tape on one corner. He lifted the lid. A scent of grease rose up. He looked closer into the box. The object inside had a dark metal sheen.

He looked at his mother in unfeigned shock. "Mom, this is a *handgun*."

Martha nodded. "I know."

"I didn't know Dad even *had* a gun."

"Yes. But I remember now. It wasn't supposed to be a gift, not really. I . . . I don't know why I wrapped it. I want you to get rid of it for me. *Don't sell it.* Please. There must be someplace they can destroy things like guns. Could you do me that favor?"

"Sure," Ian said, his shock replaced by amusement that she'd think he'd consider leaving the gun with her. After all, he'd hidden her car keys a year and a half ago. "It's fine, Mom. I'll take care of it. I was just a little surprised."

He stayed another half hour until his mother no longer insisted he stay. Then he put her to bed and left the house, stowing the shoe box in his Camry's trunk. Sliding into the driver's seat, he rested his forehead on the steering wheel.

A miserable day, ending with a difficult night. The bank turning down the loan. The malpractice suit. Dread of his coming conversation with Dennis festering in his stomach. Punctuated by his mother mistaking him for Dad. And now he got to go see a client at nine o'clock at night.

Except it *was* a client, and one claiming to have a ten-thousand-dollar retainer. There must be a good amount of work to be done. Grabbing that "up note," he straightened, started the engine, and backed out of the driveway.

Minutes later, on the freeway to St. Paul, an old memory returned—resurrected, he supposed, by the box in his trunk.

He was a young teen at the time, standing in the same kitchen he'd just left. Dinner was over and he held a wet towel in his hand. His younger sister was up to her elbows in a sink of soapy water, advocating her superior knowledge of American indie rock and nearly everything else. Half listening, Ian had accepted another wet plate and turned toward the living room, where his father sat resting by the fireplace—as his mother always insisted he do after dinner.

Connor Wells was hunched over a card table covered with a jigsaw puzzle, its borders assembled, the remaining pieces scattered about. Firelight danced over his graying hair. From the box resting on the floor, Ian could see it was the puzzle of the Minneapolis skyline, one his father had already assembled a dozen times before, like all the puzzles in the house.

As with so many things that year and in the teen years to follow, the sight plucked a chord of challenge in Ian. Dish and towel in hand, he approached his father.

"Dad," he said as he neared, "what are you doing that puzzle for? You've done it a hundred times. Why not buy a new one?"

His father's tired eyes looked up at him. Ian's judgmental tone couldn't have been lost on him. He smiled, yet his voice sounded weary. "Because, son," he answered, "knowing exactly what my efforts will produce is a rare comfort these days."

Returning unsatisfied to the sink, Ian told himself, with all the certainty of youth, that the moment had captured everything there was to know about his dad. He was a man who preferred a familiar puzzle to the fresh challenge of a new one. That image of a safe and timid man became locked in his mind, anchoring his opinion of his father forever.

Or at least until the last few months—and tonight. Because recently Ian had begun to understand how someone battered by life might long for the old and familiar over whatever new hurdle the next day could bring. And tonight his assumptions had been challenged again by something Ian hadn't seen or even imagined before—a stray piece to the puzzle that was Connor Wells that Ian *hadn't* finished as he'd imagined. One that fit nowhere in his memory of a quiet man who, for all his limits, Ian deeply wished was here now to care for Mother.

And for some reason, as he struck up a labored whistle for the remainder of the drive to St. Paul, it was that new puzzle piece—more than his mother's fading memory or the malpractice suit or the money problems—that wouldn't let Ian go.

6

Ian strode up the sidewalk to Sean Callahan's address, a three-story house with rounded windows and gables overhanging a front porch, with a wide lawn stretching down to the boulevard. He thought it probably had been majestic once, but now, in the moonlight, the lawn was sparse and spotted with weeds, the paint peeling from window frames and walls that looked decades past a serious encounter with a brush. Unusual for the upscale neighborhood where F. Scott Fitzgerald was raised. Ian wondered why someone hadn't maintained such a house, and whether what he was about to discuss had any bearing on it. He also hoped it wasn't a sign Callahan was puffing about the promised ten thousand dollars. He was in no mood for more disappointment today.

The door swung open just as he was reaching for the bell. A bulky man in a tight T-shirt, more muscle than fat, filled the doorframe. He looked to be in his thirties.

42

"Mr. Callahan?" Ian asked, surprised. Given the voice over the phone, the young man before him wasn't what he'd expected.

"No," he answered stiffly. "You the lawyer?"

Ian nodded.

"Follow me." The man turned, the entryway light revealing a six-inch Marine Corps tattoo in deep-blue ink high on his neck.

They walked down a hallway of shaded light and thick carpet into an equally dim living room with drawn shades and a tall fireplace at one end. The room was filled with thickly stuffed furniture upholstered in rich green, suggesting a faded country estate more than an urban home. The sole exception to the monotony of color was a high-backed plush chair near the fireplace done in bright orange.

An older man was standing behind one of the stuffed green chairs directly opposite the orange one, wearing tan slacks and a navy-blue polo shirt. Gray hair topped a face creased and tan. Though probably twenty years older than the Marine, he was nearly as muscular. He stood immobile as the Marine left, before gesturing Ian to the orange chair. Then he crossed the room to hand Ian a glass from a side table.

"Orange juice," he announced in a light Irish accent. "Care to 'sweeten' it?" He pointed to a bottle of Jameson Irish Whiskey on the mantel.

Ian considered for a moment, then shook his head. "No thanks," he said, taking his appointed chair. "You're Mr. Callahan?"

"Sean is fine." Callahan poured some of the whiskey into his own glass. "Cheers," he said, raising it.

Ian raised his glass. "Cheers." He sipped it carefully. Straight orange juice. He set it on a side table, atop a manila envelope.

As Callahan returned to his chair, Ian glanced around the

room, feeling uncomfortable in the scarce light. "Relative?" he asked, gesturing toward the door where the Marine had re-treated.

Callahan shook his head. "No. Aaron works in my business. And he's a sparring partner."

Ian raised his eyebrows at the boxing reference. Silence re-turned. "The green furniture," Ian said in an attempt to pick up the conversation. "Irish colors?"

"Aye. True Irish."

Green. True Irish. Ian looked down at the arm of his chair—bright orange. "Then you're from Ireland, Sean?"

"It would appear so," Callahan replied—only now his words were fully saturated with the accent he'd only hinted at before. "The man whose business we'll be discussin' brought me over from Belfast when I was twelve. Got me out of the troubles when my da died. He put me through school and gave me a job. I've made it a point to go back for a few months most every year since comin' to America." Callahan paused as he appraised Ian. "And what about you, *Ian*? English roots?"

Ian smiled. "My first name was a compromise. I'm told my mother is Irish from way back. My father had some English blood."

"A mixed marriage," Callahan responded, not bothering to match Ian's friendly demeanor. "A surefire source of trouble. 'Ian' sounds like it was the Irish did the compromisin'. If my da hadda felt like compromisin' with the English, he never would've starved to death in prison."

The words and tone jolted Ian. The "troubles" must refer to Northern Ireland back in the sixties and seventies. And starve in prison? Callahan's father had to have been a hunger striker with the IRA.

There was no safe ground in this minefield. He decided to switch topics. "What do you do for a living, Sean?"

He stared at Ian for another long moment before speaking, as though defiant about leaving talk of the so-called troubles. "I'm in construction," he finally replied.

Ian nodded, not caring what Callahan did but pleased to segue to safer ground. Mostly he wanted to get down to business, retreat from this stuffy room, and put the day to rest. "Tell me about this trust issue," he said.

Callahan set his drink aside, and with it the deeper Irish accent. "It's a simple thing, really. James Doyle set up a trust for his fortune right after his wife, Christina, passed away in '98. Some years later, Mr. Doyle followed her to his grave. The estate's funds are scattered about a few banks in the Caribbean and Belize, but Doyle's trust covers every dime of them. Our representative at Wells Fargo is the only one at present with access to the funds. And the James Doyle Trust includes his wishes about distribution."

"When did Mr. Doyle die?"

"2008."

"Alright," Ian said. "How big an estate are we talking about?"

"Nine million and some change," Callahan said with another appraising look at Ian.

Ian had personally handled estates of a million or two when cleaning up his father's files, but this was far beyond anything he'd managed before. He wavered for a moment, then reminded himself of the retainer. It didn't matter, he told himself. He'd get Dennis's help if he needed it.

"What's the problem with the trust?" Ian asked.

The Irishman squared his shoulders as if he was readying to deliver a blow. "The money's been in the trust for nearly two decades. In fact, a week from Tuesday will be the twentieth anniversary from when the trust was set up in 1998. There are three beneficiaries. On the anniversary, the funds are to be distributed to the three. One of them has children, and the trust says his portion will be split equally between him and his children. Twins. A girl and a boy."

It sounded straightforward. Simple even. Ian relaxed a bit. "So, what's the problem?"

"There's a qualification for each beneficiary in order to get their portion of the trust."

"Which is?"

"No beneficiary receives a dime of the money if they've been involved in any criminal activity since Mr. Doyle formed the trust in '98."

"You must mean no criminal *convictions*," Ian corrected. "Confirming whether a person has stayed out of all criminal activity going back so many years would be tough to do."

"No, Mr. Wells," Callahan said. "The trust definitely says any 'criminal activity,' not convictions. And as I was saying, the anniversary date is eight days from today."

"Okay," Ian replied. "And you want me to do what exactly?"

"You're to determine if the three beneficiaries qualify for the trust. You are also to take the money into your control and, along with the Wells Fargo banker, handle the final distribution."

Ian contemplated the task and the time limit. "What happens to the shares of the beneficiary with children if he doesn't qualify?"

Sean picked up his glass and took another sip of his orange juice and whiskey. "If that beneficiary fails the test, neither he nor his family gets any of the money. That beneficiary's share gets split between the remaining two recipients, assuming they qualify—with a bit set aside for the pope."

"I guess we can assume from these terms," Ian began carefully, recalling Callahan's Irish history, "that Mr. Doyle was worried one or more of the beneficiaries might already be involved in criminal activity when he created the trust."

Sean Callahan shrugged. "What's it matter to you? All you've got to do is determine whether they lived the life of the straight-and-narrow starting the day *after* the trust went into effect."

Ian shook his head. "How do you believe I could make that decision—twenty years later?"

"Any way you please," Callahan said breezily. "So long as it's done very privately, and I, as trustee, am content with the credibility of your conclusions. Oh, and to get you started, I'm authorized to pay you that ten-thousand-dollar retainer I mentioned on the phone. As I said, the trust provides for the remaining funds to go into a special account to be set up at your firm while you do the investigation. Once you, I, and the banker sign off on your conclusions, you distribute the funds. It's all laid out in the trust documents." He pointed to the manila envelope beneath Ian's orange juice.

"Eight days isn't much time," Ian said, "and I'm not a professional investigator."

Callahan rejected the objections with a wave of his hand. "You'll not be writing a book here, Mr. Wells. You'll be gathering limited information on three individuals covering a certain period of time. In fact, you shouldn't trouble yourself with any history of the beneficiaries before the trust's origin in 1998. In this day and age, eight days should be enough time for you to reach the necessary conclusions."

Ian wasn't so sure but simply nodded. He reached for the folder. "Who are the three beneficiaries?"

"Rory Doyle, James Doyle's son. Edward McMartin, who was James Doyle's brother-in-law. And myself."

"What is your legal relationship to Mr. Doyle?"

Callahan hesitated. "None, legally. A foster son, you could say."

"Well," Ian said, "the work seems straightforward enough, although I repeat that—"

"Your fee," Callahan interrupted, "for the investigation and distributions will be two hundred thousand."

In the stillness that followed the statement, Ian stared at the dust motes drifting through the hazy light of the lamp at his side—tiny globes in a tiny solar system. After a moment, he roused himself to clear his suddenly thick throat.

"For eight days' work? *Two hundred thousand dollars?*"

Callahan nodded.

Now the dimly lit room shrunk to Callahan's form in his stuffed green chair. "That's a steep fee," Ian said.

Callahan nodded again. "That's the fee Mr. Doyle agreed to pay for this service."

"Agreed with whom?"

"With the person who created the trust for Mr. Doyle. You see, that lawyer was intended to play your role, but sadly he's since passed away. In his absence, you've been chosen."

Ian hesitated, hardly able to absorb the magnitude of the fee.

Callahan drained the last of his drink, watching Ian over the rim of his glass. "Mr. Wells, I'm sure you've had a sterling legal practice these past four years—"

"Five," Ian said, embarrassed at how hollow the defense of his experience sounded.

"Aye, five." Callahan smiled. "But I'd be willing to wager that this is the largest fee you've been offered for little more than a week of work, and if you should live another thousand years, perhaps ever will. So can I assume you'll be taking the matter on?"

Ian sat motionless for a long interval. "Do the beneficiaries know I'll be doing this?"

"Aye," Callahan said with a nod. "Mr. McMartin lives in Florida and is a bit . . . infirm, but is aware the process is beginning. And Rory—Mr. Doyle's son—is acutely aware."

Ian's throat had grown strangely parched. Why was he hesitating? He reached for his orange juice, feeling moisture that could either be his hand or the cool surface of the glass.

He set the glass back down without drinking, feeling his heart pulsing in his fingertips. He looked at the manila envelope on the table beside him.

He hated what he knew he must say.

"Mr. Callahan, that fee is impossibly high. I can't accept it."

Callahan shrugged. "I'm afraid the fee is set by the trust document. If you wish, give it away. But if you're to take the case, the fee can't change."

Ian shook his head in disbelief. "That makes no more sense than the fee itself."

"I didn't draft the trust, Counselor. I didn't have any role with the attorney who did. But I can't see your objection. Have I told you a single task you see as unethical or illegal?"

Ian responded slowly. "Well . . . no."

"Then you object to being paid well for your legal services, is that it?"

The banker this morning. His mother tonight. The lawsuit that loomed. His brain tallied all the needs for money as his heart kept pounding out objections.

"That's not the point," Ian said with waning determination.

"Mr. Wells," the man said, his Irish tongue returning at the edges, "I can see you're conflicted. I tell ya what. I'll give ya until tomorrow at noon to decide."

Ian opened his mouth to say he didn't need the extra time. Closed it again.

Given all that was at stake, he'd take that night. He reached out and picked up the envelope. "Alright. I'll let you know in the morning."

Almost to Ian's disappointment, Callahan nodded impassively—as though he'd expected Ian's retreat from his resolve. "I'll await your call," the Irishman said, abruptly closing the meeting. He stood to lead them out of the shadowy living room.

At the front door, Callahan pointed to the manila envelope in Ian's hand. "In the event you agree to handle the matter, Mr. Wells, you'll find the trust in that folder as well as tax and employment information for both Mr. McMartin and myself to get you started on your investigation. Regarding Rory Doyle, you'll need to collect that kind of information directly from him when you meet."

Ian nodded.

Callahan pulled another envelope, this one business-sized, from his pocket and handed it to Ian. "Here's your retainer. Ten thousand dollars."

"I'll accept that if I take the case," Ian said.

Callahan didn't withdraw his hand. "If you say yes, I'd rather you have the funds so you can get right to it. If you decide otherwise, return the money along with the other papers in the afternoon."

Ian accepted the new envelope. Half expecting it was some kind of hoax, he pulled open the flap. Inside was a thick sheaf of bills.

"Because time's short," Callahan went on, "I arranged in advance for your first meeting with Rory Doyle Wednesday night—day after tomorrow. Rory will meet you at eight in the evening at Larry's Bar in Minneapolis, Rory's favorite watering hole. Then it's up to you how you proceed—so long as you act discreetly, within the eight days, and I'm satisfied with the credibility of the result."

Ian heard the conviction in Callahan's voice that he would certainly accept the job in the end. Through a crowd of thoughts, a question formed. "If I agree to do the work, do you get to decide if my conclusions about *your* past are acceptable?"

Callahan shook his head. "You'll see in the trust that I have no veto of any decision on your part as to whether I qualify as a beneficiary."

The client extended a hand. Ian shifted the folder and envelope to his left hand and accepted the offer with his right.

Callahan's fingers tightened on Ian's in a crushing grip. He leaned close enough to engulf them both in a breath of alcohol and citrus.

"If ya take the case, I'll be expectin' your best work here," Callahan said, his voice steeped now in the deepest Gaelic accent. "And your most careful handlin' of the trust proceeds. Let me emphasize again that there's no need to be pryin' into any of the beneficiaries' histories before '98."

Ian yanked his hand back, his vision red and his face hot. He shoved the cash and manila envelopes back at the client. "If you're worried you can't trust me," he said into the Irishman's face, "you shouldn't have called in the first place. In fact, I haven't a clue why you did."

Callahan took a step back and slid his hands into his pockets. "Mr. Doyle was always a big believer that the apple doesn't fall far from the tree," he said with a thin, unworried smile.

"What's that supposed to mean?" Ian replied, the envelopes still extended.

"Let me be more plain: Mr. Doyle admired the work of your *father*, and it seemed a natural thing to be hirin' you since he's passed on."

Ian's arm fell. He shook his head in disbelief. "What work did my father ever do for Mr. Doyle?"

"Why, I thought it was obvious," Callahan said, still smiling. "'Twas your father who prepared the trust for Mr. Doyle back in the day."

7

Under a cloudless, star-filled sky, Ian sat on a bench on a familiar knoll overlooking the Stone Arch Bridge. Behind him in the dark stood the Guthrie Theater. To one side lay the ruins of a mill that once fed the river's grain traffic. The shadows of tall trees lined both sides of the river.

The distant rushing of the Mississippi River was audible even from up here on the heights. But Ian's attention was locked on the bridge, lit with strings of lights along its edges, the solid stone structure angling gracefully over the river that frothed around its pilings.

Downriver was the University of Minnesota, Ian's law school home for three years. During that time he'd visit this spot on a weekly basis, even in the frigid depths of winter. Apart from the State Fairgrounds when it was vacant, it was his favorite place in the Twin Cities to sit and think.

Ian stretched out his legs as he pulled the trust document from the manila envelope at his side. Turning to the last page, he held it close to look to the bottom and read again the affirmation

53

clause, where the lawyer preparing a trust certified that he or she was the drafter.

This trust was prepared by Connor T. Wells, Attorney at Law, Wells & Hoy Law Office

His father's signature beneath appeared genuine. It was dated June 12, 1998.

Putting away the document, Ian settled back and closed his eyes. A breeze brushed his face. He tried to focus on his father and the new case from Sean Callahan.

Katie had worked at the office for twenty-three years before his dad's heart attack led Ian to take his place in 2013. So far as Ian knew, in all that time his father had been a spotless member of the Minnesota bar. Not prominent, but respected. Ian couldn't recall Connor Wells getting so much as a parking ticket in all those years.

Now he was told his dad had drafted this trust set to earn him a two-hundred-thousand-dollar fee simply for overseeing distribution of its proceeds. Angling for a big fee wasn't automatically wrong   or half the lawyers in the country would be disbarred. Nor was a flat fee wrong or unusual. Except his dad wasn't any lawyer. If his father had been voracious about billings, he would have earned enough before he died to at least pay off the mortgage. No, Connor Wells would never have pushed for such a high fee where so little work was involved.

Would he?

Ian's phone vibrated again in his pocket. Irritated, he fished it out.

The call was from Seattle. Why so late? Concerned, he decided to answer it.

"*When were you going to tell me?*" his sister let loose.

Ian held the phone away from his ear. This was all he needed. "We talking about Mom?"

"Who else? When were you going to tell me about Mom getting worse?"

"So you spoke to Livia."

"Yes. When I couldn't reach you, I called Livia to see how your birthday dinner at Mom's went. Right away she starts talking about Mom going nutsy in the attic and her memory sliding. So I'm thinking, Wow, this is bad. Maybe she needs to be institutionalized, maybe it's time for a memory-care clinic. And I'm wondering why my older brother hasn't even mentioned it. I'm also thinking, How are we going to pay for it? How are we going to handle *this*?"

He opened his mouth to speak, but Adrianne was already moving on.

"To have so few savings, Dad must have been the biggest pushover in Minnesota," she fumed. "Katie told me after the funeral that Dad never once brought a collection action against a deadbeat client. And Dad paid Katie way over the going rate from the day he hired her."

"Who told you that last part?" Ian asked, surprised.

"Katie did. Second to Dad, she's the most honest person I've ever known. And she adored him. She knew he was paying her well. I hope you at least got *her* pay under control when she started working for *you*."

He didn't answer that. "Adrianne, I don't know what to tell you. I'm staying with Mom at night this week. I'll let you know what I think after I spend more time with her."

"You do know Alzheimer's can accelerate from a physical or psychological trauma, don't you?"

He didn't. "You're the psychologist, Adrianne."

"Well it can. Did Mom have any big shock the last few weeks? Sources of anxiety?"

"Not that I know of. Look, it may be nine o'clock out your way, but it's after eleven here. I can't have this talk right now."

"You can't keep me in the dark, Ian. This is my problem too."

"Then maybe you should come home."

Silence. When his sister finally spoke again, her voice had calmed and carried a note of guilt.

"Ian, I appreciate what you're doing with Mom. I'd be there if I could. With my new clinical practice and all, I just can't afford to be away right now. But I still need to know what's going on."

His blood pressure shot up. He wasn't sure he wanted to let her off the hook now. For a moment he considered unloading on her about his own troubles. The moment passed.

"Yeah. I get it," he finally answered.

"Will you let me know how it goes this week?"

"I will."

"You know I love you, big brother."

Mom's side of Adrianne: always avoiding lasting scars. "Yeah, me too."

After ending the call, it flashed through his mind that he should have asked Adrianne if she knew about Dad's handgun. Or why Dad would have handled a trust with a fee of two hundred thousand. Dad had always been closer to Adrianne. But Ian had no interest in calling her back now.

Instead, he settled back once more on the bench to get back to why he was here. Could he really take this case? And for such a fee?

How could he not? Callahan was right: it wasn't like he was being asked to do anything wrong. Then there was the fact that his dad had prepared the trust that called for the large fee. Honest Connor Wells. Careful Connor Wells.

He looked down at the churning river. In the end, it all came down to how badly he needed the money—for his mom, for his practice. For the malpractice lawsuit, the monster in all this he'd mercifully forgotten for a moment.

All right. He'd talk to Dennis about the lawsuit in the morning, then make his final decision after that.

Once more he stared down at the big river's flow beneath the bridge, which seemed to wash some of the hesitation from his mind. Yep. He'd make his decision in the clear light of morning after talking to his partner.

He made his way in the dark back to the car. As he unlocked the door, he glanced back for a final view of the bridge. From this vantage point, the Mississippi was black and nearly invisible, leaving the bridge suspended in midair. Viewed this way it seemed less real. Less secure.

He almost wished he hadn't looked back as he got into his car and drove away.

8

Sales Assistant Andrew Pinz set the camera he'd just retrieved from the back room onto the counter. "You clearly have an eye for quality, choosing a Kronzfeldt," Pinz said. "Wildlife shots?"

The customer shook his head. "Sports."

It was going to be a great morning, Andrew thought. A great morning. He was about to sell a preordered, high-shutter-speed Kronzfeldt Cyber-Shot, along with a high-end telephoto lens, all totaling nearly four thousand dollars. And it wasn't even lunchtime. At this rate, by the end of the week he'd have earned enough commissions to pay off the credit card debt he'd taken on for his upcoming trip to Virgin Gorda.

"Let me take a moment," Andrew began, "and tell you about our warranties."

"No. I'd just like to pay now."

58

Better still. "Alright. Do be sure to fill out the warranty form online when you get home. Will it be check or charge today?"

"Cash."

Andrew watched the customer pull out a stack of bills from a jacket pocket. While Andrew bagged the purchases, the customer counted out a series of hundreds, a few fifties, then twenties. He laid them on the counter.

Andrew smiled as he recounted the bills; the last thirty were crisp and new. "Nearly exact. You have seventy cents in change coming."

"No need," the customer said, taking the bag. "I have to run."

As the customer left the store, Andrew turned to the register and began dividing the bills by denomination. When he came to the crisp ones, he held one up to the light, expecting to see a recent printing date.

The bills were twenties, but they looked all wrong. Not like forgeries exactly, but on the front, Jackson appeared too small.

He studied one more closely. To his surprise, it was dated 1983.

Andrew thumbed through the rest of the new-looking bills. All were twenties, and all were dated the same. Storing them neatly away, he closed the register.

Apparently the customer had raided the mattress for this purchase. But Andrew didn't care. So long as the man didn't return the merchandise, his commission was set—cash or credit card.

He could already feel the sugary sand of Virgin Gorda between his toes.

10:00 A.M.
WELLS & HOY LAW OFFICE
DOWNTOWN MINNEAPOLIS

Katie wasn't at the reception desk when Ian returned. From the cracked door at the end of the hallway, he could tell his partner was in. He forced himself to head straight there.

Dennis Hoy's office looked like tornado alley, but then Ian had no memories of it ever looking any different. Even when he'd visited the law office as a child, papers had always been piled high and strewn in all directions.

Ian's sixty-four-year-old partner was seated on a love seat in the only area not covered in papers. He scrunched his forehead as Ian came into the room with a worried look on his face.

"Dennis," Ian began, "we have to talk."

The older lawyer nodded. "I know. I found the pleadings on Katie's desk this morning. What's going on with this lawsuit?"

Ian hesitated, uncertain about how to start. "I haven't seen it yet, but Katie tells me it's some children of a woman Dad represented."

"I know that much," said Dennis, his forehead growing red. "But did you know they're claiming your father committed fraud by helping the other children? And that the Complaint is almost dripping punitive damages? Which would mean our malpractice insurance wouldn't cover that part of the claim."

Ian felt his own face flushing.

"I know the lawsuit's probably hogwash," Dennis went on. "Still, the timing couldn't be worse. I was planning on telling you I'm retiring at the end of this month." He paused, his voice tightening. "What I also haven't told you is that Charlene's asked me for a divorce, and for half of everything I've ever earned. Thirty-five years of marriage. *Thirty-five years.* A month before I retire, she wants out."

Ian's stomach fell. He had to get this out. "It's worse than that," he said. He explained about their insurance having lapsed.

The shade of color in Dennis's face turned to purple. *"What were you thinking?"* he shouted. *"You should've borrowed the money from me to cover the premium."*

Ian had never heard this tone from his even-tempered partner. "It was a miscommunication between Katie and me," Ian said. He stopped and shook his head. "No, that's not fair. Katie tried to tell me, but I wasn't listening. This is on me alone. But Dennis, you knew my dad. You know there's nothing to this lawsuit."

"No, I didn't know Connor," his partner roared as he straightened on the couch like a rocket about to launch. "We worked together for twenty-five years, and you and I have had more conversations these last five than I ever had with your dad. With Connor, this place was always an eat-what-you-kill operation—just like between you and me. Separate books, separate bank accounts. We could've been separate law firms, the way we operated. And with your father being the quietest lawyer I've ever known, *I didn't know Connor.*" Dennis closed his eyes, his anger peaking.

"I'll take care of this," Ian promised.

Dennis seemed to collapse deeper into the couch. "I'm sorry. I'm sorry. I know your dad was a great lawyer and a good man. But I can't afford this, Ian."

"I told you. I'll take care of it."

"How?"

"I've got some fresh work."

The explanation sounded hollow even to himself. Dennis dropped his face into his hands.

Staring at the partner he'd worked with these past five years, Ian remembered when Dennis offered him his father's slot at

Wells & Hoy Law Office. It was just a week after Connor died. At the time, Ian was about to graduate from law school, busily interviewing at the same places as Brook and her boyfriend, Zach—big firms with growing litigation practices. Both Dennis and Connor had been estate planners, and Ian knew the offer to replace his father carried little likelihood of help in building the criminal-defense practice he really wanted. In fact, the proposal had the trappings of a courtesy.

But the next day, Ian told Dennis in this very room that he'd join him as a partner with the same arrangement as his dad. Dennis's expression had bordered on shock, though he'd never asked Ian to explain, and Ian had never volunteered his reasons.

Now, at the end of their partnership, it had come to this.

"I'm good for it," Ian said more forcefully. "That's a promise." Then he headed back into the hallway, closing his partner's door behind him.

He stopped at the reception desk, where Katie had returned.

She looked up, worry in her eyes. "Everything okay?" she asked. He could tell she'd heard the exchange.

"Sure," Ian answered shortly. He briefly explained his meeting with Callahan the day before, not mentioning the amount of the fee or Callahan's final words. He dropped the envelope with the cash on her desk and told her to deposit it.

He retreated into his own office. Seated behind his desk, Ian looked up at his parents' wedding photo on the wall. His mother's eyes, wide and excited, looked slightly down and toward Connor at her side, conveying a wisp of caution. He'd always assumed it was concern for not tripping on the train of her gown.

But that wasn't it. Ian understood that now. Intuitive Martha Brennan, just transformed to Martha Wells, must have been worried about marrying a lawyer. And rightly so. What a profession. Architects didn't tear down other architects' buildings. Engineers didn't sabotage other engineers' bridges. Doctors didn't try to ruin other doctors' reputations. Only lawyers, sharks, and spiders fed off their own.

He looked again at the limited files on his desk. He'd best get to it. Clear away any distractions. Call Callahan and accept—tell him he had a lawyer.

For the next week, Ian would be investigating this trust and little else until he'd earned that fee.

9

The office phone jangled on its perch on the window ledge over Katie's shoulder, startling her. Setting down the firm's lease bill, she twisted to glance at the clock beside the phone.

Who could be calling at this hour? She waited several rings until finally it stopped.

Katie let out a ragged sigh. It had been a long day and it wasn't over yet. Dennis had slunk out after the explosive meeting with Ian in the morning, never to return. Ian had locked himself in his office all day, reviewing the new trust and clearing up other clients' work. When she'd finally dared to poke her head into his office, he announced the next seven days would be focused working on the trust, all the time. True to his word, he was still at it in the library. If he hadn't sent her off to finish reconciling the books for the month, she would have insisted on helping.

The phone rang again. She looked down the hall toward the

library door. Ian must not be expecting a call since he wasn't getting it. It was probably just another salesperson.

After the next ring, it stopped again.

She turned away from the window and picked up the next bill to review—when the ringing erupted again. Frustrated, Katie reached for the phone.

"*Yes?*" she said sharply.

"Hello," an apologetic voice began. "I'm calling from Wells Fargo Bank. I'm sorry to call so late, but we need to confirm there have been no unauthorized transfers from your account today. We've intercepted a hacker trolling business accounts and are contacting all our business clients who transacted business today to ensure all transfers on their accounts were authorized."

Katie shook her head at the interruption. "Hold on."

She put the phone on hold, turned to the computer, and typed in the access password. When she'd opened Outlook, she got on the internet and typed in *wellsfargo.com*. Once the bank's website came up, she entered the firm's identity code followed by the law-office password.

The security page faded, replaced by the account status page. She quickly scanned all transactions for the day, turned back to the phone on the windowsill, and took it off hold.

"Ma'am?" the voice on the phone said.

"No unauthorized transactions," Katie responded curtly.

"Thank you so much. Again, I'm very sorry for the late call, but I'm sure you understand."

The phone went dead. Katie dropped hers back on its cradle. She *didn't* understand. Why call at night when it was so unlikely they'd reach anyone?

Her back still to the computer and her piles of bills, Katie took a moment to stare out the window at the puzzle pattern of lit windows in the surrounding buildings. So many people working late. Some probably trying to impress a boss or beat a deadline, others avoiding somebody at home.

A light flickered out in an office window across the street—the sudden darkness reminding her she'd have to hustle if she had any hope of getting home before Richard went to bed. She turned away from the window and once more back to the pile of bills, the annoying banker quickly forgotten.

Standing in darkness a few feet back from the sixth-story window that looked out over the street, the photographer set down the cellphone and returned to the camera and tripod. Even without the lens's magnification, it was clear the legal assistant—her back now visible through the window across the street—suspected nothing. As the photographer watched, the light on the woman's computer screen flickered dark once more. The woman didn't appear to notice, deep into a document in her hand.

The photographer was just as indifferent as the legal assistant to her computer returning to sleep mode. He'd already gotten what he needed.

In the darkness of his empty room, the photographer reached out and adjusted the new Kronzfeldt digital camera with its foot-long telephoto lens, which rested only inches from the windowpane. With a finger touch, he switched the screen operation mode from Capture to Image Review. Within seconds the auto shots he'd just taken were ready to analyze.

The shots captured the legal assistant's keyboard and computer screen. Fortunately she'd sat with her back to the window when she operated the desktop computer. Over several weeks' time, the photographer had to slip into half a dozen offices on this side of the street to find the best view looking down and over her shoulder—from an office with no late workers to contend with.

The first set of shots engaged both the woman's keystrokes and the screen images as she typed the password gaining access to the computer. Those shots were clear and had good resolution, he saw with satisfaction.

Pulling a notepad and pen from a jacket pocket, the photographer clicked through each of the images that followed from the moment she rested her fingers on the keyboard. At ten shots per frame, covering both the screen and keyboard, the camera had captured each typed letter at a rate of one every two to three frames. He wrote down each letter the instant it appeared on the screen.

ConnorWells, it read when finished.

He shook his head. The ID displayed no imagination. He could have guessed it without the bother of the night's efforts.

He turned next to learning the Wells Fargo website User ID that followed. Since the bank's site displayed those keystrokes on the screen as they were made, there was no difficulty gaining that information: all he had to do was digitally enlarge the image on the computer screen when she finished typing.

IanWells. Just as simple.

The hard part was figuring out the law firm's Wells Fargo customer password. The photographer picked up on the digital display where the User ID shots had ended. The customer password wasn't displayed on-screen as typed letters, numbers, or symbols, but as asterisks only. That meant in the frames that followed, it was necessary to manipulate the critical images: widen and refocus each frame in order to view the legal assistant's fingers striking each key and write down the correct strokes when and where pressure was detected on the keyboard. The process was all the more painstaking because of the need to expand the frame after each keystroke to encompass her *other* hand to detect whether she'd pressed the Shift button for capitals or symbols.

When finished, the photographer's eyes were scratchy and dry from concentration. He'd written down nine keystrokes in all, visible on his notepad in the dim light cast by the streetlight outside.

7SeCrEts!, it read.

He peered back at the legal assistant in the window, still busy at her desk. Secrets? What were they? When she first started at the law office, a young eighteen-year-old with no experience, had she carried a torch for her boss, Connor Wells, just out of law school and only seven years older? Or maybe for his partner, Dennis Hoy? Or something more unexpected? Maybe she'd spent the years at the law office skimming away a few dollars each Tuesday night when she did the books.

Maybe all those notions were true.

The thought that any of the possibilities might be true made Katie Grainger much more interesting to the photographer.

He grabbed his phone from the windowsill to check the time. It was getting late. The custodian would be reaching this floor at around eleven, a little over an hour from now.

For the next hour, the photographer carefully reviewed the digital frames two more times. All three reviews yielded the same conclusion.

Another glance out the window told him she was finally packing up to leave. The photographer shifted the telephoto lens to focus on the adjacent window, the law office's small library.

Ian Wells was seated there, typing on his laptop. Whatever he was doing, the lawyer looked tired.

Fifteen minutes later, the camera and lens were packed and the room carefully wiped down. Probably unnecessary, but smart. The photographer liked smart. He left the empty office, pulling the door tightly shut to hide the damage to its broken lock. The cellphone went into a nearby trash bin, one that would soon be emptied.

The door to his elevator started to close at the same moment the adjoining elevator door opened. The wheels of a creaking cart were followed by a view of the custodian's back—just as the photographer's elevator fully closed and the car lurched its way toward the street level below.

10

A callused hand held tight to Ian's fingers. He was being led down a path toward a house. He was hot and thirsty, unsettled and afraid. Wherever he was, he didn't want to be there.

Then the path was gone, replaced by salmon-colored tile beneath his feet and twin fans swirling from a ceiling overhead. His shoes clopped down a hallway into a bright room with a grand piano, the space filled with adults with glasses in their hands and more fans whirling overhead and open patio doors facing a swimming pool. The hand that still held him slid away, and he was alone.

He passed through a door to stand beside the pool, where he knelt and leaned into the chlorine smell and the cool ripples of its surface. He wanted to swim but had no suit. He cupped the water in his hand, swirling it about like a whirlpool.

"Who are you?" a gravelly voice called out. Ian didn't like the voice, so he didn't answer.

"Who are you?" the voice asked again. This time Ian looked up at a face darkened by the bright sky behind it.

"Ian Wells," he answered.

The face still obscured, the man put his fists on his hips.

"Who are you with?" he commanded.

Ian was too afraid now to answer. After a moment, the man shaded his eyes with a hand, scanned the pool area, and moved away from the poolside.

Ian stayed, frozen in place, watching the man's retreat with fear pinching at his stomach.

———

"Wake up. *WAKE UP!*"

Ian raised an annoyed eyelid. Katie was staring down at him, a hand on his shoulder. "Wake up, Ian," she said again.

"I'm awake," he muttered thickly, leaning back in a chair pressed close to the office library table. A stack of files he'd worked on the night before still sat on its surface. His laptop was open at his elbow. His mouth was dry, his jaw stiff. "I got everything on my calendar cleared for the new case around three. What time is it anyway?"

"Eight-fifteen in the morning, hon," Katie replied. "But there's a problem." She stabbed one of the folders on the table with a finger. Ian looked at it groggily. It was the new file they'd opened for Willy Dryer.

"Wet Willy," she hurried on. "They're trying to pull his bail. They took him into custody last night. I just got the call."

Not today. Not Willy. He had to get on the trust case—the one that actually paid. A memory of the meeting with Dennis slipped back into his consciousness.

"How do we know that?" Ian grumbled.

"Judge Miller's clerk was in my Pilates class last winter, and when she saw you hadn't checked in for the hearing, she gave me a call."

"Checked in? When's the hearing?"

"This morning. Like in fifteen minutes. Apparently, Willy only told them you were his counsel this morning."

A painful adrenaline rush hit him as Ian came more awake. Why would Willy wait until this morning? Since when was Willy shy about disturbing his attorney?

"Is it a cattle call?"

"Yep," Katie said. "Starting at eight-thirty. Ten different motions lined up to be heard before eleven."

"Call the court and say I've been delayed. See if they'll move us to the back of the line. Tell them I'll be ten minutes late."

"Favors aren't Judge Miller's style, hon, you know that. But I'll see what I can do. I'll grab your coat."

Katie rushed toward the front desk like a practiced firefighter. Ian shook his head hard, driving the last shredded images of the dream away. He stumbled to the restroom to splash cold water on his face. He cupped his hands to blink more moisture into his eyes.

As he rubbed dry with a paper towel, Ian saw the lines and dark rings in the mirror looking back. He felt—and looked—like he'd hardly slept. Vague impressions of his sleeping visions came back: a pool and an angry man mostly. And an obscure sense that last night's dream was somehow related to his birthday one.

A pang of guilt surfaced. He hadn't gone home last night. Which meant he hadn't checked in on his mom since late Monday. And tonight he had the meeting with Rory Doyle that the new client had arranged.

Ian shook his head as he trotted to his office to grab a pen and pad of paper. There on the desktop was the James Doyle Trust document, just as he'd left it the night before. Out in the open where Katie could see it.

He gathered it up and knelt before the corner safe, rapidly spinning in the combination for the lock.

He'd just stood up again when Katie rushed through the door, his briefcase in one hand and suit coat from the library in the other.

"The clerk said she'd try to put you lower on the list. I told her you had a flat tire this morning. We *really* owe her."

Ian nodded. "Take her to lunch on the firm credit card. What kind of flat?"

"A nail."

Ian grabbed his briefcase. "Listen, Katie. I obviously didn't get back home last night like I'd planned, and I'm going to be late again tonight. Any way you could break away early and stop by my mom's? Make sure she's okay?"

"Of course. Now get over there and kick some poor prosecutor around the courtroom."

He rushed out the office door.

8:43 A.M.
HENNEPIN COUNTY COURTHOUSE
DOWNTOWN MINNEAPOLIS

Ian opened the door and slipped quietly into a full courtroom, trying not to attract attention.

"That may be true, Your Honor," a voice intoned from counsel table, "but it shouldn't make any difference under the law of the case."

Ian slid onto the closest bench before looking up.

Glaring down at a fresh-faced lawyer, the judge clutched a pen in her teeth. She took it out. "Shouldn't matter? That's the best you've got?"

The young lawyer grew stiff. "I mean, because of your prior rulings, which meant that—"

"Now you're going to tell me you understand what my prior rulings meant—better than I do?"

"No, Your Honor. I mean, yes, Your Honor. Only that . . ."

Judge Miller held up both hands. "Don't bother, Counselor. We're done. I'll take it under advisement. Next."

Judge Miller set the file aside. Her clerk was already pulling the next matter up on her computer screen. The young lawyer, still staring blankly at the judge, was already forgotten.

"Call the next case." Judge Miller waved at her clerk.

"*Stranton v. Pierson Electric*," the clerk called out instantly.

"No, no, no. Dryer. Willy Dryer. I just saw his lawyer, our esteemed Mr. Wells, sneak into the courtroom. I don't know how his case fell down the ladder," the judge added with a wayward glance at her calendar clerk. "I thought I had him earlier. But he's here now. Have the bailiff bring in his client."

Ian rose, feeling the stares of a roomful of attorneys jealously waiting their turn. He passed through the wooden gates of the bar, brushing by the slaughtered lamb retreating from the bench, and took a chair—with a quick glance to the other counsel table to his left.

The prosecutor at the adjacent table was Samuel Marston. Lanky, dour-faced, and older than Ian by twenty years, Marston had been the unsuccessful prosecuting attorney on both of Willy's past charges. He was proud and arrogant. Ian suspected that, twice stung, he'd *asked* for Willy's case this time.

A side door swung open, and the uniformed bailiff emerged leading Willy, who was dressed in an orange jumpsuit and handcuffs.

"I heard a rumor you had car trouble, Mr. Wells," the judge

said as the bailiff brought Dryer to Ian's side and removed the cuffs.

He got a lucky draw with this one, Ian thought as he rose to respond. Judge Miller had always liked him. Probably because he'd tried half a dozen cases before her and never made the mistake of coming unprepared. Though Ian also knew that, like him or not, she wouldn't hesitate to boil him in oil if he messed up. Mostly he'd learned that a judge's affection got you a respectful voice and patience when you had "car trouble"—and little more.

"Yes, Your Honor," Ian answered as the bailiff seated Willy beside him. "It started with a nail—"

Judge Miller held up a hand. "Got it. Mr. Marston, I understand you want to withdraw Mr. Dryer's bail. Tell us why."

The prosecutor's eyes turned to Ian, broadcasting complete disbelief in the flat-tire story. "Because, Your Honor, we received a tip that Mr. Dryer was planning a trip to California in violation of the terms of his bail. I have a statement here, if I may approach."

The judge nodded. Marston walked the paper up to the judge, dropping a copy on Ian's table as he returned.

Refusing to be annoyed by the prosecutor's swagger, Ian quickly skimmed the statement.

"So what say you, Mr. Wells?" the judge called out.

"Well, Your Honor," Ian began slowly, "as I read it, this statement claims to be from someone who is in Mr. Dryer's acting company. Doesn't say whether they're a friend or an enemy or give any foundation for why they should be believed."

Ian felt a tug on his coat. Willy had scribbled a note on a pad on the table. *Ask me about California and the guy who did the statement*, it read.

Never ask a question to which you don't know the answer: Trial 101. And Ian had no clue what Willy was about to say.

But Willy was nodding his head in strong encouragement. Well, it was his trip back to jail if he got it wrong.

"Could I inquire of my client, Judge?" Ian asked. "Maybe we can clear this up."

"Swear him in," the judge said to her clerk.

Catching Willy's gaze as he finished the oath, Ian shook his head slightly and touched his eye as though scratching an itch, mouthing the words *Don't cry*. Willy nodded.

Ian launched his exam. "You're part of an acting group, Mr. Dryer?"

"Yep," Willy said with pride. "My first one."

"We're not talking the Guthrie here, are we, Mr. Dryer?"

Willy grinned. "No, sir. Not ready for the big lights yet. It's Pandora's Playhouse in northeast. It's a new playhouse for guys . . . people just starting out. And for folks who're getting past trouble in their lives. Doesn't pay much, but it's a start."

"What's the name of your play?"

"*Macbeth*."

"Who do you play?"

"Macbeth."

Ian paused—surprised Willy could handle such a demanding role, but mostly hoping Willy knew what he was doing as they got to the key questions.

"Do you know anybody in California, Mr. Dryer?"

"No, sir, I do not."

"This statement says you told this witness you were going to drive to California. Were you?"

"No."

"Do you have a car?"

"I do, but it wouldn't make it to the Dakotas, let alone California."

Ian lifted the statement and read it again. "And do you know the person who gave this statement . . . Mr. Kyle Potts?"

Dryer nodded. "I surely do."

"He's in your acting troupe?"

"Yes, sir."

"Who is he?"

"The guy who *didn't* get Macbeth."

Snickers went through the gallery crowd. The judge smiled, but then raised a hand to bring the laughter to a halt.

Ian continued with more confidence. "When's the play open?"

"Two weeks."

"If you're put back in jail, who would take over your role as Macbeth?"

"My understudy."

"Mr. Potts?"

Willy grinned again. "Yes, sir. Mr. Potts."

Ian dropped the paper on the table and looked to the bench. "Judge, this statement, with no foundation or corroborating evidence, isn't enough to put Mr. Dryer back in jail. The fact is, Mr. Dryer has never been convicted of a crime in his life"—the prosecutor began to rise, so Ian accelerated his argument—"despite Mr. Marston's best efforts in two trials I had the pleasure to attend." Marston stood impatiently, leaning over his table. "And we all know we don't keep people in jail awaiting trial on charges like those against Mr. Dryer without a record." Marston raised his hand to get the judge's attention. "Although I'm sure Mr. Marston will argue that three burglary charges is enough smoke to fear Mr. Dryer is a flight risk, I'd respond that if a *talented prosecutor* can't

77

convict Mr. Dryer twice in a row, that's got to mean he really is an innocent man."

Ian sat down as Judge Miller shook her head and smiled.

"Your Honor," Marston began immediately.

The judge raised an index finger. "Unless you're planning on disagreeing with Mr. Wells's assessment of your skills as a prosecutor, Mr. Marston, I think we're done here. Bailiff, take Mr. Dryer down and process him out."

Ian knew Judge Miller better than to show his joy at the victory as he left the courtroom, followed by Marston. Once in the hall, the prosecutor caught Ian's gaze with narrow, frosty eyes.

"Don't expect a repeat of the last two trials," he muttered.

Ian looked him over. "Why? You have proof this time you'd like to share?"

Marston glared back. "Three burglary charges in five years and no convictions isn't a record that's going to stand on my watch."

"Unless he's got an identical twin, there's a reason you didn't convict," Ian shot back. "Willy had solid alibis both cases."

"Yeah, alibis that only 'appeared' at the last minute," the prosecutor snapped. "How convenient." Without waiting for a reply, he made his way in a near stomp down the hall.

Marston was the worst, Ian thought, watching him go. Not a sore loser. A self-righteous one.

Ian caught the elevator to the second floor and took a seat by the courthouse's indoor fountain. The area was crowded with a mix of suited lawyers, county employees in white shirts with badges hanging from their necks, and worried clients.

Willy had done better than he would have expected. Ian considered waiting for him to be released, but decided against it. He had to get launched on the trust work and had already lost half a morning to his "special client." He had a good idea on how to get started with the trust investigation.

He thought for a moment more before pulling his phone out of his briefcase and calling Katie.

"How'd it go?" she answered. He gave her a quick description, ending with the confrontation with Marston.

"Couldn't have happened to a nicer guy," she laughed.

"Yeah, well, it was mostly Willy's doing. Listen, since I'm halfway there, I'm going over to the federal courthouse to see Brook. Talk about the trust. In the meantime, start criminal background checks on a Rory Doyle, Edward McMartin, and Sean Callahan. I left McMartin's and Callahan's tax returns on my desk so you can get their socials and full names. I'll get you what you need on Rory Doyle tonight."

"Okay," Katie said. "What level?"

"National. No, Interpol too. Don't worry about the cost."

"Okay," Katie said again, sounding surprised. "And I won't expect you until after lunch. By the way, where is the trust? I wanted to put it in the new file I set up."

"I'll get it to you when I get back," Ian said, wondering how long he could delay Katie from seeing it.

Silence followed. "Alright," Katie finally said. "But I thought I'd leave early this afternoon and head over to check on your mom like you asked."

U.S. ATTORNEY'S OFFICE, FEDERAL COURTHOUSE DOWNTOWN MINNEAPOLIS

The federal courthouse was just a two-block walk from the Hennepin County Courthouse. Brook's office was located on the fourth floor. Ian made his way to the reception desk, where he was waved through.

The office door was open, so Ian peeked in. Shoes were crossed on top of the desk once more, and this time a file folder covered Brook's face. He knocked on the doorframe.

She dropped the file. "What are *you* doing here?"

"Had a hearing in front of Judge Miller."

Brook's eyes narrowed. "Okay. That gets you to the county courthouse. So what are you doing *here*?"

Ian had come planning to ask Brook a favor. Now that he was in front of her, he hesitated. "Actually, uh, I was wondering if you could get me some information for my new case."

Brook sat fully upright, noticing his pause. "This the one with that guy I heard Katie telling you about? Some kind of trust?"

"You've got good ears."

"I'm also snoopy. But I'm a criminal prosecutor. You're mixing up your two specialties again. I told you this would happen."

Ian ignored the jab. "No. The case combines the two. Sort of. I've been asked to do a background investigation on three beneficiaries to find out if they were into any criminal activity since the late 1990s."

Brook processed his words, eyeing him. "Okay. That's easy. Go back to the county courthouse. Go down the escalator. Minnesota public criminal histories are on the computers on B level."

Stretching out the request, even if she was teasing, was only making it harder. "Yeah, Brook. Believe it or not, I knew that. That's already in the works. I was hoping you could use your contacts to get me a more . . . complete picture."

Brook's voice grew cooler. "Meaning you want me to use my contacts at the county prosecutor's office to help you get arrest records and non-conviction prosecutions. Records you shouldn't normally have access to."

No point denying it now. "Yes. Something to impress my client."

"Introduce *me* to your client if that's your goal," Brook said.

"I said *impress*."

"Bold words from a man seeking a favor." She appraised him another moment. "Let's stop beating around the bush. You want Incident Case Reports."

"Yeah." Regret began to blossom in his chest.

"ICRs that are supposed to be *internal*, for prosecutors only. In fact, defense lawyers aren't even supposed to know they *exist*."

"Everybody knows ICRs exist," Ian said solemnly. "You might as well post them on Facebook."

He watched Brook's silence uncomfortably.

"Well, it's true," she sighed at last, "that those reports would let you know if someone had affiliated with gangbangers, drug sellers, scam rings—anywhere there might have been surveillance. Even if they weren't prosecuted or convicted."

Ian nodded, waiting for pushback. "Exactly what I'm looking for."

"But you've also got to know this could put me on the spot. I told you about our ladder-climbing chief prosecutor here. I doubt he'd cut me much slack if he found out."

"Then don't do it," Ian said quickly. "In fact, forget I asked."

"No, no, I'll think about it," she muttered. "Write down the names." Brook pushed a legal pad across her desk.

Ian hesitated before picking up the pen. "You sure?"

"I'll let you know if I won't do it."

He wrote down the names of the three beneficiaries. "We're

still on for dinner tomorrow night, right?" he asked self-consciously.

She nodded. "Except maybe now we're going Dutch."

Ian bowed ceremonially as he left the office. He'd never asked Brook for a favor like this before, he reflected anxiously as he walked back to the elevator. Why'd he do it now?

He stopped. Pondered returning to withdraw the request, then decided against it and kept walking.

He needed this to work. He needed to earn this fee. Now that he was in, he realized how stupid his hesitation had been. And Brook was exaggerating about getting into trouble. He wasn't the first defense lawyer to see an Incident Case Report from a friend in the county prosecutor's office. Besides, there was nothing wrong with doing the trust work, so nothing wrong with pulling in favors to get the job done.

He reached the elevator and pushed the button.

Except if he was so comfortable about the trust, why was he still failing to mention, even to Brook, his dad's connection to it or the fee involved?

11

Sitting in the quiet office with Katie gone, Ian had gotten through the tax returns covering the past twenty years, which Callahan provided for himself and Ed McMartin. Both had lived in Florida most of that time—McMartin was still there. Both had enjoyed livable but unimpressive incomes.

Nothing exciting there.

The trust had also come with a typed history of acquaintances and friends to vouch for McMartin's and Callahan's good behavior, as well as their business activities the past two decades. McMartin had been married until his wife's death six years earlier, with no children. Callahan had never married or had children. Callahan had been running a construction business the last ten years. Before that, he'd listed his occupation as assistant to the trust's creator, the late James Doyle. McMartin ran a hobby store in Port St. Lucie.

Ian spent another hour calling the men's contacts. It was

awkward at first—asking people if they knew whether McMartin or Callahan had engaged in criminal activity. Since none of the contacts so far seemed surprised, he'd finally concluded they'd all been primed for the calls. All answered with an immediate no.

Regardless, he needed to get through them so he could move to another avenue of investigation and keep this rolling. Even if it was boring him to tears. With a sigh, he picked up the list on Callahan to dial the next reference.

3:17 P.M.
MARTHA WELLS RESIDENCE
LYNNHURST NEIGHBORHOOD, MINNEAPOLIS

From under the brim of her sun hat, Martha took in the even rows of bachelor's buttons and marigolds, begonias and spiky blue salvia in her annuals garden bordering the cul-de-sac. Crouched in their midst, she luxuriated in the dissonant colors and shapes buffering the space between her yard and the street.

This afternoon she was planting the flowers she'd failed to plant the week before. She'd only finished half the job the last time she was in the garden bed, leaving some of the bulbs to die in the backyard unplanted. She couldn't recall why. It wasn't like her. Any more than it was like her to have felt so reluctant to return to the garden at all today.

She chafed at such a waste. Abandoning the garden with the planting only partly done? She hoped Connor hadn't noticed.

A red Jeep turned into the cul-de-sac, then into her driveway. Katie Grainger got out with a wide grin on her face. "Martha, doin' your magic again today, I see."

Martha couldn't help but smile back. "Doing my best, anyway. It's *so good* to see you again, Katie. It's been forever."

"I know. Trying to keep your son on task is a challenge these days. Anyway, I got 'work release' to check on you. And it just so happens I've got my workout stuff in the car—complete with sensible shoes. Make room for an assistant and good conversation."

She didn't fully understand Katie's explanation, but her smile widened. "I've got a spot for you by the marigolds," she said. "Go change."

▌4:47 P.M.

Katie groaned and lifted herself from all fours to a sitting position. "Martha," she called across the garden, "I've had enough outdoors." She lifted the sun hat Martha had lent her, rubbing sweat from her forehead with a sleeve. "I don't see how you can do it. I've gotta work up to this much sunlight after a Minnesota winter."

Martha sat back and checked her watch. "You know, Katie, it's getting near five o'clock. I can do the rest. You go on home to Richard and Nicole."

"I think you're right. I'll just go inside and wash up."

Martha thanked her—wondering, as Katie walked stiffly toward the house, how anyone could get their fill of gardening. Gardens were the only places she never felt lost.

She turned back to the soil.

Minutes later, focused on a patch of stubborn weeds, Martha heard the sound of approaching tires. She looked up.

A dark Subaru drew slowly toward her, its tinted windows drawn fully up. Her nerves began to heighten as it passed. It rolled around the circle to stop with the driver's side just a few feet away. The window began to slide down.

Clutching her hand hoe tightly, Martha straightened her back and pulled up the brim of her hat. A man's face appeared.

"It truly is a stunning garden," the man said, smiling.

Martha struggled to return the smile "Why, thank you."

"I especially like the begonias. My mother used to grow them."

She nodded, anxiously waiting for more.

"Martha," he said, "do you remember us talking a few days ago?"

Did she? Had they spoken?

Yes, the memory came suddenly back. In this garden. The last time she'd been here planting the annuals. *But why did the memory make her afraid?*

"I . . . I'm not sure," she answered.

"Well, we did. Saturday morning. I told you I needed the last painting. You told me you didn't have it. I spoke to you just like we're speaking today, right here in your garden."

A ripple of fear began in Martha's stomach and rose like a tide. "I don't know what you're talking about. What painting?"

"You said the same thing last time, Martha. And I still don't believe you. Now I need you to go get the painting for me. Or tell me where it is."

Slightly dizzy, Martha struggled for breath. "I don't know what you're talking about."

"Yes you do, Martha."

Movement caught the corner of Martha's eye. It was Katie, emerging from the house.

Katie's approach tempered Martha's fear a little, and she looked directly back at the man. "You look familiar. Like someone I used to know."

The man's face flashed surprise.

Katie was drawing closer. The Subaru's window began to rise. "I'll be back soon," he said before it shut.

The Subaru pulled gently ahead, rounding the cul-de-sac as Katie reached Martha's side.

"Who was that?" Katie asked. Her eyes widened. "Are you okay, Martha?"

Martha didn't answer as she waited for her heart to slow. "I'm fine," she said at last. "Just a bit too much sun." She waved a hand toward the Subaru as it disappeared. "That was someone admiring the garden. And talking about old times."

12

Looking around the place, Ian concluded that Larry's Bar, if a bit cleaner, could have once been a stop for the U of M law-review crowd—the top students who published the *Minnesota Law Review* journal every year. It was local enough, with no college kids in sight. A little faded. Yep. If Larry bothered to serve craft beers, the upperclassmen might've found it interesting.

Midway through his first year of law school, he'd been invited to join the law reviewers for a Saturday beer tasting. Apparently they invited out top 1Ls every year to vet for recruitment the following year. Ian accepted, and they all met at a microbrewery in East St. Paul.

Counting Ian, there were three 1Ls with the second- and third-year veterans that night. At first, Ian felt flattered by the attention from seniors nearing graduation. But around his third beer, he grew conscious of another layer to the conversation, grounded on knowing nods and insider laughs; a common understanding that law review was a stepping-stone to entitlement to the best jobs and salaries in the downtown offices of Minneapolis, Chicago, or New York—giving law reviewers a leg up on their colleagues for future careers. The beer had turned flat in his mouth as he'd thought of how many of his classmates prayed for *any* decent job coming out of the Great Recession.

Ian woke up the next day with a slight hangover, feeling stupid for judging people he hardly knew, based on simple ambition. Still, the morning-after sourness stayed with him, and that spring he didn't bother applying for law review.

The other two 1Ls with him that evening both joined the journal. Zach Harmon fit in especially well and eventually landed a position with the big-ticket Minneapolis firm of Paisley, Bowman, Battle & Rhodes. Brook Daniels, the second 1L and a new friend at the beer tasting, fulfilled her dream of a job with the Minneapolis U.S. Attorney's Office after graduation.

Neither one's trajectory surprised Ian. What blindsided him was Brook dating Zach right after graduation. Then staying at it, with a few breaks, for five years now.

Ian sipped the dregs of his second beer. What had he expected? They became inseparable friends in law school, but he'd never asked Brook out. Did he think she'd slip into a nunnery to await his exalted invitation? And what had he been waiting for? In fact, what grand, climactic event in his life did he *always feel like he was waiting for?*

He glanced at his watch. Rory Doyle was late. And apparently one beer was his limit, if two set those kinds of memories in motion.

A man slipped through the bar's entrance. Ian doubted it could be Rory, until the guy caught sight of him in the corner and approached. Sliding into his booth, he looked Ian up and down and began playing with the ring on the index finger of his right hand.

For some reason, Ian had expected Rory to be a younger, gentler version of Sean Callahan. He was neither. Sean Callahan and Rory Doyle looked around the same age—early to mid-fifties, around Ian's father's generation. But where Callahan was tall and past-his-prime muscular, Rory was short and all bones and tendons. Where Callahan appeared tightly wired, Rory was drawn and strained. Callahan seemed the predator, Rory the scavenger. The only thing they shared was a stare that made Ian instantly uncomfortable.

"You're the lawyer," Rory said curtly.

"Ian Wells." Ian extended a hand. "Rory, right?"

Rory nodded, still playing with the ring and leaving Ian's hand untouched.

It was better than the Callahan iron-grip alternative, Ian told himself as the bartender approached their booth, a dish towel in his hand. "What do you want, Rory?" he asked.

"Nothing, Larry," Rory said impatiently. "We're fine." The bartender nodded, then moved to an empty table nearby and began clearing glasses.

Ian reached for the trust document in the briefcase at his side. "I'm sure you know that your father's trust—"

"I know *all about* the trust," Rory interrupted. "You don't need to professor me."

Ian paused. "Then you know what I've been hired to do."

Rory began twisting the ring faster, as if he could unscrew his finger. "Yeah, I know. But first, I'm curious what you think about all this. Is it just about the fee to you? Or do you tell yourself you're helping my dad do a *fatherly duty*? Capping Jimmy Doyle's plan to keep his wayward son Rory out of a life of crime."

Ian leaned back, jolted by the unexpected turn of the meeting. "I don't know about your father's motives," he answered carefully. "I wasn't hired to judge. Just to do a job."

Rory laughed before sliding into a rasping cough. "Not hired to judge?" he managed to get out. "That's very good." His coughing slowed. "Very good. Because I thought that's exactly what you were hired to do. Judge if I deserve the money."

"Not exactly," Ian said, shifting uncomfortably. "I'm supposed to confirm a fact about *all* of the beneficiaries of the trust."

"There's the lawyer I expected." Rory's smile stiffened. "The thing is, Dad wasn't worried about Uncle Ed or Sean. They're just in there as a twisted way to look fair. Nope, this is about keeping me out of the money. Except I deserve the money and I'm gonna get it."

Ian opened his mouth to respond, but Rory wasn't finished.

"Tell me something—what kind of thing is a *trust* that it can let a man hide money even after he's dead? Even money that didn't belong to him in the first place?"

"What do you mean?"

Rory shook his head. "Forget it. Ask me your questions."

Ian slowly reached for the pen resting on the pad. The questions he'd written out suddenly seemed shallow and off point. "Do you have a criminal record?" Ian began.

"No. So we done here?"

Ian looked up at a hollow grin. Frustrated, he set down the pen. "Rory, I don't know what we're talking about tonight. I also don't care *who* gets the money. I get paid either way. But I do care about doing my job right. And if you don't cooperate, there's no way I can conclude you deserve a share of the money—which means it all goes to Mr. Callahan, your uncle, and the Church. You want that to happen?"

Rory stopped spinning the ring.

"I'll take that as a no," Ian went on, his mouth tasting of stale beer. "Look, I'm late for another appointment. You'll need to get me whatever can confirm the jobs you've held since the trust was created in 1998, with wage or salary information, your tax returns for those years, plus the names and addresses of your closest relatives. After that, we'll talk again."

He thought he was speaking calmly, but when he looked up, Ian saw more than one person looking over their shoulders or their drinks in his direction.

Rory's grin was gone when he looked back. The man reached into a jacket pocket and pulled out a thick handful of folded papers. "Here's a job list. The only tax returns I filed are there—or my ex has 'em. Lisa Ramsdale. She lives in Mankato. She won't do you much good beyond the tax returns, though. We divorced a few years after my mother died."

Ian glanced at the papers. "I'm told you have children."

Rory nodded. "My daughter, Maureen, lives with her mother in Mankato. My boy, Liam, I lost touch with. Haven't seen him in ten years. But the kids aren't going to know anything more than Lisa."

"How can I reach you if I have questions?"

"Same way Sean Callahan does. Leave a message at the bar."

"That's not good enough," Ian protested. "I've got only six days to finish this after tonight."

Rory shook his head. "You're reporting to Callahan, and I'm not giving him any information on where I sleep."

Before Ian could respond, Rory slid from the booth and stood to leave.

"Wait," Ian said.

Rory looked back impatiently. "What?"

He suddenly wanted an answer to the question that had been a backdrop to his thoughts since meeting Callahan. "Why was my father hired to do the trust?"

The thin man's eyes narrowed. "You serious?"

"Yes."

Rory stared for a moment longer. "You're the investigator. You figure it out."

13

Martha Wells stood in her living room with the lights out, watching through a crack in the shades as Katie Grainger's car finally drove away. The taillights were disappearing from view when she turned the inside lights back on and faced the boxes behind her.

Urgency gripped her. It wasn't the hour. It was the strange sense that her world was dripping away, as though a tiny leak were draining her pool of awareness. Instinctively she knew she soon would be incapable of what she needed to do.

She forced herself to walk among the boxes. They all looked so similar, and already she couldn't quite recall what she was looking for. A particular shape. Weight. Perhaps a color . . .

She was nearing the hallway off the kitchen when one the size of a shoe box drew her attention. Red masking tape made an X near a top corner. She brought it into the kitchen, retrieved a pair of scissors from a drawer, and cut the tape holding it shut.

A sheet of yellowed newspaper lay on top of its contents. She

94

set that aside. Beneath was a pile of random objects. She stared at them for a moment. She could no longer reason why, but she knew this was it. She put the lid back on the box.

But wasn't there another?

Yes. But she'd dealt with that . . . though she couldn't recall how.

What had she planned to do with this one?

Oh. Of course.

Beside the refrigerator was the cupboard with the shelves Martha knew her family had always thought too high for her. She opened the door and stood on her tiptoes. With her fingers she could nudge the coffee cup that had MOM stenciled on its side, making the car keys inside jingle. With her fingertips she could just grasp the edge of the key chain inside and lift it out.

Placing the marked box under one arm, she headed out the back door and onto the concrete stoop leading to the detached garage.

14

Ian opened his eyes. His old room, wrapped in early morning shadows, seemed unfamiliar. He sat up.

A stabbing pain shot through his head from temple to temple.

A stress headache. Ian rubbed his temples. They used to be common. This was the first one he'd had since high school.

Triggered by lack of sleep probably. Or stress. He looked at the white alarm clock on the nightstand. Sleep-deprived or not, he wouldn't be getting any more rest this morning, not with this headache. He cradled his head for a minute longer before plodding down the hall for an aspirin and a hot shower.

His mother's bedroom door was closed, signaling that she was still in bed. Her door had been closed when he'd gotten home from his downtown appointments the night before. On a whim he'd wanted to ask her if she knew anything about Dad's work with the James Doyle Trust—and even contemplated waking

96

her up to do so. But the better part of his nature had prevailed, and he let her sleep.

Shaving at the sink as hot water filled the bathroom with steam, he heard the distant sound of banging at the front door, followed by a muffled call. "Hello! Anybody home? Hello?"

Ian wiped the remaining cream from his face, put his clothes back on, and hurried into the hall. A police car was visible through the living room window, parked on the dark street. His heartbeat picked up as he rushed to open the door.

A stocky, uniformed officer stood on the stoop, thumbs hooked in his belt. "You can't be Connor Wells," he said.

"No," Ian stammered. "I mean, this is his house. But that's my dad. He's deceased."

The officer's eyes widened. "Do you know Martha Wells?"

"Yes. She's my mother."

"Well, then I have your mother in the squad car." He pointed over his shoulder.

"That's not possible." Ian glanced back toward the hallway.

"I'm afraid so. Looks like she was out driving all night and ran out of gas over near Children's Hospital. She's very confused. She asked us to get in touch with her husband, Connor Wells. Claimed she was driving to see him at his office last night. Does she have Alzheimer's? Dementia?"

"Early-onset Alzheimer's," Ian said through a haze of concern. "She alright?"

The officer nodded. "She's fine. A patrol found her seated by the side of the road down on Lake Street looking lost and scared. We confirmed her license was still good, so we didn't ticket her. I take it by your reaction that you didn't know she was out last night."

Ian shook his head, growing self-conscious. "She must have

97

snuck out while I was at a meeting. When I got home, I assumed she'd gone to bed."

The officer looked Ian in the eyes. "You seem appropriately concerned, so I'm returning her to your care. But you may need to look into a memory-care facility. If we have another incident, I'll have to engage State Protective Services. At the very least, my advice is that you take away her keys."

"I thought I had." Ian let out a sigh. "Thanks for helping out."

"It's alright," the officer said. "How about I drive you both to get some gas and pick up her car? Saves you from making other arrangements for a tow."

Ian repeated his thanks and rushed to grab his shoes and wallet.

His mother stared out the passenger-side window as Ian drove the back streets returning to the Lynnhurst home. Her hair was flat and dry, her clothes wrinkled from long wear. Worse, she wasn't speaking, and her eyes had a haunted look that amplified his guilt for having left her alone the night before.

After a few attempts at talking, he'd let her be until they were back inside the garage and he'd turned off the engine. "Mom," he said, finally breaking the silence, "the next time you want to hit the clubs at night, wait for me, will you? I'll be your bodyguard."

His mother didn't look his direction. "I don't know what I did last night," she said in a monotone.

"Well, it doesn't matter," he answered lightly, saddened by the uncommon self-pity in her voice. "We're home now. Why don't you try to get some sleep? I'll come in later and check on you."

She left the car, treading silently out of the garage toward the back door that led to her kitchen. Ian watched the garage door close behind her.

The instant she was out of hearing, he pounded the steering wheel with his fists. *This isn't happening!* Not now. He was *not* moving her out of her house and into a memory-care home. He'd figure something else out. Extend Livia's hours. Hire a night nurse. Move home himself . . .

His hands ached as he took a deep breath, refusing to dwell on the truth—that all options were either unaffordable or impractical.

Unless he could finish the trust work successfully.

As Ian moved to exit the car, his eye caught sight of a box in the back seat. It was shoe-box size, with a red X marked in masking tape on top. Just like the one with the handgun in his trunk. He leaned over the seat and retrieved it.

By the time he'd reached Martha's bedroom, she was already in bed, the covers rising and falling gently. Ian stood for several minutes in the doorway to be sure she was asleep. Quietly he made his way to the bathroom to resume his delayed shower.

When he returned to the kitchen dressed for work, he went first to the box on the table. He noticed the tape that once held the flaps closed had been cut away. He poured himself a glass of orange juice from the fridge, sat down at the table, and opened the box.

Inside was a folded, yellowing newspaper. Ian studied it momentarily, then set it aside. Beneath the paper was a stack of objects. He pulled them out, one by one. Five sets of thin gloves, the leather lining cracked and aging. Two dated-looking ski masks. A screwdriver. Other metal tools he didn't recognize.

All old junk. The sight only made him sadder. What possible reason was there for his parents to keep this stuff among Dad's things all these years—any more than the rest of what lined the living room? And how had this particular box made its way to the car like some special treasure? How far and how quickly was his mother slipping away?

His cellphone rang, startling Ian from his thoughts. With a glance toward the hallway and his mother's room, he answered it.

"Good," Sean Callahan's deep voice rumbled over the line. "I caught you. Meet me at the security desk in the Wells Fargo Building on Sixth Street at eleven tonight."

"Eleven? What for?" Ian asked.

"It's arranged. We can set up the special account at your firm and transfer over the trust funds."

Ian shook his head. "Nobody's going to do a wire transfer at eleven at night."

"Just meet me there," Callahan growled. "Bring an acknowledgment form for everybody to sign after the transfer."

He hung up.

Ian stared at the phone. Another strange night ahead. And he was already dragging from two nights of little sleep.

He glanced once more down the hall. He should stay home today. Take the opportunity to gauge how much his mom's decline was accelerating. But if he did, he couldn't get anything done on the trust. After tonight, he would be down to five days and nights to complete the work.

He *needed* that money. He had to keep working today. Martha would be asleep for hours, probably all day. And if she got up, she'd be fine. She'd been without nightly supervision without a single incident before today. Even during the day, Livia was there only three days a week.

Ian patted his pockets, confirming he still had the keys to his mother's car. He wouldn't make the mistake of leaving them behind again. And he'd check in every few hours, get more help from Katie if necessary.

Ian left a note for his mother on the kitchen table. *Dinner with Brook tonight, but I'll be back early enough for a game of gin if you're up.* Then he went back outside, the box of junk in one hand and the yellowed newspaper in the other, and stuffed both into a garbage can in the garage.

It'd be fine, he told himself as he headed out to his car in the driveway. He just needed to get the trust case done. Afterward he'd look into what could be done for his mom.

It'd be fine.

15

Ian looked up from Rory Doyle's papers in his hand as Katie came through the door.

"Just got back from my morning errands," she said cheerfully. "Wondering if you needed anything."

"I'm okay," Ian said. He told her about Martha's driving incident the night before. "Do you think you could break away again and stop by to see Martha? You know this is all on the clock."

Katie held up a hand. "I know, hon. Really, it's fine. Not a whole lot of work here to fret about. When do you want me to go?"

"Maybe midafternoon. I've got a late appointment, and I'm supposed to meet Brook for dinner tonight. But I'll cancel with Brook if you tell me she's not okay."

"I'll let you know. What's all that?" she asked, pointing to the stacks he'd created.

Ian passed a hand over the piles. "I met with Jimmy Doyle's

102

son last night. This is what he gave me." He dropped a finger onto one of the thicker stacks. "He's got six years of tax returns—mostly from the late '90s and early 2000s. Haven't figured out how he's made a living since then." He moved to a smaller stack. "This is a list of former employers with names of supervisors." Then he lifted a single sheet. "Here's a chronology of Rory's addresses over the years, plus information on his former spouse and his children."

Katie nodded. "You want me to look over the trust document now?" she asked breezily. "See if I recognize it?"

Should he? Ian looked up at his legal assistant's face, which signaled just how badly she wanted to see the details of the trust. "Not now, thanks," he defaulted. "Later."

"Okay." She turned and left.

That was way too easy. It was unlike Katie to let it go without questioning him. He'd have to give it to her sooner or later. Maybe getting somebody in on this would ease his anxiety. Maybe his secrecy was fueling his paranoia.

Tomorrow. Yeah, that made sense. He'd fill her in tomorrow. Things would be clearer by then.

He turned back to the nearest pile.

❚ 12:13 P.M.

The sunlight was still bright in his office as Ian finished another call. Leaning back wearily, he took a long sip from the coffee at his elbow and then picked up the legal pad to review his notes.

He pondered the few useful things he'd learned through a long morning of calling Rory's contacts. The son of Jimmy Doyle had been a real estate agent when his mother died in '98—work he soon gave up. Jobs got progressively rougher and more random after that: driving a forklift, blacktop work, replacing railroad ties for Burlington Northern, a bouncer in St. Paul—which was hard for Ian to imagine given Rory's slim figure. Then the last few years, he'd been jobless.

Several of the businesses were long gone. A few of his supervisors recalled Rory with comments like, "He just didn't show up one day," or, "I liked him, but he was a mess."

An owner of a small house-painting company described the nervous, angry man Ian had met with the night before: "Saw him nearly kill another employee one day. The guy must've known Rory, because he made some remark about his kids. Rory almost took him out. I fired them both on the spot."

If he was psychoanalyzing Rory, that story might have been useful. But that was Adrianne's job, not his. Even so, the story fed a grudging pity for the guy, who must be even more troubled than he looked.

The bottom line: no one even hinted that Rory Doyle, son of Jimmy Doyle, might be into anything "criminal" since his mother's death. There wasn't even a sign he was living beyond his means since the trust was created.

Ian picked up the sheet with Rory Doyle's family information. Lisa Ramsdale, formerly Lisa Doyle, had retaken her maiden name after their divorce finalized in 2000. She was living in southern Minnesota, just outside Mankato. Rory had given Ian her phone number and address.

He reached for the phone and punched in the number. A sleepy voice answered.

"Lisa Ramsdale?" Ian asked.

"Yeah."

"I'm an attorney from Minneapolis."

"An attorney for who?"

"The estate of James Doyle. I've been hired to help distribute some proceeds of the estate. Your ex-husband and children are potential heirs."

He expected a positive reaction—at least at the notion of her children inheriting. Instead the line went dead for an instant. "I've hardly seen Rory for ten years," she said at last. A nervous trill had crept into her voice. "Not since the kids were grown. I've got nothing to say about him."

"Ms. Ramsdale, I said that your children could qualify for the inheritance as well."

"I heard you," she muttered. "Jimmy Doyle's been dead for a decade and he's still haunting us. The money's poison, just like he was. Cursed. It ruined Rory. It's already hurt the kids. I want nothing to do with it."

"I only have a few questions," he rushed before she hung up. "Don't you want to give your children a chance at the bequest? It's a lot of money."

He'd caught her. The line was still active.

"What kind of questions?"

"I need to know whether Rory Doyle was involved in any criminal activity after his mother died."

Her voice dropped a notch. "Why that?"

"I'm sorry, Ms. Ramsdale, I can't say."

He could almost hear the calculation on the other end of the line.

"What happens if I say yes?"

"Please, Ms. Ramsdale. Just the truth. False information could jeopardize your children's entitlement to part of the money."

It wasn't exactly true. It was what Harry Christensen called "an essential untruth"—which he'd defined for Ian as "a lie necessary to get at the truth." Only Talk Show could keep a straight face at the irony of that justification.

"Mom," Ian heard in the background, "who're you talking to?"

The line crackled, as though something had been pressed against the receiver. "I can't do this by phone," the ex-wife said some seconds later. "If you want answers, you'll have to come to Mankato."

Ian thought about the time bleeding away on his investigation. Yet this was an essential witness. "Can you meet with me this afternoon?" he asked.

The phone was muted again with more crackling. "Yes," the ex returned. "Three-thirty."

"Alright. I'll be there." But the line was already dead.

Before he could absorb the idea of an unplanned drive to Mankato, the direct line on his desk phone began ringing.

"Law office," he answered.

"Let's meet early." Brook's voice this time, curt and business-like. "Make it lunch instead of dinner. Today."

Ian stiffened. "Okay. When and where?"

"Kieran's Pub. Now." She hung up.

This had to be about the ICRs he'd asked for. Something must have gone wrong.

Bracing himself, Ian grabbed his jacket and headed for the door.

12:37 P.M.
KIERAN'S IRISH PUB
DOWNTOWN MINNEAPOLIS

There was no live music at this hour at Kieran's. Only the murmurs of the lunch crowd and the competing smells of steak-and-mushroom pie, fish and chips, and burgers. From the entrance, Ian caught sight of Brook sitting at a small table near the back.

She hadn't yet ordered herself a drink, he noticed as he approached the table. Stone-faced, she watched him take a seat.

"Do you know what Ed McMartin, Sean Callahan, and Rory Doyle all have in common?" she asked immediately.

"Is this the lead-in to some kind of Scotch-Irish joke?"

Her expression didn't lighten. "Sorry, no. But don't bother; I'll tell you. *They all knew your father.*"

How could she have learned about his dad drafting the trust? And how stupid did he look now for not telling her in the first place? Before he could say anything, she slid a thick red folder across the table. Ian opened it.

Inside were a stack of Incident Case Reports. He quickly paged through them. From what he could tell, they all had Rory Doyle's name featured on top. Taking another look, he scanned the first pages of each stapled ICR. They dated from the early 1980s, detailing surveillance in northeast Minneapolis—the neighborhood, Ian realized, where his father had grown up.

"What are you telling me here?" he asked.

"That's only the first batch I've come across so far," Brook said. "Now look through them more carefully."

Ian tried to ignore her worrying tone as he turned his attention back to the reports before him. Each one described an event targeted for surveillance—mostly teenage parties at a house or houses in Columbia Heights. Each had a list of the persons identified at the event.

Ian looked up again, shaking his head. "I still don't get it. What is it you want me to see?"

She grabbed one of the reports and opened it up in front of him. "This," she said impatiently.

Her index finger was pressed against the list at the back of the first report. His eyes went to the end of her polished red nail.

22. *Connor Wells.*

Ian made it a point not to show his concern. "Huh," he said evenly. "That's a surprise."

"Yeah. And this," she said, sliding her finger further down.

37. *Rory Doyle.*

Ian could feel Brook scrutinizing him as she continued on. "You'll also find Sean Callahan at most of the same parties the police were surveilling. And four of the parties took place at the home of Ed McMartin, your other guy. The reports don't explain why, but it appears McMartin lent his house out for the teenage parties. The point is, that's the trifecta of your beneficiaries—plus your dad. Apparently Rory Doyle, Sean Callahan, and your father all ran with the same crowd in their teens, a crowd with possible gang ties that warranted surveillance."

Ian nodded, swallowing his reaction.

Brook's expression tightened. "*C'mon, Ian*. Don't act so non-chalant. You tell me you've been hired to check out a bunch of guys' criminal histories for a trust, and out of the blue you find out not only that they were under potential criminal surveillance but that your own father used to run with them. Mild-mannered Connor Wells. Aren't you just a little shocked?"

"Well, yeah, I'm surprised," Ian said, working to stay calm. "But first, I was only hired to look for criminal history on these three going back twenty years, and these reports go back over thirty. Second, like you said, this looks like gang-related stuff.

Just because my dad was at the same parties that included some gangbangers way back then doesn't mean he was one of them—or even that he knew them. Dad grew up in Columbia Heights. That's probably why they crossed paths."

"Knock it off," Brook said dismissively. "You're not arguing a motion, Counselor. You're talking to a friend. A friend who just took a big risk to bring you this information. Aren't you just a teensy-weensy bit curious why your father is showing up with these guys, people somebody thought warranted a criminal check before handing them trust funds? Who also hired *you* of all people to do the investigation?"

"That's not my concern," Ian mustered weakly. "I'm just making a report and distributing cash. If my dad and they were teenage acquaintances, maybe they hired me because of name recognition."

Brook looked about to explode. "Stop lawyering me—and stop sounding so defensive. Also, stop holding out on me. What's going on with this case? How's your father connected to this James Doyle Trust?"

"I'm not sure," Ian said abruptly.

"Really? Okay, show the trust to me."

Ian hesitated. "I can't."

Brook shook her head, then reached across and gathered up the reports, putting them back in the folder.

"You're making me nervous, Ian. First, you used our long friendship to get information. I was okay with that. But then you tell me the contents of the trust are none of my business?"

"Brook, I don't know why you're getting so excited. It's nothing sinister, I promise."

"Really?" Her tone grew cool. "It doesn't bother you that you're using our friendship and won't even explain why? You and I have known each other for eight years, and now you play off it to get something like this—knowing I'll do it but keeping me in the dark."

"You're going the wrong way here."

"Why didn't we get past this in law school?"

"Get past what?" he said.

"The flirting. The friendship. Why didn't you ask me out?"

Ian looked around the room, thrown at the shift in the conversation. "I don't know . . ."

"*That* I can believe," she stabbed back. Ian looked up at eyes that had grown distant. "Listen to you. Asking me Monday how Zach was doing. Like you cared. What's *wrong* with you? And what are you doing with your life? You graduated with honors from law school, then took your dad's little practice in his little office—even tying in with his old partner, making it near impossible to do the kind of legal work you claim you want to do."

A server approached their table, saw their faces, and quickly swerved away.

Ian leaned forward, keeping his voice low. "I'm not sure what's going on here, Brook. I'm sorry about the ICRs. I didn't want you to get into trouble, and I'm sorry I asked. But this trust thing isn't a big deal—at least I don't think it is. I just can't talk about it yet. And I'll admit, my dad being in these reports with the others—that's a surprise, okay? I admit it."

Her eyebrows rose.

"And I'm not ignoring the personal stuff. The truth is . . . I've wondered about what you said too. Really. But I don't have any answers. Not just now."

"You've never liked my dating Zach. So why haven't you ever said anything?"

She wouldn't relent. The pressure boiled over and came out.

"Maybe because I could never picture you interested in me if you'd date somebody like him."

His anger flattened at hearing his own words. It was, he knew instantly, a very bad summary and a half-truth at best.

"Really?" Brook said, dropping to a near whisper. "Well, that's a little late, and weak since you never offered me an alternative. But how about this: maybe I dated Zach all these years because he might be ambitious, but he's never used our friendship to get something for a client. Even if you've never approved of him, Zach's got some notion of where he's going with his life. Anyway, it doesn't matter. Zach and I broke up two months ago."

Ian was stunned. "You said—"

"I know what I said. It was none of your business on Monday. You never made it your business."

"Did you break up because of me?" The words hung, stark, in the air.

Brook closed her eyes and shook her head. "Somebody's thinking way too highly of himself."

Ian finally succeeded in keeping silent. Brook opened her eyes and shrugged despairingly. "At least before this you were a good friend with a decent sense of humor."

She got up and walked away. Ian numbly watched her leave.

He looked back at the table. She'd left the folder lying there. He stood, tucked the folder under an arm, and followed her out of the restaurant.

The streets were more crowded now as he left Kieran's Pub for the blocks of walking back to his office. In the sunshine, people were abandoning the overhead skyways for a breath of fresh air at lunch or maybe some exercise. Ian unconsciously dodged hurrying pedestrians as he walked.

Waiting at a red crossing light, he stopped and pulled the top report from the folder, his chest still aching over his conversation with Brook.

He stared down at the page until someone bumped his shoulder as she passed. He looked up to notice the light was green. Despondently, Ian put the report away.

Why had he been so reluctant to tell Brook the truth? What he said was correct: his father knowing the beneficiaries didn't necessarily mean anything. Then why would he hesitate to explain what he was doing?

Two hundred thousand dollars in fees maybe. Or maybe because he'd met one beneficiary who looked like he wanted to strangle him, and another who ended their first conversation with a threat.

No, the question wasn't why he'd kept the details of the trust from Brook. It was why he wasn't running for the hills himself.

16

Wrapped in a blanket of humidity, Ian felt panic building in his chest. He looked around.

Behind him was a pool. In front, an open patio door. Around each were grown-ups, talking and drinking and paying him no attention.

A man was walking away. Though frightened, Ian felt compelled to follow. He weaved through an ocean of pant legs and dresses as though being dragged in the man's wake.

Ian came to a black piano, which stood like an island in the crowd. By the keyboard was a jowly man with an iced drink in one hand. He glanced down, then raised a stubby finger to point in a different direction.

The crowd parted the way he'd been directed, and Ian took the gap, soon finding himself standing before a closed door. He hesitated. Then he turned the knob and entered, closing the door behind him.

It was a square bedroom with a single window with drawn

shades. A bed occupied the middle with chairs scattered about. A man was seated on the bed.

Ian stared at the seated man. He knew who he was. It was Rory Doyle. To one side of the bed were an old man and a large man, the old one seated with a hat in his hands, the large one leaning against the wall.

A voice stated, "What're they doing here?" Ian turned to see the speaker, a fourth man who he knew instinctively was the man he'd followed from the pool.

"This is my house," the man went on. "They're spitting on her grave by being here."

The old man with the hat in his hand spoke. "Nobody else knows them," he said. "And we've business to handle."

"She was my sister," the man from the poolside said.

"Let it go, boyo." It was the large man, speaking for the first time.

Ian also knew the large one, he realized. He'd seen him in a cemetery—and elsewhere too. His name was Sean Callahan.

"Ian," a voice called from the dark corner by the shaded window. "Be a good boy. Go back to the pool now."

This was a dream—or maybe several dreams shaken together and poured over him all at once. But the voice from the shadows instantly gilded it with a firmer sense of reality.

Fear began bubbling from Ian's every pore. He wanted to run to the voice—for protection or to protect, he wasn't sure. Even if he couldn't see her, he knew it was his mother speaking, and that from her dark corner she was the only possible source of safety in this room.

Ian also knew, with a son's certainty, that his mother was very afraid.

Ian opened his eyes tentatively. The tension headache was drilling into his forehead again this afternoon. He looked about, gaining his bearings.

He was lying on the love seat in the office library. The ICR reports were on the floor beside him. He'd lain down to rest after his meeting at Kieran's with Brook and before heading to Mankato.

Within seconds of awaking, he could recall only the vaguest details of his dream. It was enough, though, to know he was creating a mosaic in his sleep around the people and events confronting him in this case and in his life.

It wasn't a pleasant picture.

Katie's heels approached down the hallway an instant before she appeared in the library door.

"Good," she said. "You're up. You said you wanted to get going about now."

Ian rubbed his face. "Yeah. Thanks."

Katie shook her head. "You want me to stay overnight with your mom?"

"No," Ian said. "I'll do it. Maybe I can get caught up on my sleep this weekend. If you could just cover the afternoon like we talked about."

Katie nodded. "Done. Oh, by the way, those criminal background checks came back this morning. Nothing on Ed Mc-Martin, Sean Callahan, or Rory Doyle."

"No criminal records at all?"

"None. Nada. I'd asked for only twenty years back, but they reviewed them back to 1985. On all three guys."

Ian was taken aback. Before his nap, he'd reviewed the ICRs Brook had given him. Given the surveillance, he'd expected at least one of them to have an adult criminal record. What did that mean about his concerns?

"Okay, thanks," he replied.

Ian rose and went into his office to grab his sports jacket.

Maybe he shouldn't be so worried. Maybe he was letting Brook's accusations make him too touchy about the case.

He headed back into the hall. As he passed her at the reception desk, Katie looked up.

"Got everything you need?"

"Yeah," Ian said. "Get ahold of Harry and ask him if he can find time to call me on my cell. Tell him I want to find somebody on the 'other side' of the criminal defense business."

Katie nodded. "He'll know what that means?"

"He should."

Ian took the stairs down to the parking garage. He'd made real progress today. If things went well with Rory's ex and Harry came through, he might get his report done despite the short time limit. Take the money and move on to other priorities— like what he could do for his mother with the cash and how he should handle the malpractice case.

He slid into the Camry.

And what he'd do about everything personal Brook had resurrected at Kieran's.

17

"So how's the referral working out?" Harry asked the instant Ian accepted the call via the Camry's Bluetooth.

Ian was watching for the exit into Mankato. Distracted, it took a moment to remember what Harry meant. "You mean the woman you referred on Monday? She hasn't called yet."

"That's a surprise. You got her retainer I sent over, though, right?"

Ian thought for a second. "Haven't checked. I'll confirm with Katie."

"Good. Oh, before I forget, my legal assistant has a sister you might hit it off with."

Just like Talk Show, turning one conversation into three simultaneous ones, without the complication of anyone actually joining on the other side.

Ian ignored the blind-date offer. "I've got a situation," he began instead. "I need somebody who knew the crime scene in the Twin Cities going back to the mid-1990s or before. Somebody

117

on the street level who'd be willing to tell me if they recognized some clients as having been active in crime back then."

"That's easy," Harry snorted. "Anthony Ahmetti."

The name rang no bells. "Who's that?"

"I don't blame you for not knowing. He goes back a ways. Got his start when Elvis was doing *Jailhouse Rock*. He's got to be pushing his mid-eighties now. Just got out after a long-overdue, late-in-life stretch in Club Fed."

"Could he help?"

"Sure. He had his fingers in everything at one time. If anybody alive could recognize your clients, he could. The question is whether he'd be *willing* to help you."

"How do I find this Ahmetti?"

"He's private. I've tapped in a few times when I needed a history lesson for a case. I always came away with a slimmer wallet. But I can reach out. Anything more you can share?"

"I can't explain much," Ian said. "You can tell him none of the guys I want checked out are in trouble, as far as I know. In fact, they know I'm doing the search. I need the history due to a strange condition in a trust for someone named Doyle. And it's urgent. Very urgent."

"Okay," Harry answered. "Look, I've gotta go. Give me the full name on the trust and I'll try to set you up with Ahmetti."

"James Doyle," Ian replied.

"Okay," Harry said. "I'll see what I can set up for you. And think about my assistant's sister."

Twenty minutes later, Ian's GPS announced he was nearing his destination, a little green rambler on the outskirts of Mankato. Ian was struck by the contrast with Callahan's Summit Avenue house in St. Paul. Callahan's place was a small palace in decline, while this modest house was neat as a pin—the lawn carefully mowed, garden hose neatly coiled near the front stoop, a new roof.

He sat for a while in the car, gathering himself before heading to the door. On his second knock, the door swung open.

The young woman who answered had crimson hair falling across her cheeks to her shoulders. She wore little makeup on pale, freckled skin, which only accentuated the redness of her hair. Dressed in a red T-shirt and tight jeans, Ian guessed she was just a few years older than him.

She stared at Ian. "Yes?"

"I'm looking for Lisa Ramsdale."

The woman nodded. "You must be the lawyer. Yeah, she had to run some errands."

Ian felt his face grow hot. "I drove straight here from Minneapolis because she told me she could meet with me at three-thirty."

"Well, I'm Lisa's daughter, Maureen. Rory's too. Mom said I should meet with you instead." Maureen turned away, leaving the front door open.

Swallowing his anger, Ian followed. The living room was sparse but immaculate. He took a seat on a small sofa. Books were piled neatly on several tables, one lying open next to a notebook. Maureen sat across from him, a glass at her elbow. She picked up a notebook beside the glass with her right hand, a pen with her left, and began doodling.

After a moment of silence, she looked up to catch Ian's eyes boring into her as he tried to figure out what she was doing. "I'm working on a nursing degree," she explained. "That's why I'm living with my mother. And don't mind this—I doodle to relax. So, Mother tells me you were hired to represent my grandfather's estate. Go ahead with your questions."

Ian shook his head as she looked down at her pad.

Well, he was here. "What you said isn't exactly true," he began. "I told her I was hired to investigate your father on a matter related to the estate."

She looked up at him again. "I always thought lawyers should be taller. And heavier. And have shorter hair."

"Sorry to disappoint," Ian said, smoldering. "They let all kinds into law school."

"Oh, I'm not that easily disappointed. I just assumed that no matter how they went into law school, they all came out pretty much the same."

He wasn't sure how to respond to that, so he said nothing.

"Mother believes my grandfather's money is dangerous," Maureen said. "Isn't that a strange notion? She's always thought that. Now she thinks I shouldn't take any of it. Like it's part of something bad."

The words resonated uncomfortably with Ian as he recalled Rory's comments. He wanted to get to his questions, but instead found himself asking, "You believe that?"

She set the pad and pen on a side table. "I believe it's not that easy—giving it a label and then just walking away. Some people think *all* money's bad. Well, what if my grandfather's money *is* cursed? Maybe I can lift the curse, use it in better ways than somebody else. Maybe I'm *supposed* to have the money. Maybe I *deserve* the money." Her eyes tightened on Ian. "What do you think?"

Ian shook his head at what he was being drawn into. "I don't believe in curses. Just actions and consequences and some credit for good intentions."

She smiled and leaned back. "Wow, you sound like a lawyer *and* a philosopher."

"Not really." Ian's irritation was morphing into embarrassment. "Could I get to my questions now?"

"Sure, but I already know what you're going to ask," said Maureen. "Mother told me. You want to know if my father committed any crimes after my grandmother died. I was only twelve when that happened. That was just two years before my parents divorced."

"Sometimes parents confide in their children," Ian said, "especially in a divorce. And sometimes children know more than their parents would ever suspect. Even at age twelve."

Maureen smiled. "Isn't that the truth? But here's the thing—I can't tell you about anything criminal my dad may have been involved in. And before she went out, I asked Mom what she would tell you. She said she didn't know of anything either. Mom's always said that Grandpa and Dad did some messy things, and Dad never recovered—and it finally killed their marriage. She's never explained what it was and I don't care. To me, Rory was just the dad who disappeared when I was still a teenager. Except for gifts on my birthday and at Christmas, and the occasional guilty call, he's been gone, out of our lives. But as for Dad being into any real crime after Grandma's death? No. My mother said she didn't know of any."

Ian thought about the amount of money that made up the trust and Rory's comment about its source. "Did you ever hear that your father or grandfather might have been involved in any criminal activity *before* your grandmother's death?"

Her smile grew coy. "Now you want to know about my grandparents. That goes back even further. How much do you remember when you were that young?"

Ian shrugged. "Not much. But even twelve-year-olds see things, hear things. Or maybe you've heard family rumors?"

Maureen shook her head. "I don't listen to rumors, even family ones, and I certainly don't pass them on. And even if I did, ten minutes' conversation with a philosopher-lawyer doesn't make you family."

Nothing was coming of this, Ian realized. He glanced at his watch. "Would your brother, Liam, have any more information? Was he close to your father?"

"Very close, at one time," she answered. "But he left town years ago, moved to California. He's only in touch once in a while."

"You're twins, right?" Ian recalled Callahan's description.

Maureen nodded. "But Liam never got over the divorce, even after all these years. Mom's always said he was another casualty of a dysfunctional family."

"I'm going to need any tax returns or financial records your mother has for Rory," Ian said.

"There are none. I helped Mom clean out all that stuff years ago."

After a ninety-minute drive, this was all he got? He could have covered this ground on the phone.

"So how much money are we talking here?" Maureen asked.

Ian considered giving her a figure, but after the runaround he decided against it. "A lot," he replied. "But there's no guarantee."

She shrugged. "I've learned not to believe in guarantees when it comes to money." Then she smiled again. "But just in case the money comes my way, why don't you leave a card so we can talk about how you define 'good intentions.'"

18

Ian's phone rang just as he reached St. Peter on his route back to the Twin Cities. He glanced at the screen's readout, saw it was Harry Christensen, and pressed a button to answer through the Bluetooth. "Yeah, Harry."

"Hey, I heard back from my man Ahmetti."

"That was quick. What'd he say?"

"He'll take a meeting with you."

"When?"

"Tonight at eight. Doggy's Bar on Hennepin Avenue."

Not tonight, Ian thought. Not with the meeting at the bank at eleven and needing to see his mother. And really, not Doggy's.

"C'mon, Harry. Doggy's was probably a dive back when John Dillinger still came to town. How about a club in the Warehouse District? Any place that opened *after* Kennedy was president."

Harry laughed. "It's where he said to meet. I think he's old-fashioned. And be prepared to negotiate. He said yes so quick I'm sure he's got a price in mind."

123

"How will I know him?"

Another bark of laughter. "I described you. Scrawny lawyer, in over his head. He'll see you coming, trust me."

"Wiry, not scrawny," Ian replied.

"Hey, confirm you got that retainer for me."

Ian said he would, then ended the call.

Another long night. At least after the first meeting he could still sandwich in some time to spend with his mother.

The phone rang again.

"Willy's here at the office," Katie said when he answered. "He's brought over the original charging papers and more information about his case. Says he can meet with you when you're ready to talk."

Not tonight, that was for sure. "Maybe tomorrow. Or tomorrow night. Maybe we can meet someplace. Ask him where he's living now."

Silence. "He's living over on the northeast side." She gave Ian an address.

It was near Larry's Bar. "Okay. Tell him I'll give him a call." How much could he cram into a single night?

He accelerated the Camry as he left St. Peter in the rearview mirror.

A knock on her doorframe pulled Brook's eyes off the computer screen displaying the brief she'd been trying to write the last four hours since "lunch" with Ian. Brook looked up to the office's newest law clerk from St. Thomas Law School, diminutive and fresh-faced, holding a stack of papers in her hand. Chloe something. Chloe Moore.

"I heard you were looking at ICR reports on a few people," the young clerk said eagerly.

Brook flinched. She'd had her legal assistant retrieve the reports from a buddy at the Hennepin County Prosecutor's Office, but it was supposed to have been confidential. How did the law clerk learn about it?

"Yeah. Doing a favor for someone. But keep it to yourself, will you?"

"Sure," Chloe said. "But I saw the names you were checking and dug into anything the FBI or Federal Strike Force might have shared with us on the same names." She held up the stack of papers.

Brook groaned inwardly at the expansion of this mess. "That's great, but I'm good."

"Oh . . . you don't want these?"

Brook forced a smile. "Sure. Thanks. Leave them on the desk."

Clearly disappointed, Chloe turned and slipped from the room.

She was getting nothing done, Brook fumed. All thanks to Ian. It ticked her off in a serious way that he was getting to her. Why should *she* be the one bothered about the scene at Kieran's when it was Ian who was displaying the emotional intelligence of a maple?

Except it was *she* who'd turned a talk about ICRs into an autopsy of their friendship and its limitations—even bringing up Zach, for heaven's sake. Stupid, stupid, stupid—

Another knock startled her.

"What is it?" she said, looking up.

Eldon Carroll, her boss, stood in the doorway.

"Brook Daniels! Glad to see you're in."

Brook forced another smile. So her long walk after lunch with Ian had been noticed. "Sorry for the outburst, Eldon. I'm a little . . . behind today. And I had a long lunch with a friend."

Eldon nodded tersely. "Fine. Fine. You're here now. Which is good because I want to bring you in on something." He stepped into her cramped office and took a chair, a thick folder in his hands. "You may have gotten wind that I've put together a team on a new case."

"Heard rumors, yes," she replied.

"Well, it's really not a new case. It's actually a cold case that's gotten new life." Eldon's eyes began to light up. "This one could get some attention. Certainly the *Star Tribune* and *Pioneer Press*. Maybe national."

Emotionally winded, Brook had trouble mustering the expected enthusiasm. "Okay" was all she got out.

"Last week," he went on, "the FBI let us know they'd learned of some bills being circulated. Twenties going back to a theft and murder at a small art gallery thirty-five years ago—in St. Louis Park."

"How do they know the bills are related?" she asked.

"Because the gallery got some cash at the bank before the heist, and the proprietor noticed they were fresh bills—as it turns out, sequenced. He pocketed a few that didn't get stolen, enough to put out a bulletin on any related twenties after the rest of his cash and some big-time art was stolen. Anyway, last week a Wells Fargo branch got an anonymous call about 'hot twenties' coming in. They started scanning all the Jacksons they were collecting and, lo and behold, half a dozen came up from the old watch list."

Eldon looked at Brook as though awaiting a reaction.

"That's pretty exciting," Brook said, a little too late.

"*Exciting?* It's a lot more than that. Then on Tuesday, we got another big hit of the bills." Eldon shook the file in his hands. "This is serious business, Brook. The St. Louis Park job was, and still is, the *largest art theft in Minnesota history*. One that's had everyone clueless for over three decades. We catch the bad guys on this, it'll be a big mark for all of us."

He sounded as though he was ready to measure the Minnesota Attorney General's office for furniture, Brook thought. Or maybe even a Senate office.

But he was right. This could be a career maker. "Who are we working with at the FBI?" she asked.

"The stolen art section's a little shorthanded for a couple of weeks, but we got a young agent assigned: Special Agent John Soukup. I said we'd pitch in. I've already got Cassidy Morrow doing legal research. You know Cassidy, right? And I want you to follow up on this." He handed Brook a portion of the file.

She opened it. Inside was a multi-page FBI memo titled Deposits. "You say there was a tip about these deposits?"

"Yep. Somebody called it in."

"Isn't that a little strange? Who spends hot money, then calls in a tip about it?"

Eldon's voice dropped a notch. "Could be a perp with a grudge. Maybe an anonymous store clerk who handled a bunch of old bills that still looked new. They got suspicious but didn't want to get involved."

That last one sounded like a stretch, Brook thought. Who suspected a crime just by seeing a handful of thirty-five-year-old twenties?

Still, she could hear the cracking of thin ice underfoot from her last question. "So you want me to follow up on trying to trace the depositors who might have handled the twenties?"

"That's right," Eldon said. "Reach out to them and see if we can narrow this down quickly based on the age of the depositor, businesses versus personal, that kind of thing. I'm also putting Cassidy to work combing the list of suspects from the investigation back in the day—seeing who's still alive and in Minneapolis. We'll then cross-reference with each one you find. As a starting point, Wells Fargo has helped by narrowing the deposits to two hundred seventy-seven potential cash depositors at three possible branches."

Brook thought it over . . . 277, several days of grinding work at least. "Okay, chief. I'll get on it right away."

Eldon grinned. "Put your heart into it, Brook. This could be *huge*. For everyone involved."

Brook nodded enthusiastically. "*Got it.*"

Only when he was gone did Brook let out a sigh. She reread the memo. The list of depositors had been broken down by branch. She scanned the list, wondering where to start.

The good news was that maybe this would get her focus off Ian in a way her brief hadn't. Maybe.

Pushing aside the stacks on her desk—including the new one from Chloe—she spread out the depositor list and reached for her phone.

19

Ian approached the scarred wooden door of Doggy's Bar. Beside the door was a glass display case featuring tonight's acts.

He shook his head. He was too young to have known Hennepin Avenue in the days when clubs like this ran from end to end, mixed with flophouses and bars. But he'd seen pictures and read the stories about when this strip was the center for sports betting in America, with speakeasies and worse as thick as flies, and bank robbers like Dillinger and Al Karpis walking the street unafraid. By the time Ian was old enough to venture downtown alone, those days were long gone. Places like Doggy's were the stubborn bits of driftwood in a gentrifying sea of new stadiums and office buildings from Nicollet Avenue to the Warehouse District, from the Mississippi River to the Basilica of Saint Mary.

Taking a deep breath, Ian pushed open the door and stepped inside. The bar looked a lot like Larry's except in deeper decline. Its now-empty stage was set back to one side of a wooden bar, scratched and in need of polishing. A stale smell hung in the air. The low light suggested dinginess awaiting a wrecking ball.

As Ian's eyes slowly adjusted, he saw there were only a few people camped out at the bar and tables—an older group, with hardly a face under fifty.

He felt somebody come up from behind.

"Excuse me." A massive hand circled his body with a metal wand.

Startled, Ian asked over his shoulder, "This some kind of a frisk?"

There was a snort, followed by a low rumble. "You're not the kinda guy likely to come in here with a gun. You're the kinda guy likely to come in here with a tape recorder." The thick hand slapped his shoulder. "Mr. Ahmetti's in the corner booth."

When Ian glanced behind him, the man had already slipped into the shadows beside the entrance door.

He walked to a booth in the back. No one was sitting nearby, as though a ring had been drawn around the table defining a no-man's-land. Ahmetti sat with his back to the wall, a clear drink on ice before him. White hair crowned a lined face and sharp, appraising eyes. Like an ancient accountant, Ian thought. He looked up as Ian approached.

"I appreciate your meeting me, Mr. Ahmetti," Ian said, taking a seat.

"Sure. I've got plenty of time these days."

Tired as he was, Ian didn't try to make small talk with an eighty-year-old, recent ex-con. Instead he launched right in. "I need to know something about a few people I'm told you might have known."

"Yeah. Don't tell me. We're talking about Rory Doyle, Sean Callahan, and Ed McMartin, right?"

"Right," Ian said, surprised. "How'd you know?"

"'Cause Talk Show told me something about beneficiaries of a trust and Jimmy Doyle, and that's the likeliest crew to be involved in something like that."

Apparently Harry had picked the right guy. "I need to know if any of them was involved in criminal activities from 1998 up to the present."

Ahmetti settled back and crossed his arms. "Care to tell me why that question?"

"I can't," Ian said. "Attorney-client privilege." A necessary lie.

Ahmetti shook his head. "That's a load. But I don't really care."

"Then will you help me?"

Ahmetti settled in deeper, looking unhurried. "So you're pegging this around the time Rory Doyle's mother died, huh?"

Another surprise hit Ian.

"Don't look so wowed," Ahmetti said. "I nearly went to Christina's funeral. Couldn't make it because of a business matter. But I knew Jimmy."

"You knew James Doyle?"

"Everybody knew Jimmy. Everybody in the know, anyway. Jimmy kept his head down, under the radar. Still, he was high in the business."

The conversation was taking a turn Ian hadn't prepared for. "What are we talking about here?"

Ahmetti smiled grimly. "Ever heard of Kid Cann?"

He had. Ian felt his stomach clench.

"Jimmy was part of the Kid's system," Ahmetti went on. "The liquor racket that replaced prohibition. You must know this, in your line of work. The Kid cornered the market on liquor licenses, with the help of a lot of grease and easy-to-buy officials. Anybody wanted a license to sell liquor in the Twin Cities, they'd go to the Kid. The system held up into the seventies. Of course, by the time Christina died things were very different. Minnesota guys like the Kid and Davie Berman, who'd been respected back in their day, they were gone. At their height, they were like Meyer Lansky out East, or Capone in Chicago—who left the Twin Cities alone out of respect for Cann and the rest of 'em. But by the eighties and nineties, they were all like old smoke. Nobody knew where they'd gone. The average person around town never even heard of 'em."

"You're saying James Doyle worked for Kid Cann," Ian said, stunned, "that he was operating in organized crime here in the Twin Cities?"

Ahmetti's expression slid into disappointment. "I thought you were Talk Show's friend. 'Organized crime.' Lawyers love labels. Lawyers organize an industry charging five hundred an hour to people who don't want to hire them. Kid Cann gave services people desperately wanted for a tenth of the price. And Cann was the 'organized criminal.' Since your generation doesn't like hurtin' people's feelings, let's use the phrase *undocumented money transfers*."

Ian stared across the table, his original questions all but forgotten. "Did James Doyle build his estate with illegal money?"

Now Ahmetti looked amused. "So you're adding Jimmy Doyle to the list of characters you want to know about? Let me see: Jimmy Doyle, Rory Doyle, Ed McMartin, Sean Callahan. I'm gonna need a scorecard. And we haven't even talked about compensation."

Ian paused. "What do you want?"

"I'm a simple man these days, Mr. Wells. Life gets that way after eighty."

"What do you want?" Ian asked again, keeping his tone respectful.

Ahmetti shook his head. "You're young and haven't got a ring. But someday you'll see: children are the joy and the bane of life. Great to age ten, a crapshoot after that. You can raise 'em to respect themselves and still they disappoint."

Ian nodded quietly.

"My brother's grandson, my grandnephew," Ahmetti said, "he got caught selling oxycodone at his high school. Quite a thing, don't you think? An eighteen-year-old selling a prescription medication to get high. I suppose it's higher class than glue. Anyway, I want the charges dropped."

"I'm not a prosecutor," Ian said.

"Yes, but your friend Brook Daniels is. And she's gotta have friends at County."

This time Ian didn't even try to hide his surprise. "I don't know how you learned that, but I can't get that for you. Trust me on this."

Ahmetti shrugged. "Another disappointment. For both of us."

Answers he wanted felt inches away. "I can't get any favors from Brook Daniels, but I can get your grandnephew free representation. I'll do it myself if I have to. And if he hasn't got a record, he'll walk without jail time. Probably need a program, but no jail time."

Ahmetti's eyes seemed to cloud over. "You'd promise that, would you? Don't underestimate me, Mr. Wells. Old as I am, making me a promise you may not be able to fulfill could still be risky."

Ian felt his stomach churn some more. "I can make it happen," he said, wondering if his three necessary lies in a day were bad luck.

"What I'm asking—what you're offering—it's nothing," Ahmetti said. "But I'm going to take it anyway. Mostly because I don't care what happens to Rory Doyle or the rest of 'em, but also because now you have me curious to see if you can deliver for my grandnephew. We've got a deal. Now, what do you want to know?"

Ian quickly sorted his priorities. The last question came spilling back. "Was Jimmy Doyle's estate made up of illegal money?"

Ahmetti paused. "Come back to that one. Ask me another."

Ian hesitated. "Tell me about Rory Doyle. I need to know whether he was into anything criminal after the mid-nineties."

The elderly man turned thoughtful. "What happens to Rory if I say yes? His old man plant some poison pill in his will or something? 'Cause that would have been Jimmy all over."

Ian's discomfort deepened at Ahmetti hitting so near the truth—again. "I thought we had a deal," he replied.

He leaned toward Ian and nodded. "The young Doyle had a habit of taking things that weren't his own in his day."

Ian felt unexpected disappointment. "How do you know that?"

Ahmetti smiled. "Did you know that Ahmetti's an Albanian name? People think I'm connected, but how many connected Albanians are there? Still, what people assumed about me brought me business. As a middleman."

"You fenced," Ian said.

"I helped with 'undocumented asset transfers.' Before my retirement, not a stereo, gemstone, or sports cars got resold in the Twin Cities that I didn't know about."

"What kinds of things did you help Rory Doyle resell?"

Ahmetti pursed his lips. "This. That. Things removed from homes and businesses when the owners weren't around."

"Burglaries."

"Your word."

"After his mother died?" Ian asked.

"I wasn't keeping a timeline. But yes. For a while after his mother passed."

This was it. This would satisfy Callahan. "How about Sean Callahan or Ed McMartin?"

Ahmetti shook his head. "They were employed with Jimmy back in the day. But after '98? I know nothing about those guys being in the business in that time frame."

"And you knew about everything that moved?"

The smile again. "I knew everything that moved."

"So, back to James Doyle's estate—"

Ahmetti held up a hand. "I don't know every way Jimmy made his money. He started as part of Kid Cann's organization back in the fifties, and Cann or his people were still operating into the seventies. That's all I can tell you. But Jimmy was one of the smart ones, never spent a day in the state pen or Club Fed. What money he saved and where it came from, I don't know. I can tell you this, though: by the early eighties, with Cann out of business, Jimmy was looking for work. Cann's liquor business had dried up and, like a lot of guys from Cann's organization, Doyle was hurting for money. Later I heard he'd retired in Florida."

Retired with nine million dollars—or a nest egg he grew to nine million.

Ian took a deep breath. All this begged another question he was almost too worried to ask. "I've got another name for you. Connor Wells. Was he mixed up with Kid Cann's organization?"

Ahmetti wrinkled his brow. "Connor Wells. Relative of yours?"

"My father. Ever heard of him being mixed up in the Cann rackets?"

"Can't say that I have," Ahmetti said. "Nope. And now, it's getting late. If we have nothing else—"

"What about Rory?" Ian interrupted. "About him being into

. . . undocumented transfers after his mother's death—what proof can you give me?"

"You doubt my word?"

"My client may want more proof."

Ahmetti looked to his drink again. Then he looked past Ian's shoulder and cocked his head.

A mountain of a man appeared just seconds later. Ian noticed his thick hands and knew instantly he was the guy who'd checked him for recording devices at the door.

"Prima," Ahmetti began, "tell Mr. Wells here whether Rory Doyle was still bringing us product after his mother died—after 1998."

The man looked like he was in his mid- to late forties, which meant he could have known Rory back then. He turned his big head and stared at the ceiling for a moment before nodding dutifully. "Sure," he said. "He was."

Ahmetti nodded. "And tell Mr. Wells how you know he was still engaged in the business after '98."

"Because he told Mr. Ahmetti he was getting out and then sold some product the same day. That was the fall of '99."

"Now tell Mr. Wells how you know it was '99."

The big man's face grew more animated. "'Cause that was the year Fernando Vargas beat Winky Wright to keep his IBF light-middleweight crown. Wright had just dumped the Acaries brothers as managers. Vargas opened up in the bout with—"

"That's fine, Prima," Ahmetti cut in. "Thanks, you can go now."

With a look of disappointment, Prima turned and ambled away.

Ahmetti smiled. "Prima's a regular savant with dates and events, so long as he can tie 'em to boxing. Satisfied?"

Rory was into crime a year after Christina Doyle's death. It wasn't real proof. It was hearsay. No solid details, just the recollection of a boxing-obsessed giant. Even so, it was the kind of proof Callahan would likely accept.

"Just one final question," Ian said. "My father—Connor Wells—he represented Jimmy Doyle's estate at one time. If he wasn't associated with . . . Cann's business, do you know why Jimmy Doyle would hire him?"

For a moment, Ahmetti looked as though he was going to refuse to answer. Then with a nod, he said, "Since it's about family, this one's on the house. Your dad and Jimmy, they may have had a family tie. I stress 'may have.' Just a theory. But I say it because, in his corner of Cann's business, Jimmy *always* worked with relatives. Rory. Sean. Ed. Jimmy didn't trust anybody who wasn't blood—or very, very close."

9:15 P.M.
MARTHA WELLS RESIDENCE
LYNNHURST NEIGHBORHOOD, MINNEAPOLIS

Ian parked the Camry next to his mother's car in the garage this time, circling outside to pick up the paper. The headache was gone, replaced by deadening fatigue so powerful that he nearly missed the note tacked at eye level on the front door:

> *Gardened with Martha till after dinner. She got a little cooked, but was her usual joyous self. Let me know what else I can do.*
>
> *Katie*

He doubted his mother had been up for much gardening after her long night. The note must have been there since the day before, missed when he'd come home in the dark. Regardless, Ian was swept with gratitude for Katie. He'd call to thank her again later. But now he wanted to focus on Mom.

He found Martha sitting on the back porch, staring distantly across the yard. Her expression quickly cleared as she looked up at his approach.

"Ian! I didn't hear you come in."

He took off his sports jacket and dropped onto a deck chair. "Sorry I've been so busy. I know I've been neglecting you this week. Everything okay?"

His mother shook her head dismissively. "Fine. Katie was here for a couple of hours but left before supper."

Ian nodded, pleased at his mother's better mood and memory after the adventures of the night before. Her eyes seemed clearer than he'd seen in weeks. Maybe, he told himself hopefully, the driving incident was an aberration.

For several minutes, he tried to prime a conversation around their usual subjects. Despite her improved mood, nothing seemed to catch.

"Mom," he said at last, "can you handle getting beat at gin by your oldest child?"

His mother's eyes smiled back. "I'll play if you're prepared to shed tears, tough guy."

The season was too early for bugs yet late enough to avoid a chill. Evening shadows veiled Martha's face until Ian could imagine being back in a time when they'd play cards on nights like this after Father and Adrianne disappeared for sleep—sharing sights and sounds that his early-to-bed dad and sister never knew. Like thin, gray clouds drifting across the face of a spring moon. The horn of a distant locomotive on quiet summer air. Dried leaves clattering across the yard in a fall breeze. The memories eased him, though he recalled that back then his mother rarely lost except on purpose. Now he was passing on winning cards to let his mom enjoy an occasional "gin."

"You know," his mom piped up as she sorted a hand, "my grandmother used to be quite the poker player."

Ian looked up. "Poker?"

"Oh yes. Your great-grandmother Netti lived on a farm near Madelia, and she and her husband, Orville, would have folks over for cards. She loved poker, so they'd usually end up playing five-card stud. Anyway, she had a glass eye, you see, and when the playing got a little more serious, she'd take it out. Didn't even put on her patch."

"Why?"

"She said it kept her opponents from noticing her tells."

Ian laughed. They so seldom talked about his mother's parents or grandparents anymore. "You knew her growing up?"

"I did. Heard some great stories. I was so sorry you didn't really have any relatives around growing up."

He hadn't. Martha had been raised by her mother, a single parent who, Martha long ago confessed, had borne her one daughter out of wedlock—a great stigma in her day in an Irish Catholic family. Maybe that contributed to her passing before Ian was old enough to know her. His grandparents on his father's side had also died young. Neither parent had siblings, so cousins, aunts, and uncles weren't part of his and Adrianne's experience.

He reached for a card, deciding that, with the mood high, now would be a good time to broach the trust. "Mom," he began, "you worked with Dad at the office in his early years. Were you aware of Dad doing a trust for a James Doyle?"

"Your father handled hundreds of trusts," she replied.

"This would have been different. Dad not only did this particular trust, he also got assigned the job of distributing the funds after a period of time. We're talking lots of money, with a very big fee attached."

Her face swung toward him. He tried to read her blank eyes. "Why are you asking, dear?"

"Because I've been hired to do the work instead."

She looked down and picked up his discard. "Are you going to do it?"

"I already am. But it's getting . . . strange. Strange people. Strange circumstances."

"Then maybe you should stop. You know what your father always said. '*Actions have consequences.*'"

Ian hesitated. "Actually, Mom, that was your saying."

"Was it? Well, it's just as true. It sounds like you should stop."

Ian heard the gong of the grandfather clock in the living room and pulled out his phone to confirm the time. Ten-thirty.

He set his cards down on the table. "You win, Mom, I've gotta go. But think about whether you remember anything on the James Doyle Trust, will you?"

"Of course. And you missed gin by a card," she said, laying down her hand.

Ian slipped his jacket back on and went out the front door to a choir of tree frogs across the street serenading the moon.

He was anxious to get this bank meeting over with and then get some sleep. At least he'd had some time to spend with Mom, as well as a chance to see her doing better tonight.

Almost her old self, he concluded as he circled the cul-de-sac and headed up the street past a darkened Subaru.

20

A heavyset man in a suit appeared on the opposite side of the glass doors of the Wells Fargo Building, a security card in his hand. As Ian watched, he slid it through a card reader. The door unlatched with a click and Ian walked through.

Sean Callahan was standing in the empty lobby beside the vacated guard's desk, arms folded across his chest.

"Randolph Fordham, this is Ian Wells," he said curtly.

Ian shook Fordham's limp hand. The squat banker said nothing but immediately began walking toward the elevators.

On the fortieth floor, the banker didn't bother to turn on the lights as Ian and Callahan followed him down a dark hallway that felt like a long, narrow vault. Near the end of the hall, he led them into a room and flicked on the lights of a windowless office, empty but for a desk, a computer, and a few chairs.

"This is a guest office," Fordham explained. "The bank keeps it for visiting execs."

"Isn't this all a little strange," Ian said, "doing a wire transfer at night?"

Fordham took a seat in front of the computer. "My counterpart in Grand Cayman was only available at this hour," he answered matter-of-factly.

"Mr. Fordham," Callahan explained to Ian, "made the arrangements for this service with Mr. Doyle twenty years ago when the trust was set up. I'm sure you've read the trust and know that besides makin' tonight's transfer to a new account, after your investigation, with you and I agreeing on who's to receive the money, you'll be directin' Mr. Fordham concerning the final distributions."

"I also saw," Ian said, looking back to the banker for confirmation, "that if we don't agree, Mr. Fordham casts the final vote."

Fordham eyed Ian with a blank expression. "That's correct. Now, I've taken the liberty of setting up a new account at your law firm in which to hold the trust money. Do you have the acknowledgment form?"

Ian pulled the folded sheet of paper he'd prepared earlier from his coat pocket. Fordham read it quickly, then slid it back across the desk with a pen and several other documents. "Mr. Wells, please sign these forms to formalize the new account, and both of you will need to sign your agreement to move the trust proceeds into this account."

Callahan took the pen and scribbled his name on the acknowledgment. Ian signed the account forms and, with much less certainty than his client, did the same with the acknowledgment.

"I've got another question," Ian said. "Why does my firm need to hold the money at all? Why can't it stay where it's at till the distribution?"

"Because those were Mr. Doyle's wishes," Callahan growled.

"I'd say it's a compliment, Mr. Doyle thinkin' his lawyer could do the best job of carin' for the cash."

"Very well," Fordham said, focusing on the computer screen. "Over the past six months, per agreed-upon procedures, the trust funds have been accumulated in a bank associated with Wells Fargo, the First Trust Bank of Grand Cayman." He looked up at Ian. "Your predecessor approved of these arrangements when he drafted the trust."

"You mean Connor Wells," Ian confirmed uneasily.

The banker nodded as he typed.

Would his father also have agreed to this arrangement? Ian wondered, glancing into the dark hallway. A wire transfer in the middle of the night?

"Twenty years is a long time," Ian said aloud. "What if you'd been hit by a truck, Mr. Fordham, or changed jobs? Who would have done all this then?"

"Provision was made for a successor to handle the transactions," the banker said. "Just as the trust provided that Mr. Callahan, as trustee, could select your father's replacement."

"Yeah," Callahan said offhandedly. "Fortunately, Mr. Fordham and his wife are great fans of Grand Cayman, isn't that so?"

The banker cast a nervous glance at Callahan. "Yes, that's true." He typed for a few more minutes. "Gentlemen, I will be transferring the entirety of the proceeds to the Wells & Hoy Law Office Trust Fund Account, routing and account number as follows." He read off the bank account information. "At that point," the banker continued, "the funds will be under your care, Mr. Wells. Once you've completed your investigation of the beneficiaries and you and Mr. Callahan concur on the results, you will each confirm distribution to the appropriate recipients. In the event you disagree, I will make the final decision. Is that understood?"

Callahan nodded.

Ian cleared his throat. "Yes," he replied.

"Good." Fordham typed a few more lines, then pressed the Enter button. "The wire transfer is in process. The funds will be in your new account this evening."

"How much?" Ian asked.

"Nine million, two hundred and thirty-six thousand, two hundred and seventy-two dollars and eighty-six cents," the banker said. "That's the contents of the trust, net of certain transfer fees."

"Which I'll be looking at closely," Callahan said firmly.

"Yes," Fordham muttered. "Of course."

Fordham walked them back to the lobby, where he shook each of their hands with the same soft, now-sweaty handshake. He turned eagerly away and retreated back toward the elevators.

Callahan looked Ian up and down. "So that's handled," he said calmly. "How's the investigation comin'?"

"It's coming," Ian said, nearly claustrophobic in the dark lobby.

"Tell me about it."

Ian considered the Irishman and the man's complete comfort with the strange process they'd just completed. He took a breath and briefly explained the results of the criminal background checks he'd ordered, his review of McMartin's and Callahan's information, and his meeting with Rory Doyle. He quickly went through a summary of his talk with Rory's daughter. "I've also met with a source who knew the Minneapolis underworld in the '90s," he finished.

"Who's that?" Callahan asked.

Ian told him.

Callahan's eyebrows rose. "Anthony Ahmetti? I'm impressed at your initiative, Ian. And what did your source have to say?"

144

Ian looked Callahan in the eye. Callahan had said the Albanian's name as though it was familiar. "He just gave me some suggestions on getting more information. About Rory in particular."

Callahan studied him as if catching a hint of Ian's restraint in not sharing all of Ahmetti's news—or even the ICRs. "Well, cheers to all that," Callahan said. "That's progress in just three days. That last bit especially. Though I doubt the rest of your inquiries with bosses and family will get ya anywhere with Rory."

Ian grew defensive. "What do you mean?"

"I mean I doubt Rory would've told his bosses he'd been sellin' meth the night before or that he came home at night to tell his missus, 'Had a great day. Robbed a Holiday station and stole some credit cards. Pass the peas, will ya, sweetie?'"

Defensiveness gave way to anger, amplified by Ian's fatigue. "So where else would you suggest I look after twenty years?"

"No, no, do your lawyerin', son," Callahan said, shaking his head. "Really. Go ahead. I'm sure you'll do a fine job in the end."

Ian wanted to wipe the smugness from the Irishman's face. "You know I'm handling each of your background investigations the same way."

"Of course, son," Callahan said with a smirk, his accent in full swing. "Why, if I didn't have such a high opinion of ya, I'd think you were implyin' I'm more interested in a larger share of the estate than the truth. The thing is, though, you've been thinkin' about the trust for a few days, while I've been at it for twenty years. I know the players a bit better than you do. So do your job fairly. That's what you're bein' paid for. But in the end, if you tell me the counterfeit son of Jimmy Doyle and his family are entitled to a third of the trust money, you'd best have gone a far sight past a criminal background check to prove it before I'll sign off."

Ian didn't bother responding.

Callahan grinned and slapped Ian on the back with a blow hard enough to bruise. "Have a good night, Ian. I'm truly lookin' forward to your report. And take good care of that money now, boyo."

Ian watched him leave the building and walk out into the night. He looked back toward the elevator, where the banker had disappeared, digesting the odd scene he'd witnessed upstairs. Then he recalled Ahmetti's comment about Jimmy Doyle working only with family, or the nearest thing to family, in the days he'd been associated with Kid Cann and his illegal enterprises.

Though exhausted, Ian decided he couldn't go home to bed just yet. He pushed through the doors and turned up the street in the direction of his car.

21

Amidst shadows painted by starlight, Ian sat with his back against the cold brick of the Grandstand. The vacant Giant Slide was in front of him. Overhead hung the Skyride's cables. The top of the Coliseum could be seen in the distance, down a street that, in the monochrome of night and the absence of State Fair crowds, looked as wide as a highway.

Ian looked again at the glow of the Ancestory.com website on his laptop. He'd joined their highest level of access as soon as he settled into this thinking spot two hours earlier. He'd begun by typing his father's name and birthday into their search field.

In the two hours since, he'd checked every branch of Connor Wells's family back five generations and a mile on either side. He followed that inquiry with a review for James Doyle, father of Rory Doyle, and came up with nothing. James Doyle's family and his dad's could just as well have been from different galaxies.

Next, Ian moved to his mother's side of the family using her maiden name, Martha Brennan. The search was narrower

147

since *her* mother was registered as a single parent. But no connection popped up with the Doyle family there either. The Brennan family came to America from Ireland in the late nineteenth century, Doyle's the same. Besides that, they didn't cross paths.

Ian kicked at a stone near his heel. Why had he felt the need to stay up half the night to do this research? What did it matter if his dad was related to Doyle? He may be burning to know why his dad got chosen to work the trust, but that wasn't the problem. Whether Connor was or wasn't a blood relation to Jimmy Doyle didn't change Ian's situation.

Until tonight, the big fee he needed so badly had him overlooking the strange clients, the ICR reports, and the unusual job he'd been asked to do. He'd even thought he could justify going on after Ahmetti's hint that the estate might hold illegal money from the Cann rackets—since he wasn't being asked to steal it and had no way to return it to any victims, fifty years on anyway.

But how did he interpret walking into a bank in the middle of the night and watching a wire transfer take place in an empty office? It smelled like laundering. And money being laundered meant money that was *still* dirty. Even if his dad had drafted the trust with the big fee, he wouldn't have knowingly been a part of something like that. Not the dad he knew, right?

Right?

Self-assurances that would have been rock solid a week before felt shaky now. Ian looked up at the fairgrounds he loved. Gazed to his right, toward the silent Midway.

Connor Wells didn't like crowds. That was why Mom—and never Dad—took him and Adrianne to the State Fair every August. Mom would inch their car through traffic up Larpenteur

Avenue to battle for a parking spot. They'd step out into the hot morning sun to follow the same route every year: start at the Pet Center, do the rides at the Kidway, take an air-conditioned break in the Merchandise Mart, hit the Dairy Building for a towering bag of chocolate chip cookies with all the milk they could drink, have something fried and on a stick, and take in the Coliseum and barns to watch the horses. Then came the climax: spend their last dollars and energy on the Midway carnival rides and barkers' contests before limping sore-footed and exhausted back to the car.

It was a predictable annual rite of passage, never missed until they grew too old to be seen in public with either parent.

Except, Ian now recalled, for that one summer. The summer his dad had substituted. He hadn't thought about it for years.

He must have been ten when Martha came down with the flu and broke the news that Dad had been persuaded to go in her place. That Fair visit, he and his sister had left the car to find themselves in a death march behind their father's long and relentless strides. They barely stopped for the kids' rides. The cookie and milk lines, Connor declared, were too long to endure. Their walk through the barns left no time to pet horses, let alone watch them show. The rocket speed was spoiling it all.

Then they reached the Midway.

The full memory came back to him now. In the flurry of their dad-driven pace through the Midway, he and Adrianne had been allowed to use up their remaining dollars on the Spider ride, Tilt-A-Whirl, and attempts at winning stuffed animals. Water guns, softballs, and ring tosses followed—all for nothing. Every single ticket gone in a heartbeat. Their disappointed faces couldn't have been missed, even by a man rushing to get home.

In mid-stride to the exit, Connor stopped them in front of a pistol-shooting gallery. "Wait," Dad ordered. "Wait right here." He disappeared into the crowd. Minutes later he returned with a handful of fresh tickets.

He handed a bunch to the barker. Ian and Adrianne picked up pistols next to each other and rapidly fired away. Nothing. Ian didn't hit the target once, and his sister did no better.

Ian set down his pistol and turned to his dad. Two lanes down, the barker was handing Connor a stuffed animal big enough to be in a zoo. Dad passed it to an astonished Adrianne without a word, then gave the barker the last of the tickets. Picking up the pistol for another round, he aimed and squeezed off ten popping shots in quick succession. Each was perfect, each a bull's-eye. Connor passed another giant stuffed creature to Ian. Afterward they resumed the hurried pace to the exit and the car.

It was a moment when the rules of the universe were briefly altered, enough for their predictable father to do the unpredictable. Yet even that shocking interval at the Fair had been too solitary, too much of an aberration to shake Ian's worldview of his father's limitations. After a week, the matter had been forgotten.

Ian looked down at the laptop that had gone to sleep, wondering again what he really knew and didn't know about the man.

Maybe there was no blood connection to explain Connor's selection to perform the trust work. But that selection wasn't random. There was some reason Jimmy Doyle had chosen his dad. Somehow Ian had to find out.

In the meantime, though, he was done with the case. In the morning he'd call Callahan and tell him he was withdrawing. He'd figure some other way out of his money problems.

Walking away from the fairgrounds toward his car, Ian cast a final glance over his shoulder. The space was so silent this night that he could hear the wind in the trees—an impossible feat on crowded Fair days.

And for an instant, in the midst of the silence, he could imagine the popping of his father's pistol at the distant Midway, scoring an incredible twenty for twenty before his children's astonished eyes.

22

Brook leaned her head back, took a deep breath, closed her eyes. She stretched her fingers and opened her eyes once more to the list her boss had given her the day before.

"Hello?"

Chloe was standing in the doorway, her eyes bright. Brook was so bored that for an instant she was actually glad to see the Energizer Bunny of a law clerk.

"How's it coming?" Chloe asked.

Brook shrugged. "Two hundred seventy-seven potential individuals and businesses that could have deposited twenties at a Wells Fargo branch on Tuesday. I've called eighty-eight so far. No luck."

"Isn't this detective work?"

"Usually it is," Brook said. "But Agent John Soukup is our assignee from the FBI stolen-art section, and he's been out in-

terviewing tellers at the branches where the bills were received.
So Eldon asked me to do this."

"Did they check the bills for fingerprints?"

Brook's initial pleasure at an interruption was already fading.
"Yes. Nothing."

Chloe had to have detected the tone, but pressed on anyway.
"You know, I could look over the list if you'd like. Take some of
the names to call."

"No," Brook answered instinctively, then more civilly said,
"No, I really shouldn't do that. Eldon dropped this on my plate.
It wouldn't look good to assign it to anybody else."

Chloe looked like she might question that logic, but didn't.
"Okay," she said. "Let me know if you change your mind." She
turned and disappeared.

Guilt trickled in at her treatment of the clerk—even one
she found annoying. Something about Chloe made her reluctant to get involved in another project with her. Ambitious law
students came and went, but there was more to it with Chloe.
Definitely more.

Still, she could probably muster more patience for Chloe if
she was having any luck on her new project. Finding a depositor who recalled receiving and depositing a group of twenty-
dollar bills, based on nothing more than that they were stiff
and over thirty years old, was proving very hard. So much so
that Brook's heart was barely in the effort. The task had also
proved too boring to push from her mind the previous day's
encounter with Ian.

With an effort, she picked up the master sheet of depositors
once more.

All right, where was she? Until now, she'd simply been working her way from the top of the page down, dialing depositors.

That method took no imagination at all. Maybe there was a way to organize the list to reduce the number of calls required, eliminate the obviously weak contenders.

Brook began reviewing the entire list. An ice cream shop. Unlikely. Probably not a lot of twenties there. She made a mark. Car dealer? Not a lot of cash transactions there. Her eyes stopped at an entry:

Wells & Hoy Law Office—6/5/18—4:27 p.m., $12,000

Weird, she thought. The biggest share of the hot money deposits they were investigating went into the downtown Wells Fargo branch on Tuesday, June fifth. This showed Ian's firm depositing into the same branch that same day.

It also happened to be just after she'd visited Ian's office. That was a strange coincidence.

That was the day Ian got the new client with the trust, the one she'd overheard Katie and him discussing. Then on Wednesday Ian stopped by to ask her for investigation reports he had no business seeing. It was for the trust case involving beneficiaries who might have been involved in criminal activity.

She looked again at the deposit list. Retainers were typical with new cases. If Ian had just gotten this case on Monday, this could be the deposit of a new cash retainer from that client the next day.

Brook opened the desk drawer where she'd kept a copy of the ICR reports she'd given Ian. The pile was thicker than she remembered. Until she recalled that Chloe had delivered a few new reports after her adventure at Kieran's. Strike Force and FBI papers, she'd said.

Uncertain what she was looking for, Brook started paging

back through the pile once again. Nothing piqued her interest as she neared the bottom.

The final report was an FBI memorandum dated June 9, 1998. Brook hadn't seen it before. Clearly it was one of the records Chloe had delivered after Brook was with Ian at Kieran's. The summary page was titled *St. Louis Park Robbery and Homicide—January 14, 1983.*

Brook stopped abruptly. That was the cold case she was working on for Eldon. She kept reading, more slowly now.

Surveillance of Potential Suspects—Funeral of Christina Doyle—Port St. Lucie, Florida.

Her pace began to increase.

Particular attention has recently been directed to Rory Doyle as a person of renewed interest, based upon reports of spending inconsistent with his present employment. Mr. Doyle arrived at the funeral in a late model Mercedes . . .

She skipped to the bottom of the report and its conclusion.

Persons attending the Christina Doyle funeral who have been positively identified and were previously persons of interest include . . . Rory Doyle . . . Edward McMartin . . . Sean Callahan . . .

She felt her pulse picking up. These were the three names Ian had asked her to check. Names that likely represented the beneficiaries of the trust Ian was working on.

Brook looked up at the open door of her office. She rose and closed it, then returned to sit again. Reluctantly she lifted the phone, her other hand hovering over its keypad.

This was relevant information to the art-theft case. No, *critical information*. Eldon had to be told immediately.

She paused. Dropped her hand. Raised it again.

Punched in a number. No answer.

She tried a different one. This time a familiar voice answered. "Wells and Hoy Law office."

"Katie," she said softly. "This is Brook. I have to talk to Ian. *Right away.*"

23

FRIDAY, JUNE 8
2:03 P.M.
WELLS & HOY LAW OFFICE
DOWNTOWN MINNEAPOLIS

"Katie. This is Brook. I have to talk to Ian. *Right away.*"

The legal assistant stiffened at the soft but urgent tone. "He's not here now," Katie said. "It's just me and Dennis. Is everything okay?"

Several deep breaths filled the line.

"What's wrong, Brook?" Katie asked, her alarm rising.

"Do you know where he is?"

She wished she did. He was like a ghost these days. "No. I can try to reach him on his cell."

"I already tried," Brook said impatiently. "And I can't try again. It's . . . complicated. Katie, you've got to tell me about the trust case you got on Monday."

This time Katie remained silent.

"I've got to see that document," Brook went on. "I need to know where Ian got the case. And I need to know whatever you can tell me about the beneficiaries of the trust. Anything."

Katie's worry deepened. "Listen, Brook, let me try to find Ian for you."

"I can't wait. I'm coming over to your office now. And I have to see the trust when I get there." The line went silent.

Katie set down the phone and stared at her computer screen. After a few minutes it went blank. Katie continued staring, her fingers intertwined atop her desk.

She stood and glanced down the hall. Dennis was still in his office. She locked the front door to the suite and headed into Ian's office, closing his door behind her.

It took only a few minutes to page through the piles of papers on his desk, bookshelf, and couch. Next, a search of the drawers of his credenza and desk. Nothing. Which meant the trust had to be in the safe. Or he was keeping it with him, probably in his briefcase.

Katie crossed the room and knelt in front of Connor's ancient safe. Quickly she spun the lock to the right combination until she heard an audible *click*. Gripping the safe's handle, she pulled open its heavy steel door.

Early afternoon sunshine through the window lit the interior of the safe, filled with stacks of files and papers. The files on the bottom looked familiar: wills, trusts, and accounting records. Katie reached in and grabbed only the papers stacked on top. She stood with a grunt and took Ian's chair.

On top of what she'd removed was a sheaf of papers, folded in half. Beneath that lay a manila envelope. She glanced first at the envelope. *Hennepin County Attorney's Office* was printed on a label. Setting that aside, she unfolded the papers and saw the caption JAMES DOYLE TRUST.

Smoothing the document on the desktop, she settled back and began reading.

Ten minutes later, Katie had finished. She then took out the contents of the manila envelope. It took another ten minutes before she was through the reports contained within.

She returned the envelope and folded papers to the safe just as she'd found them, closed the door, and spun the combination lock. Then she returned to her workstation as though wading through a fog.

The James Doyle Trust. Ian hadn't told her the half of it. It was dated 1998, years after Katie had started working for Connor. Yet she'd never seen it before today. Connor had definitely prepared it; it was his style and was certified at the end. She even picked up a couple of whited-out type-overs, which meant he'd probably done it on the Selectric typewriter he used to keep in the office.

Except, unlike any trust Katie had typed for Connor, this one set him up for a fee of *two hundred thousand dollars*. He'd never earned more than five to ten thousand for the most complex trusts in all the years she'd worked for him. It made no sense at all.

Then there were the reports from the Hennepin County Attorney's Office. Half a dozen of them, all with highlighting over Connor's name and the names of the beneficiaries of the trust. The highlighting was probably done by Ian, yet it was no big leap to assume the contents of the folder, all police-surveillance reports, had come to Ian through Brook.

What did it all mean? What had Brook so shaken?

There was pounding on the front door. Startled, Katie recalled that she'd locked it. She rose, smoothed her dress, took a deep breath, and went to open it.

The door swung back to reveal Brook Daniels, a briefcase in her hand. Her face was stern and colorless.

"Sorry about that," Katie said. "I must have locked the door by mistake."

Brook's eyes didn't waver. "Where's Ian?" she demanded.

Katie took a half step back. "Like I told you, he's not here."

"Where *is* he? I've got to talk to him now."

"I told you: I really don't know."

Brook's stare was measuring her for a lie. "Then you and I have got to talk," she said, her tone only feeding Katie's alarm. "I know you're protective of Ian, but I have to see the trust document he told me about. I have to know where you got the cash you deposited on Tuesday into your client account. And I've got to see your bank records."

Katie looked anxiously away as she cataloged the contents of Tuesday's deposit in her head. She looked back at the young prosecutor, thinking as she remained planted in the doorway. This was obviously about the trust deposit. Something about it was touching on something illegal.

The first time she'd met Brook Daniels was near the end of Ian's first year at law school. Ian brought her to his father's office, introducing her as a classmate. She was cute with abundant personality. Full of life. Brook had joked and kidded Ian. Touched his elbow. A shoulder. Ian hadn't touched back that first day—it was clear he was too shy for that. But he'd noticed. He'd liked it.

Why hadn't it gone anywhere? Even with Brook still stopping by the office every few weeks all these years? Still joking. Still playful.

Ian never talked about it, so she didn't know and she didn't pry. But she did know that even if Brook kept flirting, the prosecutor in her had grown more serious underneath. It didn't take a mind reader to see that Brook took her role at the U.S. Attorney's Office very, very seriously.

So which was more important to Brook, Ian or her job?

Katie's mind flashed away again—to Connor's safe and its combination, which she'd known since her first year working here. Nobody could have kept that secret long from the eyes of a young woman both curious and insecure. Hardly trying, she'd worked the combo out a number at a time, stepping into his office and glancing past Connor's shoulder while he knelt in front of the safe.

But she'd used the secret only twice before today. The first time was her first summer working for Connor. She was eighteen then, and too foolish to trust the man or believe in herself. A word of praise from Connor for some other lawyer's assistant sent her snooping into the safe late that night, sure she'd find her imaginary rival's résumé.

There was no résumé. But she'd found the letter. It was addressed to the firm's accountant and dated the week after Katie had been hired. Signed by both partners, Dennis Hoy and Connor Wells, it said Connor would pay an extra fifty percent over Dennis's share of Katie's salary, under a deal that was to remain secret. It added up to young Katie earning half again more than most every legal assistant of her experience in the Twin Cities.

Connor must have typed that single-page letter on his own IBM Selectric too. But however he did it, with raises over the years Katie and her family had enough money to send Nicole to Carleton College, cover Richard's bouts of unemployment, even pay for a decent retirement home for Katie's mother last year. All for a girl from a single-parent home, hired right out of high school, by a lawyer willing to train her himself.

She'd gone into the safe a second time a month after Connor died. Ian was her new boss on the heels of his father's sudden death. The boy was mostly still a stranger. Worried that Ian and

Dennis would replace her and her high salary, Katie had convinced herself she had a right to know what they were planning.

Again, the safe was empty of anything about giving her a pink slip. But on top of Connor's undisturbed files lay a new letter, signed by Ian, typed on the computer this time. In this one, Ian confirmed he was going to keep secretly paying the extra fifty percent toward Katie's salary—just like his father had.

She'd stayed too insecure over the years to break the secret and ask why, or even to properly thank Connor or Ian. But she'd tried to show her appreciation with long hours, often without recording them for the pay. Volunteering to help on family matters. Being available. And she'd loved them for it. Father *and* son. All the more because they'd never even expected gratitude.

Those events replayed in seconds as Katie stood her ground in the office doorway, looking Brook in the eye. Prosecutor or friend? she wondered. Which one was standing there? How could Katie possibly know for sure?

She couldn't.

"I haven't got a clue what you're talking about," Kate said at last with a shrug. "But I'll tell you this. *Nobody* is looking at Ian's client files without his permission. And *for sure* nobody's looking at his bank accounts. Nobody. Not even you."

24

FRIDAY, JUNE 8
4:19 P.M.
FEDERAL COURTHOUSE
DOWNTOWN MINNEAPOLIS

Brook lifted her briefcase from the metal-detector belt and moved rapidly toward the elevators at a pace that matched her frustration. A pounding frustration. She felt like screaming.

She'd driven everywhere after facing off with Katie at the law office. Ian's apartment. His mother's house. That place she knew he used to go to think during law school, by the Stone Arch Bridge. Even, by some bizarre logic, the last place she'd seen him, Kieran's Pub.

Nobody had answered the door at the apartment or house. He wasn't at the bridge. And of course he wasn't still hanging out at Kieran's waiting for her to return.

He was nowhere she could find him.

She couldn't even telephone him or his office again or consider a text or voicemail. If he became a target or witness in the stolen money and art investigation, they'd almost certainly subpoena his phone records. If Eldon ever learned the depths of their friendship, or saw phone calls the day she discovered a possible link between his law office and the art heist, he would think she'd tried to warn him. And he'd be right.

Then there was the quandary about confiding in Ian's legal assistant, Katie. She just didn't know Katie well enough to take the risk—any more than Katie was willing to trust her. Brook would have admired the lady for her Alamo stance at the door, if she wasn't so worried about Ian.

"Brook!"

Only a few steps from the open doors of an empty elevator, Brook sped up. In three strides she was in the elevator, the doors closing.

It wasn't fast enough. Chloe threw a hand into the gap the instant before the doors closed.

"Brook!" the law clerk repeated excitedly as she took a place at her side. "I've been trying to catch you!"

Brook tried to smile apologetically. Actually, by the tally on her cellphone, she'd ignored two voicemails and three emails from the law clerk in the last few hours while searching for Ian. "Sorry, Chloe. Lots of errands."

Chloe pushed the button for their floor. "Oh, that's alright. But I was looking over that list of depositors Mr. Carroll gave you yesterday in the art-theft case. The deposit list from Wells Fargo?"

Brook's head snapped in her direction. "How'd you get that list?"

"After you mentioned how long the list was," Chloe said, smiling, "I went and asked Mr. Carroll if I could help out. That's one of the reasons I was trying to find you earlier. So we could coordinate our efforts."

"I thought I mentioned it wasn't a good idea for me to ask for help on this," Brook said tightly.

"Oh, sure. That's why I asked Mr. Carroll myself."

Brook paused as a vein pulsed in her temple, wondering if the clerk could be that vacant—or really that ambitious.

"Okay," Brook said reluctantly. "Find anything?"

Chloe nodded. "That's the other reason I've been trying to reach you. You must not have gotten far with the deposit list yet, but I noticed the Wells and Hoy Law Office was there. Did you know that *Connor Wells* was a founder at that law firm? And did you also know he was on some of those ICR police-surveillance reports you have?"

"You looked over the surveillance reports?"

"Why, yes," Chloe said sweetly. "I mentioned to your legal assistant I was going to be helping you and asked if she'd kept a copy of the reports, and she had. Anyway, you *especially* should take a look at all the connections in that FBI memo I gave you. You must have read that by now, right?"

Ice was forming in her stomach. "I looked it over," Brook said.

"Really? Well, then you agree it can't be a coincidence, can it? I mean, first an FBI surveillance of a 1998 funeral of people possibly linked to the St. Louis Park art theft shows Sean Callahan, Rory Doyle, and Ed McMartin *all at the funeral*. Second, those same guys are associated with Connor Wells in old ICR surveillance reports done right here in Minnesota. Third, Connor Wells's former law office deposits money at Wells Fargo on Tuesday, *the same day* that money linked to the art theft is deposited there."

Chloe stopped to take a breath. "Come on, Brook. That's way too coincidental. And you *must* have suspected those connections between Connor Wells and the theft or you wouldn't have asked for the ICR reports in the first place, right?"

Brook forced a smile and a nod as the elevator door opened

on their floor and they stepped through together. "Just following a hunch," she said.

"Wow. Too modest," Chloe went on. "Well, did you look over any of the other people the FBI listed as attending the funeral? See if they could be linked in any way?"

"Not yet," Brook replied as they reached her office.

"Have you told Eldon about this?"

"No," Brook said quickly, noticing how fast *Mr. Carroll* had turned into *Eldon*. "Eldon doesn't like theories unless there's something to back them up. I'm . . . going deeper now."

Chloe looked her over. "Makes sense, I guess. So what can I do to help?"

"You've done enough—finding me that FBI report, I mean," Brook said as warmly as she could manage. "I'll tell you what, though. Since you already got started, why don't you take the last hundred people on the deposit list and dive into those?"

The petite law clerk's eyes flickered with dismay. "Really? I mean, shouldn't we be focusing on the Wells and Hoy Law Office and Connor Wells—after what we just talked about?"

"No. It's still too thin," Brook responded firmly. "We shouldn't narrow the search too early. A defense attorney would have a field day if we ignored other possible suspects so early on."

Chloe stared at Brook for a moment as though deciding whether to protest. "Okay," she said with a final smile. She turned and disappeared down the hallway.

Brook sat down behind her desk, her skin crawling with sudden worry. She pulled her copy of the FBI surveillance report out of a drawer and stared at it once again.

There had to be an explanation for it all, some simple reason she and Ian would later laugh about. One that explained how Ian's quiet father got linked on paper to a bunch of guys once suspected in the St. Louis Park theft. *Crazy stuff*, they'd say. Then they'd run through how it was all because his dad grew up in the same neighborhood as those guys, or played on the same baseball team. That kind of thing.

Except what if the stolen cash really did come from Ian's office? And why, as this was hitting the fan, was Ian suddenly nowhere to be found? And why was Katie building a wall around the office?

Brook reached back into the drawer and pulled out another thick folder of her own.

She was very glad she'd gotten this folder herself before heading to Ian's office this afternoon, not even using her legal assistant. It was a copy of the final summary report on the 1983 art-theft investigation, prepared by the FBI before the matter was transferred to low priority "cold case" status in '97. Eldon, she suspected, must have the original of this report somewhere in his office.

Brook read the report carefully. It chronicled the years of investigation after the theft. Thousands of leads and hundreds of suspects trailed or interrogated were detailed, eventually touching on almost everyone involved in organized crime in the Twin Cities. She read the summary file through twice. Afterward she took a breath and did what she did with any new case assignment. She closed her eyes and tried to picture exactly how the crime unfolded.

On that cold January night in 1983, the proprietor of the small St. Louis Park gallery on Excelsior Boulevard was staying late. He was excited and understandably so: they were on the first weekend of a Norman Rockwell exhibition, with nearly a third of the paintings and sketches on display available for purchase. Getting this gig had been a coup. The proprietor's commissions on sales for the two-week showing could reach deep into six figures.

The gallery had closed early at eight-thirty because of a monster Minnesota snowstorm settling in. Two security guards had already canceled, unable to make it through still-unplowed roads. The owner's only employee offered to stay on until the one remaining security guard arrived at midnight from his day job at the Southdale mall. The proprietor had declined. Get on home, he'd told his assistant. As it was, he'd be slogging through deep drifts for hours.

The grateful employee had slipped away.

The owner went to his office to count receipts while he waited for his security guard to arrive. Those receipts were bolstered by a surprising cash payment on an early sketch, Rockwell's *The Scoutmaster*. Nearly fifteen thousand in cash needed sorting. It was a very good start to the exhibition.

Until everything exploded.

It was shortly after eleven when two men appeared, coming through the back wearing ski masks. They quickly bound the owner's hands behind him and put tape over his eyes and mouth. Then they lowered him with surprising gentleness onto the wooden floor.

Within seconds, the owner distinguished three more voices and sets of footfalls in the gallery. He lay shaking from adrenaline, fear, and a flow of cold air along the floor from outside, listening to the zip of knives slicing paintings from their frames, counting the departing artworks by the crash of the frames to the floor.

The tearing finally stopped. The last frame fell. They were packing up. The guard would be there in another half an hour after they'd left, the owner told himself. The ordeal would soon be over.

Six rapid gunshots punctured the silence. Unable to cover

his ears, the owner twisted spasmodically into a fetal position, certain that now they would return for him.

They didn't. He was still curled in a defensive ball when the police arrived to free him, summoned by a neighbor who'd heard the shots. He walked, heartbroken, back into his gallery strewn with frames where he saw the blood splayed across the floor like brushstrokes leading outside onto a canvas of snow.

They found the guard's incinerated body an hour later in a burned-out garage a mile away. It lay beside the escape car—a stolen Mustang seen leaving the scene by a taxi driver going the opposite direction on the empty streets. The thieves had taken the only shots. The guard had arrived early and, once wounded, was likely taken alive from the gallery because the thieves feared he might identify them if left behind. His murder was the strangest piece of the puzzle. The two shots to his chest were a brutal act by a crew that had otherwise operated with complete professionalism.

The thieves had gotten away with over fifteen thousand dollars cash money and eight Norman Rockwells, the most valuable of which, *The Spirit of 1776*, was worth in excess of eight million on the open market at the time. If fenced right after the theft, the thieves might have garnered a quarter of that amount. If they were able to wait years or even decades to sell it, they could have gotten much more.

Apparently they were patient. One of the biggest barriers to tracking down the thieves and murderers was that none of the paintings surfaced in the fifteen years of active investigation. That, combined with the absence of any meaningful evidence at the scene, had made the criminal pursuit a dead end.

Rory Doyle and Jimmy Doyle, Ed McMartin and Sean Callahan. None were ever serious suspects because none had any experience or history of robbery, let alone stealing art. But Jimmy Doyle had been a soldier in Kid Cann's liquor racket for over thirty years. Given the thin leads in the case, he and the people around him got spotlighted along with every other person in Twin Cities organized crime in 1983. The only reason they stayed under surveillance longer than most was a stray report that Rory Doyle was spending money out of line with his known income. Even so, the focus on those four by FBI's special art theft unit had waned long before Jimmy Doyle's death in 2008.

Until now, Brook thought.

She opened her eyes.

What was her next step? How did she warn Ian that he might be helping distribute the proceeds from a thirty-five-year-old robbery that ended in murder?

Because he couldn't already know. Not Ian.

Brook was just picking up the deposit list again when she sensed someone at her open door.

It was Chloe once more. "Hey, I almost forgot to tell you," she said with her maddening pixie smile.

"What's that?"

"I gave Eldon a memorandum earlier this afternoon explaining all that stuff we talked about on the elevator."

Brook blinked. "You put all that in a memo to Eldon?"

"Yes."

"Including about the FBI report? About the possible connection with Connor Wells?"

"Uh-huh. Since you and I hadn't had a chance to talk, I thought I'd get him what I knew right away—especially since he's so anxious to solve the case. I drafted a written memo and dropped it by his office. I haven't heard back, but thought I'd let you know."

And you didn't *email* it to Eldon. That way it wouldn't be as obvious that you'd failed to cc me with a copy, Brook thought.

She pretended to smile back. "Well, that's fine. Great initiative. He'd have wanted to know."

Chloe returned the smile as she backed out of Brook's office and left.

As soon as Chloe's footsteps faded up the hall, Brook hurried in the direction of Eldon Carroll's corner space on the far side of the floor.

That ambitious little troll. Going around Brook to make sure she got credit for linking the missing money to Jimmy Doyle and the Wells & Hoy Law Office.

Eldon usually took his meetings in the afternoons, so he may not have seen Chloe's memo yet. If she could just retrieve it from his office, maybe she could delay things for another half day or more. Enough time to find and talk to Ian privately. After all, memos got misplaced all the time in these offices. Especially ones hand-delivered instead of emailed.

She turned a corner and ran hard into the chest of a man six inches taller than herself. Stumbling back, she looked up into Eldon's red face.

"Brook, I'm sorry," he said.

"That's okay," she replied, out of breath.

In his hand was a stapled report. He held it out before him. "Have you seen this from Chloe?"

Brook nodded thoughtfully. "We were just talking about it."

"Well, it's a stretch, but interesting and worth following up, especially without any other leads. I checked, and Special Agent Soukup can't get to it right away. I'd like you to go and interview this Ian Wells. Chloe's memo says he's Connor Wells's son and runs the office now."

"Yes, sir," Brook said dutifully, thinking how she'd been trying to do that for hours.

"Good," Eldon said, and then he grew more stern. "Actually, you know what? Send out a Marshal to get him and bring him *here*. I want to be with you for the interview."

25

Sean Callahan. Rory Doyle. The angry man from the pool. The old man with the hat. They were all there in the room with Ian.

And his mother too. Hidden in the darkness of the corner by the shuttered window.

No one was speaking—then they all were speaking, words and thoughts ricocheting through the room.

"You can't take my money." That was Rory, Ian thought.

The old man set his hat on the floor, shaking his head.

"How about what you did on the job?" Sean Callahan's growl.

"You never should have involved them." Rory again, waving his index finger at the old man.

The old man pointed to Ian. "Get him out of here."

A hand grabbed him roughly. Callahan looked down at him with eyes as cold as dead flesh.

173

"GENTLY." His mother's voice at last. Callahan's hand loosened instantly.

Then he was staring at a door, shut tight before him, and hearing the click of a lock.

Ian moaned. The moan rose until it was a cry. He banged on the door, though he knew he couldn't batter through.

She was all alone, with them in there.

He had to get through.

"Ian, wake up, dear. Wake up."

His eyes opened to see his mother's face. He looked around, startled.

He was in his old room, on his old bed. A wave of relief shot through him at seeing her there. It was only a dream, he repeated to himself. Another dream.

"Thanks, Mom."

"You must've been having a nightmare," she said. "You used to get them as a little boy, do you remember? I thought you'd outgrown them. I hope that being back in your room didn't bring them up."

Ian shook his head as he sat up. "No. It's probably just stress from work. What time is it?"

"After four in the afternoon. I slept in myself. I didn't even know you were here until I heard you call out. Your car isn't in the driveway."

"I've been parking it in the garage." His mind was clearing. He had to call Callahan about dropping the case. He'd do it from the office. "I've really got to get going."

"Of course. Oh, but dear, I almost forgot. *Happy birthday*."

4:19 P.M.
WELLS & HOY LAW OFFICE
DOWNTOWN MINNEAPOLIS

Katie stared at the screen, feeling her stomach rumble like it always did when she got upset. It'd been rumbling all afternoon, though it just got worse.

It was no mistake. She'd checked it three times. Gotten onto the website. Input the password. Gotten out again only to do it all over.

Somehow the firm had a new bank account. And there was over nine million dollars in it.

What in the name of everything holy was going on?

She'd gotten waylaid by Dennis for a project right after Brook left. Agitated as he already was about the malpractice lawsuit, thank goodness Dennis hadn't come out of his office while the prosecutor was still there. But as soon as Katie could manage it after Brook's visit, she'd sat down to her computer to check the Wells Fargo account.

And found this unbelievable sum of money deposited into a new account.

She picked up her cell again. Punched in Ian's number *again*. Nothing, again.

She'd tried calling Martha's house once, but no one answered. She was probably out in the garden. But she had to reach Ian to warn him about Brook. And now to find out what this bank account and cash meant.

Wait. What if her cellphone was tapped by Brook's office? Could they even do that? Or what if the office phone was tapped? She knew they could do *that*.

She set down her phone.

Even if she couldn't call him, she still had to find Ian. If he wasn't home, maybe he was with that new client.

She grabbed her keys and headed for the door.

5:07 P.M.
SUMMIT AVENUE, ST. PAUL

Katie drove slowly by the large house on Summit Avenue with the big picture window. She'd half expected Ian's Camry to be parked out front. Even if he wasn't here, on the drive over she convinced herself she'd knock on the door and find out about this new bank account from the client. After all, the money had to be related to the trust. And once she was looking him in the eye, she'd also tell this Callahan he had no business giving stolen money to Ian, no business *messin' with her boss*. If she had to, she'd drag him around the block until he confessed.

She was still imagining what she'd do as the house retreated in her rearview mirror for the fourth time.

Sean Callahan's home wasn't how she'd pictured it, she brooded. More shoddy. Less sinister. The place looked unworthy of Connor. She felt betrayed to even imagine Connor sneaking to the place to create the James Doyle Trust without telling her.

Except Connor was better than that. He had some reason for what he'd done. She just hadn't figured it out yet.

She'd left a note for Ian at the office, but that was almost an hour ago. Her inability to reach him was beginning to leave her unsteady with helplessness. It was a sensation that had been a second skin growing up, starting the day her mama had told her that Daddy was gone. Until she woke up on the first-year anniversary of her job at Wells & Hoy really believing something good was going to stick.

She was rounding the block again. This time she was going up to the door. Katie accelerated hard toward the middle of the block to park.

A black flash startled her. She slammed on the brakes and turned the wheel to the curb as a car veered past and pulled to a stop in front of Callahan's house. Before she could touch the gas again, a gangly man got out and marched up the steps she'd planned to take.

The man knocked on the door. A moment later, it swung open and he disappeared inside.

Katie let out a sigh of frustration and relief. Whatever she was hoping to accomplish, it wouldn't work now. Gripping the wheel angrily at her own weakness, she turned the car around.

Fine. Then she'd drive to Martha's house.

She had to do *something*.

"Sean, that car went by again," Aaron said, picking at the Marine Corps tattoo on his neck as he looked through a gap in the front window shades.

Sean Callahan nodded without looking up from the book in his lap. "See who it is?"

"No. A woman driving. Maybe she's lost."

"If she goes by again, get the license."

Aaron grunted. "Wait. Another car's pulling up and parking. There's a guy getting out. *It's Rory.* I didn't even know he owned a car."

Callahan dropped the paper. "Rory call ahead, did he?"

"Nope, boss. I'd have told you. You want me to get rid of him?"

Callahan shook his head. "This was going to happen sooner or later. Bring him in when he gets here."

Minutes later, Rory was staring at Callahan, seated in the orange chair by the fireplace, twisting the ring on his finger.

"You look even leaner than the last time I saw you," Callahan said. "Pick up some bad habits?"

"You sent him to Ahmetti, didn't you?" Rory declared.

Callahan shrugged. "Okay, let's back up a bit. I sent *who* to Ahmetti?"

"Stop it. You know I'm talking about the lawyer. Ian Wells."

"Where'd you hear that?"

"Somebody told me Wells met with Ahmetti at Doggy's last night. Somebody who was there."

Callahan looked to the cold fireplace for a moment before answering. "Then to answer your question, no. I can honestly say I didn't send Wells to Ahmetti—though he told me after he'd gone. But what have you got to worry about? You told me you qualify for the trust money, that you've stayed out of crime. So why care who the lawyer talks to?"

"Because Ahmetti's a liar and you know it."

"Well, you used to work for him, so you'd know better than me."

Rory slid forward in his chair, gripping the arms. "I may have, but I stopped working for him after Mom died."

Callahan nodded. "Yeah, your da worked that first part out at the funeral, ya may recall," he said, sliding into his Irish inflection. "It was pretty disappointing as I recall, him finding out you were payin' for the car and the clothes by being a punky little burglar and sellin' pills on the side. That's why we're dealing with this trust business in the first place. But at least that last part's good, isn't it? You going the life of 'straight and narrow' after Christina's death? Because that's all that Jimmy asked of you. 'No more criminal activity,' he said, didn't he? 'For the protection of us all,' he said. Put it right there in the trust. So you should be in good shape, eh, Rory?"

"You know I didn't do any of that before," Rory said. "Dad didn't even let me into his business before the job. I'd never held a gun before that night. It was the job that changed me."

Callahan shook his head. "*Ohhh, it changed me*," he sneered. "You weak little snot. And you call yourself Jimmy Doyle's son."

Rory's hand grabbed the lamp at his elbow. In a single motion, he threw it into the fireplace and rose to his feet. Callahan straightened at the crash, reaching toward the edge of the seat cushion.

Behind him, Aaron came stomping into the room from the hallway, his footsteps halting behind Callahan's chair.

"It's okay, Aaron," Callahan said, raising a hand and holding the thin form of Rory in a glare. "Our friend was makin' a last point before takin' his leave."

Rory stared. "I don't care what you think of me. I'm having what's mine and my family's."

Aaron's weapon was still in his pocket, Callahan saw with satisfaction. Good. The last thing they needed was something bloody at the house.

Rory looked at each of them a final time, then rounded past both as he headed toward the hallway.

Aaron followed him out. There was the slamming of a door. The Marine returned and pointed to the fireplace. "I'll clean that up, boss."

"No hurry."

"It seems Rory is upset," Aaron chuckled.

"Aye," Sean said. "And unfortunately that means the man may not be rational when the inevitable comes to pass."

26

The office was empty and quiet as Ian picked up the note on his desk. It was Katie's handwriting, but uncharacteristically scribbled and rushed: *The new matter is in your safe.*

Ian read it several times. What new matter? And how could Katie put anything in the safe?

He knelt before the black metal box and spun the dial. In his hurry, it took two tries before the lock clicked free. Inside, another note lay on top of the trust and the folder of ICRs.

Brook was here and said we may be mixed up with stolen money. I think she must mean the trust retainer. She didn't give any details. She was very upset. I told her nothing. But we've got to talk. What is this new account we've got with all the money in it?

Please, please, please call me. Right away.

Katie

180

Stolen money. Sean Callahan's cash retainer.

And now the trust money in his control. Ian pictured the banker's pudgy fingers running along the keyboard in the borrowed office, transferring all those funds into an account in his law firm's name.

Ian reached for his office phone. Stopped.

Who should he call? Brook? Katie?

Callahan?

Callahan. Except he wasn't going to call. He was going to confront him in person.

Ian put the trust back into the safe, then thought better of it. He slid it into his briefcase.

He reached the office suite door and pulled it open—and straightened in surprise. A suited man with ramrod posture stood just on the other side.

"Mr. Wells?" the man boomed.

"Yes."

"I'm with the U.S. Marshal Office. I've been asked to invite you over to the federal courthouse for a talk."

Ian's hand tightened on the briefcase. "Who's inviting?"

The officer pulled a smartphone from his belt and tapped the screen a few times. "It's Assistant U.S. Attorney Brook Daniels. And she requests your presence right now."

6:47 P.M.
FEDERAL COURTHOUSE
DOWNTOWN MINNEAPOLIS

Ian fumed behind a mask of casual indifference. He prayed the mask would hold. Because across the table, Brook and the boss she'd introduced as Eldon Carroll were locked in a whispered discussion. He had no idea what Brook and her boss knew, or what they thought they knew.

From Katie's note, Ian had arrived prepared for a grilling about the trust money and some link to stolen cash. So far, in an hour of questioning, Brook hadn't come close to those topics. But what else could it be?

"Mr. Wells, you're not a suspect," Brook had said in a strangely formal voice when he asked why he'd been summoned. But that was no consolation. Because if the trust money *was* stolen, his status would change in a heartbeat when they traced it to his firm's bank account. Worse, if his dad was linked to stolen money from the trust—even innocently—his estate could be subject to federal forfeiture. Possibly including Mom's house.

Ian took a deep breath to slow his heart. Like so many clients he'd coached, his first instinct was to open his mouth and tell everything to broadcast his innocence, especially with Brook across the table. The details of how and why he was hired by Callahan. The limited role he'd been asked to play. What he'd learned. How stupid he'd been to take on the case in the first place.

Except it wasn't Brook, his friend. It was Brook, Assistant U.S. Attorney, sitting next to Eldon something, U.S. Attorney. And Ian knew how statements offered to prove innocence had a strange way of doing the opposite. Prosecutors didn't get paid to find people innocent. "Don't *lie*," he'd tell his client. "Don't say a word. Not until you know what's going on, and the proof the prosecutor thinks she or he has."

It was all tearing him apart. But he wouldn't dig the hole any deeper. He wouldn't step forward until he could talk with Harry Christensen.

Brook and Eldon were still quietly going back and forth. Maybe he could've figured out where this was going if Brook hadn't spent the last perplexing hour asking him things she already knew. Like the nature of his father's legal practice, Ian's background up through law school, and where his parents grew up. Typical stuff for an interrogation yet odd when she already knew every answer he'd give.

Wait. That had to mean her boss must not know they were friends. Which could also mean this formal interrogation wasn't Brook's idea—especially the way she'd stopped by the office and confronted Katie earlier in the day. Brook might still be in his corner.

The brew of anger and worry cooled slightly in his chest. Still, friend or foe, real questions had to be coming. Brook couldn't interrogate him in front of her boss forever and keep avoiding anything relevant.

Brook finished her conference and turned back to Ian. Her forehead was flushed now. She gripped her pen more tightly as she leaned into the table. Ian felt the stronger attention of Brook's boss like the tug of a magnet.

"Did your father have any association with the Kid Cann crime syndicate?" she asked.

Here they came.

Ian wouldn't lie. If he could help it, he wouldn't even appear uncooperative. But if he was going to avoid a fall, he'd have to do some serious ledge-walking now.

He crinkled his forehead, answering Brook's question immediately and with an uptick of wonder. "Seriously? No. Not that he ever told me."

Brook circled that question with related ones, all of which Ian could truthfully deny.

Then her eyes grew edgier. "Were there any sudden changes in your family's wealth or lifestyle as you were growing up?"

"Not that I recall."

"How large was your father's estate when he died?"

Ian related the number. A few softballs followed.

"What personal knowledge do you have about any association between Connor Wells and either a Rory Doyle, a Sean
Callahan, or an Edward McMartin?"

She was drawing from the ICR reports she'd shown him.
But she'd asked 'personally,' which meant *firsthand*. If she
asked about what was in the ICRs, he would have to admit
he'd seen them. But he had no firsthand knowledge about an
association.

"I don't have any personal knowledge of that," Ian answered.

She let it pass. So she *intended* to limit the scope of her
questions.

"What about a James Doyle?"

"What about him?"

"Was your father a friend or associate of James Doyle?"

"I have no personal knowledge of my father being a friend or
associate of a James Doyle." He slowed his breathing, sweating as he anticipated the question he couldn't avoid—whether
James Doyle was ever his father's client.

The question didn't come. Brook was giving him room to
maneuver. She couldn't get away with this much longer, not
with her boss at her side.

"Did you deposit a sum of cash on Tuesday of this week into
a Wells Fargo account?"

"Yes. My legal assistant did so for the law firm."

"And where did that money come from?"

"Clients."

"Who?"

"That's attorney-client privilege," he replied, a bit irate.

"No, it's not," she shot back. "We can get a warrant to gain access to your bank records."

"Well, you can try. You can also just tell me what this is about and let me decide if I can cooperate."

She'd led with the punch line on the last one. She could have crept up on the money issue, boxed him in first. Coming straight had allowed him to dodge and her to confirm he was here because of Sean Callahan's cash retainer.

Brook leaned over and whispered to her boss again. "Mr. Wells," she said after they separated, "money was deposited at your Wells Fargo branch on Tuesday, June fifth, which was associated with an art theft of a group of Norman Rockwell paintings in St. Louis Park in January 1983. Your firm was one of the cash depositors at that branch the same day. That's all we're prepared to tell you at this time."

Ian's mind rolled. "How much was stolen?"

"Paintings with a potential value between eight and twelve million dollars, depending on when they were sold," she answered, watching him carefully.

He immediately started sweating again, gripping his thigh under the table. "Okay . . . thanks for sharing that. But I still won't reveal my client at this time. I have to ask him or her before doing so."

Brook nodded. She looked almost relieved. "Please do so," she commanded.

Eldon Carroll whispered something in her ear and tapped hard on one of the documents at her elbow. Brook pulled it front and center and nodded.

"Mr. Wells," she said, holding out the document, "you say you have no personal knowledge of your father having a relationship with James Doyle. I will inform you we have information that your father was, in fact, associated with James Doyle's son, Rory Doyle, in his youth—as well as the other gentlemen mentioned earlier, Sean Callahan and Ed McMartin. I will also inform you we have a partial list of attendees at a funeral that includes Rory Doyle and those other men—"

Brook stopped, her eyes scanning the report in her hand. She looked up at him, and a spark of deepening worry had taken over her expression.

"Did you know," she said more slowly, "this same Sean Callahan, Rory Doyle, and Edward McMartin attended the funeral of Jimmy Doyle's wife, Rory Doyle's mother, in 1998?"

"I don't . . ." Ian began, trying to grasp the question.

"Do you know any other persons who attended that funeral?" she interrupted, pressing on.

This was really out of left field. Ian struggled to get his bearings. Even Eldon looked puzzled. "No," he answered.

"The FBI took the following names from the sign-in register at the funeral home that day. Do you know a Sherman Calhoun?" she said, reading from the list.

"No."

"A Buddy Provenzano?"

"No."

She turned the page toward him, slowing her cadence. "Please look at this list of people and tell me if you know *any* of the others attending the funeral."

Ian puzzled at her emphasis on "any" as she slid the document in front of him. How could he know any of these people at a funeral twenty years ago? What did she expect him to say?

Martha Brennan.

The name was halfway down the sheet. Surprised, he glanced at Brook. He'd told her his mother's maiden name on Monday in his office. There it was on the funeral guest list. And Brook clearly recognized it; her eyes burned with the knowledge.

She tilted her head at a slight angle away from her boss. "The funeral took place in Port St. Lucie, Florida," she continued as Eldon looked on. "You would have been nine or ten years old. According to the report, it was a rainy day . . . June 8, 1998. Twenty years ago today."

The dream that visited him every year. A gravesite under palm trees. A rainy day. The funeral of Jimmy Doyle's wife?

This wasn't possible.

"I already told you," Ian said slowly, sliding the report back to Brook. "I will not reveal potential clients and their actions." His next words slipped out in a fog of apprehension. "But June eighth—today—happens to be my birthday."

27

Sitting on the back porch with Martha in the fading twilight, Katie glanced at her watch. She'd stayed at the Wells residence embarrassingly long, nearly three hours, and Ian *still* hadn't shown up. Martha had even gone to nap at one point, inviting Katie to stay. She had, pacing the backyard like a cornered rabbit.

But now Martha was back and making conversation again. Which was, Katie thought, the only positive of this long wait— the chance to see Martha more clear-minded than she recalled her being in a long time. They'd spent the late afternoon into evening facing the vegetable garden that stretched across the far end of the yard, as Martha demanded to hear everything about her daughter, Nicole, and husband, Richard. She'd even recalled Nicole's age and schooling and thought to ask about Richard's job prospects. Katie had answered, doing her best to hide her worry about Ian. But through it all, Martha was calm and present. If Katie hadn't seen her early memory lapses for

188

herself, she'd have sworn Ian was crazy, that Martha was unchanged from the old days when she'd organize parties on this very porch and play the host with so much energy and charm that Connor's quiet manner was hardly noticed.

"Did Ian tell you," Katie asked, pulled irresistibly back to her worry, "whether he'd be out late tonight?"

Martha shook her head. "No. He hasn't told me much about his business lately."

The shadows were deepening. Katie heard a robin call from a willow in a corner of the yard.

"Do you miss our Connor?" Martha asked abruptly.

Katie turned toward Martha, startled by her serious tone. The woman was facing away. "Yes. I do."

"There are times I ache so bad it makes my chest hurt." Martha's voice had grown weak.

Katie wondered if Martha was sharing her pain because it was the kind of sentiment a mother couldn't talk about with her son. Or perhaps fatigue was the reason for her sudden openness.

"Of course you do," Katie replied.

"We shared his heart, you and me," Martha said, turning toward her with a sad smile.

"Oh, Martha," Katie answered through her own sadness. "Connor really was a wonderful boss. But you know his heart was all yours."

Martha didn't respond. Instead she was focused on the vegetable garden, where the greens and reds were fading to gray in the failing light.

"You know," Katie said, trying to conjure an excuse for staying later, "Richard's out with Nicole tonight. How about we tackle those boxes in the living room before it gets any later? You said it's a lot of Connor's office stuff, and I know more about Connor's practice than Ian ever will."

Martha shook her head. "Too much work. I couldn't ask you to do that. And frankly, I haven't the energy right now."

Katie knew she couldn't stay here all night; she'd have to figure out another way to connect with Ian. "Okay, Martha," she said, standing. "Then I should probably be going."

Martha nodded but didn't stand. "Katie, Ian told me he got a new case recently."

The trust. Katie froze. "Yes, he did."

The older woman smiled over concern in her eyes as she reached out to squeeze Katie's hand. "Before you go, could you tell me a little about how it's going? I really want to know."

10:10 P.M.
FEDERAL COURTHOUSE
DOWNTOWN MINNEAPOLIS

Ignoring leaden fatigue, Ian came out of the courthouse at a slow trot headed toward his office. Without breaking stride, he pulled out his cell and retrieved the phone number for Sean Callahan he'd placed there only three days earlier, punching it in.

"C'mon, c'mon," he repeated as he moved. "Answer your phone."

The ringtone broke. "Yeah," Callahan's familiar voice answered.

"What's the source of the trust money?" Ian asked.

"This Wells?"

"Yes. I need to know the source of the trust money and my retainer."

"Whaddya mean? It's Jimmy Doyle's estate."

"*Where* did the money come from?"

190

Callahan's tone dropped a notch. "Are you interrogatin' me, son?"

"I've got to know how Jimmy Doyle made the money."

Silence. "Jimmy was a saver. And this isn't a discussion I'm havin' over the phone."

Ian neared his office building. "When can we meet?"

"Tomorrow morning at my house. Eleven."

"I'll be there."

"Fine. Oh, and Counselor? Something to think about: your da never felt the need to ask these questions of his client."

The line went dead.

His dad never asked? Ian felt a renewed tightening in his stomach.

The questions raised by Brook's interrogation circled through his head like stones in a tumbler. Callahan and the rest of the beneficiaries being at the funeral of Jimmy Doyle's wife made sense. *But his mom being there?* And had she really brought Ian along as a child?

If she was there, what did that say about his parents' relationship with Doyle and the rest of the bunch? What did it mean about Dad's knowledge of the source of the trust money? Did it really come from this old art theft?

He reached the parking garage and hurried down the concrete steps to the lowest levels, furious that he'd been too slow to withdraw from the case and return the money to Callahan. He still had to do it, then figure out how to approach the prosecutors. But moving the cash now would look like he was covering his tracks.

He'd driven halfway home when his phone buzzed in his pocket. Ian punched the Bluetooth to accept the call over the car's speakers.

"Yes," he answered.

"We need to talk. Now."

The voice was muffled and hard to make out over talking in the background, but the caller ID said LARRY'S BAR. "Rory?" Ian asked.

"Yeah. Meet me at Larry's. Midnight."

The line went dead.

Now what? Had Callahan told Rory about their meeting in the morning? There was no way Rory could have gotten wind of his interrogation by Brook. He deliberately hadn't mentioned that to Callahan.

This was turning into a circus. But he had to go. Not to answer Rory's questions but to confront him about the trust money.

His weariness was fueling a new headache as Ian pulled the car into his mother's garage and strode up to the kitchen door. He headed to the living room, where his mother was sitting on the couch in her robe. On her lap lay the photo album she and Livia had brought down from the attic the weekend before.

She looked up.

"Mom," he said, shedding his coat, "we've got to talk."

She didn't answer. Her eyes were blank.

The planned questions melted away. "You doing okay?" he asked.

She nodded, smiling. It was a child's smile, and one he'd never seen before on his mother's face.

On the table at her elbow was an envelope with his name on it, propped against a lamp. He picked it up. Katie's handwriting. Inside was a note:

Ian, when you get this, call me right away. We have to

talk. Brook is looking for you. If you haven't seen my note at the office, you need to know that Brook seems to believe the cash retainer from the new client with the trust could be stolen money. And I've got to know about that new bank account. CALL ME!

Katie

P.S. I spent the evening with your mom. She was fine until just before I left, when she asked about the new case. I didn't tell her much because I don't know much, but then she started to fade fast. She became confused and even forgot my name for a bit, so I encouraged her to call it a night and go to bed. You may want to check on her.

Ian looked at his mother, who'd resumed paging through the photo album. "Mom, I think it's time to get you to bed." She continued smiling vacantly.

Ian helped her to her room and into bed, drawing the covers up around her. As he reached for the light, there was a tug on his shirt.

"Katie was here today," Martha said in a far-off voice. "She's such a nice girl. You were right when you insisted on hiring her, Connor. It was the right thing to do. But I think now she's worried about *you*."

Ian stared at her face, cradled in the pillow. "Why is she worried?"

"Because of the trust," Martha said quietly.

Ian paused, feeling guilty for prolonging the pretense of being his father. "Why is she worried about the trust?"

She didn't say anything more for a long interval. Then she frowned. "It's not safe."

Uncertain what to ask next, Ian hesitated.

His mother tugged on his arm to pull him closer. "Connor, I need a special favor."

Ian sat down on the edge of the bed. "What is it?"

His mother's eyes were milky in the soft light. "I want you to say no. Tell him you won't manage the trust when it needs to be distributed. I know you've already written it up and you can't undo that. But no matter what he says, just tell him you won't touch it again. Tell him we're through—really through this time."

His mother turned on her side, facing away from Ian. She began to hum a song he didn't recognize. A few moments later, her breaths grew even and deep. He considered waking her and asking more, but didn't.

Ian returned to the living room and sat on the couch. Lifting the open photo album, he set it on his lap and began paging through it aimlessly in a chaos of emotions.

A favor asked of "Connor." Including Dad's surprise handgun to be destroyed on Monday, that made two indulgences his mother had sought surrounding his departed father in the last week.

He recalled how few favors his mother had asked of anyone in the past, himself included. The one in the fourth grade—that he mow their neighbor's yard after the man broke his leg. Their neighbor was a glowering giant whose presence terrorized Ian for years but who gentled overnight at the sight of Ian with his mower. Another favor, his senior year, with no girlfriend in sight, when she'd asked him to invite his shy younger sister to the prom. It was the only prom either of them would attend. He never fully admitted to his mother afterward what a great time they'd had.

And the last one when he finished law school, just weeks after

Connor died. They were sitting at Olive Garden over a subdued brunch, celebrating his graduation. Adrianne had slipped away to the restroom. Martha chose that moment to lean close and ask Ian to take over his father's practice for five years and keep paying Katie the "special way" Dad had—and not tell a soul she'd asked him to do so. She couldn't explain why; she begged Ian to trust her.

On the verge of launching his career, the request was a blow. Because he couldn't refuse her. It didn't matter that he didn't know what the "special way" meant at that moment, or what drove the request. He instantly knew he'd do as she asked, bypassing offers by big firms where Zach and Brook were being courted, putting his own plans on hold. Because this was a special favor asked by his mom, who had just lost her husband. And hard as it was, he trusted that she wouldn't ask such a thing if it wasn't very important, somehow, for both of them. That was the nature of all her favors after all.

He could still recall Brook's odd look when he'd told her, inventing an excuse for his decision that he no longer remembered. Something had broken in their relationship that day. Brook started dating Zach a month later.

And now here they were, five years on.

For his part, since he was a teenager Ian could recall asking only one favor of his mom. It was the same summer his dad died, on the back porch of the house, when he asked her to find another man to love and marry. She'd said that more than once, Connor had asked the same favor were he to die, and she'd promised to do her best. Before her memory failed, she could have had her pick.

Now she was asking "Connor" to refuse to manage the trust distribution. That meant she knew about the trust itself and how it was to be handled—though she'd acted ignorant about it before. It also meant the trust frightened her.

The implications of this new favor roiled in Ian's stomach like a drumroll, especially after the day's interrogation.

There was a stirring in the hallway. Ian looked up. His mother was standing there, her eyes wide.

"What is it?" he asked, startled. "I thought you were asleep."

"Connor, there's something more I have to tell you. I know you told me not to. I know you said it could be dangerous. But I did it anyway."

"What did you do, Mom?"

She didn't even notice it was her son's reply. "Connor, I . . . I spoke with Mr. Ahmetti. I told him what he wanted to know. I paid him back for his information. He said we're even now. Please forgive me, but I couldn't owe that man any longer."

28

Rory Doyle drove the struggling car to the curb a block short of his destination, wanting to walk the remaining distance. The sidewalk was empty at this late hour. He passed a mattress store, a neon-red *Closed* sign in the window. A small deli. A computer-repair shop.

Just ahead he saw what he was looking for. Or at least he saw what was there now.

Rising from the corner lot behind a protective wire fence was the skeleton of a new building under construction. A painted sign declared it would be a combination of residential and commercial when done, with a coffee shop at street level and condos above.

Rory stepped closer to the fence.

His cigarette craving was especially strong tonight. Maybe because being here was another in a long line of promises he'd broken to himself. Another sign of the "weakness" Sean accused

197

him of. But he told himself he didn't care. With the trust payout nearly complete, he'd had to see the spot again.

Had the lot been vacant all these years before this new construction? Or had they rebuilt the garage that was on the corner the last time Rory was here? He had no way of knowing. He hadn't been back for thirty-five years.

Staring at the site in the dark, Rory tasted bile rising deep in his throat. He grabbed the fence and closed his eyes, spitting out the rush of fluid in his mouth. It happened again. And again.

The nausea eased. He spit once more and took a breath, then looked up at the steel girders. And suddenly he remembered it all *so well.* . . .

Like how bitterly cold it was inside the garage that night. "Cold as a meat locker," his dad had muttered when they'd all stepped out of the Mustang into the abandoned repair shop. One of their crew shut the bay door behind them, making the place more still than a coal mine.

The Mustang's headlights that night were crusted with street salt, scattering weak light and a wavy shadow of an oilcan onto a wall. They'd emptied the car in the dim light, including the trunk's contents. Then the rest of the crew slipped out into the snowstorm, leaving him and his dad alone in the garage.

An instant later, a sudden *plop* on the concrete floor made Rory jump.

He looked up, his heart racing. Chunks of snow were tracing streams off the car's still-warm hood, sliding around the leather case his dad had propped against the windshield. The plops kept coming, like the cadence of a melting clock. He shrugged at his own jumpiness.

The place was full of smells that night, he recalled. His own sweat through his jacket. Gasoline fumes mixed with old grease. A sharp bite of iron. The iron he especially remembered.

"Wipe down the passenger doors," his dad had ordered, tossing him an oily rag. Rory's body was shuddering so hard he cursed out loud through his teeth, making his dad call over the hood, "Minnesota winter could freeze the marrow in a charging bear." Yeah, Rory had thought, that had to be true. Because he could feel his own marrow freezing solid—though some of that, he knew, was the realization of what they'd just done. What *he'd* just done.

Rory glanced across the Mustang's low roof at his dad, working the other side. Always the cool Jimmy Doyle. Moving deliberately, blowing frost clouds as he wiped his side of the car, cold as Rory but showing none of it. "We can't take any chances with prints tonight," his dad called out, calm as a cornfield after a snowfall. Like any hurry was pure choice.

After a time, Jimmy raised his chin to listen, and Rory followed suit. All he could hear was buffeting wind gusts. No sirens. No screaming alarms. His dad let out a familiar grunt of satisfaction before he pounded his feet on the hard floor for warmth.

Rory was just finishing up his side when his dad came around the front bumper and looked him up and down. "You did okay," he said to Rory's numb surprise. "Yep. Everything's going to be fine."

It would've felt good, the rare praise. Except it was a lie. His dad even lied when he encouraged. Rory knew he didn't do so well. The memory of what he'd done burned in the back of his mind like a brand even as Jimmy spoke the words.

In that moment, Rory thought he'd seen regret in Jimmy Doyle's eyes—right in the middle of the lie. Rory knew it wasn't regret for what he'd said. But maybe he regretted that he'd taken his kid through a door that got locked shut behind all of them. Or that he'd broken the vow to Mom that he'd never involve Rory in his business. Over the years, Rory had thought a lot about that brief, uncommon look, because his dad had said more than once that regret was a cancer that made a man weaker and his enemies stronger. Maybe it wasn't regret at all. Whatever it was, Rory never saw it again.

Then Jimmy pulled a gray plastic bag filled with bills out of a coat pocket and put it in Rory's hand. "That's your part of the cash we got tonight," Jimmy said. "Take it. But be careful. They feel stiff. They're probably new and traceable. Spread 'em out. Never bank 'em."

Rory took the bag. Jimmy nodded approvingly and pointed at the leather case still propped against the Mustang's windshield. "It'll be years," his dad said, "a lot of years before we can fence the real take for value. That's okay. It'll be your inheritance, Rory. So you're gonna be smart like we talked about. Get a real job. Take no shortcuts. Be patient. Put this behind you. It'll all be okay."

Rory had nodded, but the strange idea that it would all be okay drew his eyes to the place he'd avoided looking until then: the floor behind Jimmy, where they'd laid the burden from the trunk. Even twenty feet away, Rory could smell the iron from that spot, floating like an accusation in the air.

His dad grabbed his shoulders. "Listen," Jimmy repeated until Rory's attention was focused again. "What happened tonight was one time. We had some bad luck, but we'll put it behind us. Remember that someday that case is gonna be your inheritance. A very big one."

The words had sounded as thin to Rory as the oilcan's shadow. His stare wandered past Jimmy's shoulder again.

A slap from a bare hand pounded his face, sending his vision red. Another blow caught his other cheek.

"Tell me you understand," his dad demanded, in a voice as calm as if they were walking in the park.

His face stinging, Rory heard the first far-off call of a siren rising above the wind, followed instantly by banging on the wall. "C'mon!" came a muffled shout. "What're you doing in there?"

Jimmy didn't move. "Say you understand," his dad repeated.

Above the welt forming on his cheek, Rory replied, "Sure. I understand." He'd wondered if his eyes showed the hate as he said it.

The sirens grew louder.

Jimmy snatched up the leather case from the hood, Rory's arm in the other hand, and dragged him around the front of the Mustang. In two strides they reached the spot where the iron smell was strongest. Jimmy took a high step over the uniformed figure curled there on the floor, surrounded by a freezing pool of rust brown.

Rory slowed, until Jimmy yanked him over the body in a single tumbling step. Two more strides and they were at the side door. Jimmy pulled it open into a face full of snow and wind.

The others were at the van outside, its engine running. Past flapping wipers, Rory saw one in the driver's seat and another in a rear seat. The third was by the car door, snow covering his shoulders and a ski hat. A metal gas can was at his feet.

"Who's gonna do it?" the snow-covered man said.

Jimmy turned back to Rory. "Light it up," he shouted over the wind.

The regret was still absent from his dad's eyes, along with the encouragement.

Maybe ordering him back in there with the guard who'd been

breathing half an hour before was to pay for his mistake, Rory had thought at the time. Or to pay for what his eyes said in the garage. Maybe making Rory incinerate the guy with all the rest of the evidence was supposed to be an act of atonement to his dad.

He wouldn't do it, Rory told himself. The orders stopped there. That was where he'd draw the line.

Except he didn't. He hardly hesitated before stepping to the gas can, picking it up, and doing his father's bidding. Jimmy Doyle's bidding.

The long memory faded. Rory blinked twice. The frame of the condo and retail building returned in the darkness.

He remembered it all. Better than he remembered last week. He wished he didn't.

Rory turned to walk away. He'd never come here again. Never. And he'd get what he deserved from that night. For his kids. Because heaven knew he'd paid for the inheritance. Paid for it every day of his life since that distant night.

29

Ian checked his watch again as two men came into Larry's. One was filled out, the other slender. Both were far younger than the rest of the patrons hanging around the bar. One of them gave Ian a long stare while the other picked up beers and cues. Soon they were circling the pool table, racking the balls.

Ian looked away. He'd been waiting at this table for thirty minutes and still no Rory. He didn't have the energy to stay much longer. What could Rory know—or want?

The money. Rory was about the money. He'd want assurance he'd get his share and want to know how soon. Of course, two days ago, this had been about the money for Ian too. And it wasn't like his money problems had gone away. They'd just gotten smothered under things even worse.

But it didn't matter. He didn't come to answer Rory's questions. He came to ask his own.

The bartender doubling as a waiter came by again. "Another beer?"

"No. Diet Coke, please."

The bartender looked at him like the order wasn't worth the walk, but he went away, returning a minute later with a glass half filled with something dark and carbonated.

He had to know where the trust money came from and Connor's connection to it. Not only to know how best to extricate himself and his family from Brook's investigation but also, in light of his mother's words tonight, to figure out how his parents' and Ahmetti's worlds had somehow overlapped. What could Martha Wells possibly have shared with the fence that had any value to him? What could Ahmetti have told her that put her in his debt in the first place? And what did it all have to do with the trust?

His phone began to vibrate with a text. He pulled it out and stared at an unfamiliar number on the screen.

Are you coming tonight to talk about the case? the text read. Below the text was the name *Willy Dryer*.

Through his haze of fatigue, Ian tried to recall where he'd left things with Willy. He'd told Katie on the phone that maybe he could meet with him soon. But he'd never confirmed for tonight, had he?

I didn't think we firmed it up, he texted back.

I thought we were on came the reply. *I'm rehearsing for my gig. After tonight, it will be hard to get together for a long time.*

He was so tired. *Another night*, he texted.

Please, man. Worried about this one.

A quick meeting would salvage something from this day. And he was close. *I'm in northeast already. Send address again. I've only got a few minutes.*

The address popped onto his screen. Only eight or nine blocks away.

Soon, Ian texted, ending the exchange.

He was putting away his phone when he heard ringing near the bar. A moment later the bartender sauntered back. "You Ian Wells?"

Ian nodded. "Yeah."

"I just got a call from Rory Doyle. He says he can't meet you after all. Says he'll call tomorrow to reschedule."

Great. Ian looked at his watch. Nearly twelve-thirty. "Thanks," he muttered. Ian dropped a ten-dollar bill on the bar and started toward the door.

As he neared the pool table, the bigger of the two latecomers set down his cue. Ian was coming abreast when the man stepped directly in his path.

Thick as a freezer, a wiry mustache on his upper lip, the man looked down at Ian with surly eyes. Before Ian could speak, he bumped Ian hard with his chest, sending him stumbling backward.

Arms came around him from behind.

Ian's weariness was lost in a sudden rage. He twisted out of the encircling arms and launched himself at the big one, who took a surprised step back.

A blow hit the top of Ian's head. The room flashed bright then dark then light again. He tumbled down.

On his hands and knees, Ian's vision cleared slightly. He looked up.

Kneecaps were six inches from his face.

Ian launched himself with his legs, driving a shoulder into the nearest knee with all his weight. It inverted with a cracking sound.

A howl like a wounded bear filled the bar. The big man above him tottered backward, dropping into a chair and gripping his kneecap in both hands.

Ian looked over his shoulder at the second man still behind him. To his surprise, that one was standing back. He pushed off the floor to his feet unsteadily. "You guys friends of Rory's?" he demanded angrily.

Neither one answered. Ian took a cautious step toward the door. The freezer hugging his kneecap looked up and let out a final roar of pain but didn't try to stand.

That was lucky, Ian thought blearily. Barely able to balance, he stumbled through the front door into the fresh evening air.

12:05 A.M.
UPTOWN DISTRICT, MINNEAPOLIS

Brook sat coiled on her couch, staring at the mounted television her parents had gifted her a month earlier. It was tuned to a show she didn't care about. There weren't many shows she'd recognize given her work hours, which was why she'd never needed a TV that took up half the wall.

Her cellphone called out a tune. She lunged for it on the table.

It was a friend from work. Disappointed, she declined the call.

When was Ian going to show up or call her? He had to know she couldn't call *him*. He'd become a key witness in an investigation, maybe a key suspect. Ian knew she couldn't create a record by telephoning him.

So *where* was he?

She picked up from the coffee table the rap sheets she'd printed out earlier, covering James Doyle, Sean Callahan, Rory

Doyle, and Ed McMartin. Only two had arrest records. James aka "Jimmy" Doyle had an adult conviction from back in the 1950s. Sean Callahan had two assault charges from the '70s, but they were youth charges. There was nothing at all on Ed McMartin or Rory Doyle.

What was Ian doing? How did he know these guys? Was it his own connection or was he linked through his father?

In law school, Ian had been shy, occasionally brooding. *Always* overprotective of those he cared about. Smarter and kinder than any man she'd ever met, and the first one to get her humor every time.

That Ian Wells couldn't be connected to the Doyle bunch. He couldn't even have known his dad was connected to them— and to the biggest art theft in Minnesota history, one involving murder. If she needed more proof, it was that he'd asked her help getting the ICR reports. If he was hiding that connection, why would he ask her to gather evidence that linked the Doyles with Connor Wells?

She walked to the window. Lake Calhoun was just a few blocks up the street. She considered taking a walk there. It was warm enough, and there'd be plenty of people on the walking paths, even this late. It would be nice to have other people around just now.

Except then she'd miss Ian if he came by.

What should she make of the FBI report on Martha at the funeral of Christina Doyle? And how it fit Ian's dream? The strange dream he'd told her about while in a funky mood one morning the spring of their 1L year?

Nothing. Even if Ian really was at the funeral as a young boy, it didn't prove he knew about his parents' connection to Doyle and the others. And she'd seen Ian's look when he read his mother's name on the funeral attendee list. Nobody could have faked the surprise she saw in his expression.

Brook looked around her two-bedroom Uptown apartment. Ian knew where she lived, but he'd never been inside her place before. She'd been too embarrassed to invite him in. With her father a partner at Abrams & Milliken, her mother at Stunsel & Grey, she'd worried how Ian would react if he came inside and surveyed the many trappings of *their* success on display. Like the Italian leather couch and love seat. Or the new high-end television hanging on her wall. He'd always seemed disdainful about such things. Not above it—just not driven by it.

The massive TV suddenly blared a commercial. Brook grabbed the remote and turned it off.

Then she'd gone and ambushed Ian at Kieran's Pub about how he'd mishandled their relationship since law school. She wasn't wrong. But it was her, not him, who'd run so fast when Ian told her he was taking over his dad's practice. She'd taken off like Usain Bolt, picturing him morphing into the image of the father and his stolid practice Ian always described. Like if she stuck around, sooner or later she'd be dragged into the quicksand of his limited ambitions.

She couldn't conjure the power of those fears anymore. Five years had passed and Ian was still Ian. Still protective. Still following some agenda known only to him. Still getting her jokes.

And though they'd still gotten together for meals and the occasional walk through these years, she missed him. Missed really being with him.

Brook set down the remote, picked up her cellphone, and headed toward the bathroom to prepare for bed. "If you're not coming, *then call*," she said aloud.

She was brushing her teeth when the image in the mirror

looked back at her with questioning eyes. Would she ever tell Ian more about her final breakup with Zach? Would she ever mention how it happened the third time she'd turned down Zach's ring?

Probably not. And it was even more unlikely she'd ever have reason to tell him that the last time, as the question was posed, her mind had flashed to Ian.

Just like it had the two times before.

12:45 A.M.
NORTHEAST MINNEAPOLIS

Ian rounded the corner and trudged up the side street the half a block toward his car. His sight was blurred at the edges; his head and neck pulsed pain. Maybe a concussion, he thought vaguely. It seemed the least of his worries at the moment.

His Camry was just ahead. Pulling his keys from his pocket, he stepped around the back bumper to the driver's door.

The car was listing—too much to be the flaws in his vision. Ian leaned carefully forward and squinted at the nearest tire. The hubcap rested nearly on the pavement, the rubber crushed to a few inches deep.

Ian let out a loud curse, looking angrily back in the direction of the bar. The guys who'd attacked him. They must have done it before they came into the bar.

He'd never be able to get the tire changed the way he was feeling now. How likely was it he'd find a tow this late? He reached into his jacket pocket for his phone.

It was gone.

He searched every pocket. Nothing. Ian looked again toward Larry's Bar.

A figure rounded the far corner in the direction of the bar, big and limping heavily on the leg Ian had injured. One of his hands was thrust into a bulging pocket. As he drew closer, Ian could see a grimace of pain accompanying every step.

Ian looked up the long street going the other way. Empty as far as he could see.

He had no interest in knowing what was in the man's pocket. With a rush of adrenaline spiking the pain in his head, Ian began a stumbling walk away from the approaching man.

30

A slash of light from the low moon angled into the alley off the street, illuminating it like the center stage spotlight Willy Dryer imagined it to be. Deeper in, the light tapered and disappeared. But where Willy stood, only a yard from the street end, it sparkled off flecks of broken glass, painting the brick with a soft white glow.

He loved this spot, just a few blocks from his friend's apartment where he was crashing. Quiet. No stores or clubs nearby. The hint of an echo that made it perfect as a practice stage.

"'Stars hide your fires,'" Willy muttered, pacing the narrow width of asphalt. "'Let not light see my black and deep desires. The eyes wink at the hand; yet let that be which the eye fears to see.'"

He stopped. "'Yet let that be which the eye, when . . . it . . . is . . . done . . . fears to see,'" he corrected.

He shook his head, disgusted. How could he muff the lines? This was *Shakespeare*.

211

Footfalls approached along the street that crossed the alley's open end. Willy looked up.

The overhead streetlamp was broken, leaving moon shadows of surrounding buildings stretching across the pavement like fallen pillars. Only a narrow strip of moonlight split the dark road.

The road had been empty a moment before. Now a man was moving up the far side of the street, half a block to Willy's left. Wearing a disheveled suit, he was walking erratically. Like he was drunk, Willy thought.

Willy stepped into darker shadows out of sight. There, he began his lines again in a near whisper.

Heavier footfalls began on the street. Willy stepped close to the end of the alley again and peeked out.

The drunken man was nearer, but a second figure had appeared behind him. This one was big and walking with a limp, with one hand thrust into a pocket. The other arm swung like a pendulum to balance his awkward gait. He was closing in on the drunk.

A sound pulled Willy's attention the other way.

A third man had appeared from the opposite direction, coming toward the drunk from the front. It was a skinny man holding something in his hand. Passing through a strip of moonlight, the object glinted twice, as though he was spinning it. It was a long, narrow knife.

Willy began whispering the lines again. "'Stars hide your fires . . .'"

The drunk was almost directly across the street from the alley, his steps labored. He looked up and saw the third man nearing from the opposite direction. He slowed.

The big guy closed quickly from behind.

Twenty feet from the drunk, the big man pulled his hand out of his pocket. In a hefty fist he held a handgun.

"'STARS HIDE YOUR FIRES!'" Willy shouted.

The big man's head pivoted toward him.

Willy pulled from his pocket a short-barreled Smith & Wesson. The big man's gun was angling toward Willy when it began filling the street with barrel flashes and explosions.

Willy squeezed the gun's trigger, unleashing a deeper-toned thunder.

The big man gave out a short grunt. His bones seemed to melt, and he collapsed to the ground. Then he came to life again, pushing off the ground onto his one good leg. Thrusting his gun into a pocket, he hobbled away in the direction he'd come, a hand gripping his side.

Willy looked the other way. The man with the knife had halted, staring at the scene. As his companion limped off, he turned the other way, disappearing in a run around the corner.

Willy looked back to the drunk, who stood there frozen. The noise still ringing in his ears, Willy lowered his gun and crossed the street.

The drunk sat down on the edge of the moonlit strip that had become a harsh stage light. Willy squinted to make out the man's face.

"He was surely going to shoot you," Willy said. "Never fired my gun at anybody before. But I had no choice. It all happened so fast."

The drunk looked up.

"Willy," Ian Wells muttered, "as your lawyer, I hope you have a permit for that thing."

The moonlight strip had slid farther up the street. Willy had returned the handgun to his pocket. The scene was so surreal, and Ian's head so muddled, that he had to keep looking at his client to stay grounded.

"I always do my prep up here," Willy was saying. "This alley, it's perfect. And it's only a block from the apartment I gave you the directions for, straight up the street. I figured I'd wait for you here."

Ian nodded silently.

"So why were those guys coming for you?" Willy asked.

Ian shrugged. "Maybe a mugging. Maybe an angry client put them up to it. Trying to intimidate me."

"Got somebody in mind?"

Ian nodded again.

"Hey, if this guy's after you, you think it's a good idea to go home?"

Ian's thoughts were hard to assemble. What if he was being followed? He didn't want to draw anybody to his mom's place where he was staying. "You got somewhere I can sleep tonight?" he asked.

Willy ran a hand through his long, unruly hair. "Not where I stay, man. I sleep in a corner of a living room, but there are four of us as it is."

Ian didn't think he could drive just yet. "It's okay. Maybe I'll find a hotel downtown."

"That's silly, man," Willy said. "Pay two hundred bucks for a few hours' sleep? Hey, I've got a buddy in my acting group who's got a place on Medicine Lake. His parents' place, actually. They're gone now. He told me I could crash there if I wanted to. It'd be safe. His parents are out of town and won't be back till July."

"Any chance you could drive me?"

"Not in my car. It broke down yesterday. Told you it wouldn't have made it to California. I could drive yours, though."

"Flat tire."

"I'll help you change it. Where is it?"

"A few blocks from here."

Willy reached down to help Ian to his feet. Their slow walk to the car took fifteen minutes at a pace Ian could manage. When they arrived, the street around the Camry was silent. Ian popped the trunk.

In the middle of the empty trunk was the cardboard box with a red X on top. Ian looked up at Willy at his side, then took the box out and set it on the back seat while Willy began wrestling the jack from the trunk.

Nearly an hour later they pulled up a long gravel driveway leading to a two-story house surrounded by trees. The drifting moon cast sparkles over the surface of Medicine Lake, partly visible down a slope below. Willy got out and retrieved a key from under a rock near the front door.

"Bedrooms are upstairs," Willy said.

Ian retrieved the box from the back seat and thanked him. "You take the car. I'll call tomorrow about getting it back."

Willy drove away as Ian unlocked the door and made his way upstairs, settling for the first bedroom he could find.

He didn't bother to remove the covers or his clothes. Setting the box on a side table, he lay down, thankful that at least the spinning was gone.

He wanted to reach out to Brook. Or Katie. To confide in somebody. Get help sorting through everything.

But he shouldn't, not yet. It could get either one of them in trouble. He should stick with the plan he'd made earlier, when he was thinking clearly. Meet with Callahan. Talk to Harry about how to drop the case. Return the money—or hang on to it and go to the prosecutors. Harry would help him figure it out.

He'd help figure it all out, including how to protect Mom.

He closed his eyes.

Dreams, schemes, money machines, in pieces on the ground. Connor . . . Dad. What in the world did you do? How could you drag the family into such a mess?

His surrender to sleep was laced with images of his dad before the fireplace, his mother confessing to her dead husband in the hallway, Brook's disappointed eyes at Kieran's, and a cameo of an Irish setter barking incessantly at an orange harvest moon.

31

Richard groaned as Katie twisted in bed again. She lay still. His breathing smoothed over. With all the worrying about Ian, she wasn't getting to sleep anytime soon. All she'd do is disturb Richard if she stayed in bed.

She rose, quietly put on her robe, and left her husband, heading toward the kitchen.

Since Brook's visit to the office, she'd called Ian five times. He hadn't answered any of them. Four texts got the same treatment.

Learning the terms of the trust and dealing with Brook and her story about stolen funds had been strange enough. The huge client deposit hitting their account even stranger. But Ian's disappearing act was the strangest of all. It was driving her crazy. If Brook had more luck finding him, she could blindside Ian at any minute.

The light was on in the kitchen. Nicole was seated at the breakfast table with a bowl of cereal and a smartphone in one hand.

217

"Mom!" she said, looking up. "What are you doing up? You're never up after ten."

"What are *you* doing up?" Katie replied. "It's way after midnight."

Nicole set down her phone. "I'm twenty-four, Mom. If I was asleep at this hour, I'd likely be depressed, very lonely, or both. I was out with some friends. I've got a free morning to sleep in. But I'm heading to bed now. What's your story?"

Katie wanted to talk with Nicole, talk with anyone about what was going on. But she wouldn't drag her family into this mess. "Nothing, hon," she said as she sat across the table. "Just worrying about a few things at work."

Her daughter nodded her understanding, then came around the table to kiss Katie on the head. "Get to bed soon, young lady," Nicole said.

Katie smiled. "Good night."

Alone in the kitchen, Katie pulled her laptop from a bag on the floor. Opening it, she prepared to send yet another email to Ian.

A message alert from Wells Fargo popped onto the screen. Katie opened it.

You have made an electronic transfer, the transaction receipt confirmed.

No, I didn't, Katie thought. She brought up the Wells Fargo website and typed in the ID and password. Once the account's home page opened, Katie went to the account summaries.

The firm's account summary for Ian's practice looked untouched since earlier. So did the clients' funds account. She scrolled down to check the new account with the large deposit of money.

Account balance: $00.00

Katie stared for a moment. This wasn't possible. There was over nine million dollars in there this afternoon. Katie glanced down to the list of transactions: only one, and it was just fifteen minutes ago. Someone had gone into the new account at 2:05 a.m. and made a withdrawal.

Katie shook her head. Now what did that mean?

She still had no clue where the new account and money had come from—and wouldn't until she reached Ian. But now she had even more news to share.

Because in a single transaction, all the funds in the new account had been completely withdrawn.

32

Brook came down the hallway toward her office with a loggy headache. She never recovered well from restless nights, and last night had included less than three hours of actual sleep. Even a long, hot shower hadn't revived her.

The office was quieter than on a weekday, of course, yet she could hear she wasn't the first one in. She rounded the corner.

Chloe was coming out of Brook's office, shutting the door carefully behind her.

"*Hey,*" Brook called out. Chloe stopped and turned.

"Hi, Brook!" Chloe greeted her with excited eyes, as though she had no clue why Brook was glaring. "You haven't heard?"

Her anger slid away as Brook sensed a new train coming at her. "Heard what?"

"That guy you and Eldon interviewed late yesterday? Ian Wells? You gave him the usual instruction not to leave town without checking in with our office, right?"

"Yes, it's routine," Brook said.

"Well, we got a tip on voicemail last night that he's left. Somebody called to say Wells was seen driving out of the Twin Cities."

She wanted to wipe the clerk's smirk from her face. "A tip from who?"

Chloe shrugged. "It was anonymous. Anyway, Eldon's got people trying to figure out if it's true and where Wells might have gone. The message said the caller would get back to us with more information."

"Who'd give an anonymous tip about something like that?" Brook asked—wanting to add, *Like who would give a tip about stiff twenties being deposited in a bank?*

Chloe shrugged again. "Who knows? But they're going to check it out."

Brook nodded, suddenly deflated. "Okay. Keep me in the loop. Really, I mean it."

The law clerk flashed one of her broad smiles. "Of course, Brook. You'll know whatever I know."

Muffled voices seeped through the locked wooden door in front of Ian. The voices were all he had, as he had no way to get to the other side. Fear filled him. His mother was on the other side of the door, and he desperately needed to rejoin her.

He wandered down a hall to a room where a group of adults towered over and around him, talking and drinking, paying him no attention. Couldn't they see he needed to get back into the bedroom?

Across the room stood a young girl with red bangs. She looked straight at Ian. She raised a hand and crooked a finger in invitation.

He walked toward her, weaving through the grown-ups to her side, then followed in her wake as she led him down another hallway. They reached a door, where she raised the same finger to her lips before turning the knob and going in.

It was a dark room with glass aquarium walls floor to ceiling, the panels filled with whales and dolphins swimming in shadowy circles about them. In front of the panels was a forest of bamboo, creaking and swaying in an unfelt breeze. Beneath his feet was a plush forest floor.

If only for an instant, Ian wanted to watch the sea life swimming by. But the girl was leading him at a tiptoe pace across the floor to the double doors of a closet. With a gentle pull, she drew the doors open.

Moths came rushing out in a fury like a flight of escaping bats. Then they were gone, leaving behind a row of suits and dresses hanging above a small wall of neatly stacked shoe boxes.

Ian approached. The clothing and shoe boxes had been parted to create a path to another wall. In that wall was a thin crack through which light filtered from somewhere beyond.

The girl motioned Ian closer and stepped aside to make way. Ian obeyed, leaning forward to look through the crack to the other side.

He was seeing into a room. It was the one behind the locked door. Young Rory Doyle sat on the bed in the middle of the room. Sean Callahan leaned against a far wall beside the old man, who was seated with a hat in his lap. A fourth man stood nearby, the one by the pool. Instinctively he knew it was Ed McMartin.

His mother was nowhere to be seen.

Voices from the room twisted and twined like a choir's harmony, no single voice distinguishable. "Rory's fault . . . When do we distribute . . . Danger . . ."

The choir stopped, and Ian heard a voice he knew was the old man's. "A while longer."

The chorus renewed, rushed and frantic, until the old man spoke again, silencing them all once more.

The words were less distinct this time, but impressions flowed to Ian like flavors washing over his tongue. Of trust. Or a trust. Of money in a safe. Or until it was safe. Of paintings or a painting. Of choices or one choice.

And over it all, a command of patience.

Ian blinked. In that instant the room emptied. All except for the old man with the hat, and now his mother standing nearby, the skin of her face rich and young.

Desperate to join her, Ian strained to focus on each word and gesture.

"We won't take the money." It was his mother.

The old man raised his hands as he spoke. "They won't trust you then," he said. Then he added, "There's only one painting left."

More impressions streamed through the crack. The secrecy of the remaining painting. A year of significance. That the man was entrusting something to his mother's care.

Ian blinked.

And his mother was gone. In her place, Sean Callahan stood before the old man, hands deep in his pockets. They were discussing Rory. "Don't harm him," the old man was saying. "No matter what, you must never harm him." Callahan acknowledged the command with a dip of his head.

Their conversation then shifted to "Connor and Martha."

"Watch them" was all the old man said this time as he reached down to tie his shoe.

Ian was about to turn away when movement pulled his attention to the floor near the bed.

And he saw it. He saw it.

Ian pivoted away from the crack toward the bamboo-filled room behind him to ask the girl about what he'd just seen. As he twisted, his foot caught on something and he began falling onto the shoe boxes, rattling them like tenpins across the ground. He landed and instantly struggled to get to his hands and knees, but the forest floor had become ice and his hands and feet slid in all directions.

Then he was rising, rising, rising—off the floor and into the air. Staring into the face of Sean Callahan.

Ian sat up from the hard bed, feeling as if he hadn't moved for hours. His shirt was wet. The dream was fading. He began an unsettling slide back to reality.

The images were mostly gone—except for a single painting. A year associated with the painting. And something he'd seen before a fall that he could no longer recall.

Emotions filled the place of the lost images. Panic. Dread. Anger. His youthful mother.

Danger.

He took several deep breaths. The emotions congealed into one. A powerful compulsion to reach Martha.

Ignoring a stab of pain in his neck, Ian rose from the bed. The shoe box with the weapon inside still sat on the bedside table. He opened it, removed the gun and slipped it in his belt, then walked to the open bedroom window.

Orange pulses of light skipped across the surface of the lake below, visible through the trees. Sunset. He'd slept the whole day away. He went downstairs to the front door and out into the dusky yard. The driveway was empty. Of course it was, he recalled. He'd given Willy his keys and let him drive away. And him without a phone.

Great move. He returned to the house and searched the place for a phone. There was none.

He had to get a ride to his mom's home and check on her, make sure she was safe. Afterward he'd follow through on his plan to extricate himself from all of this.

He was returning to the front door when he felt the weight of the gun at his back. He had no registration for it—or a permit to carry any handgun, for that matter. All he needed now was to get arrested on a weapons charge.

Ian walked around the outside of the house to the back, where it faced the lake. The home was a walkout, the basement opening onto a wooded slope topped by a stairway that led down to a beach. Ian took the stairs, moving toward the water below.

Near the base of the stairs, a short dock reached out over the lake, its surface stirred by a soft breeze. A wood-chip trail followed the water's edge toward the neighboring home about fifty yards away.

Ian began walking the trail.

Half the distance to the next house, he stopped. A rotted log lay just outside the trail in the shelter of the woods amid taller grass. Ian stepped over it. The log was cracked on the side opposite the trail, hollowed inside. Ian wedged the gun into the space and covered the place with brush.

He rose just as a flock of mallards launched themselves off the lake's black surface into the darkening sky, startling him. The birds lifted higher, one letting out a loud call as they slid into formation and lofted away. Ian watched, his worry accelerating about his mom. He wished he could launch himself into similar flight to Minneapolis.

He hurried back up the trail.

At the top of the stairs, he heard the sound of gravel popping under approaching tires. Willy must be wrong, he thought, momentarily panicked. The owners must be returning to the house after all. Either that or Willy had come back for him.

Calm down, he told himself. If it was the owners, maybe he could give some kind of explanation and then borrow a cellphone to arrange a ride into Minneapolis.

Ian walked to the top of the driveway and waited.

A gray car came around the nearest curve, its headlights off. In the growing darkness, the face of the driver was invisible. The car drew near and parked. A large, familiar figure stepped out.

The man scratched his neck with one hand as he strode purposefully toward Ian. His other hand reached into his belt.

It was Sean Callahan's assistant, the Marine. In the instant of Ian's recognition, the man raised the biggest handgun Ian had ever seen and pointed it at his face.

"My man!" the Marine said. "You remember me, right? Aaron Ziegler? Well, I am *so glad* to have found you here, son. So glad. And let me tell you, Sean will be too."

33

Seated on the porch, Ian licked dry lips. His eyes flickered to the gun that rested, along with a cellphone, on the Marine's lap. "I don't understand," Ian said again. "Just tell me why you're here."

The Marine gestured toward his phone. "Sorry. Can't say anything until Sean texts me back."

Just seconds later, the phone in his lap buzzed. Aaron picked it up and read the screen. "Okay," he said. "I guess we're headin' to St. Paul."

"Is this about the money?" Ian asked. "Because I don't want it. I'm not going to represent the trust anymore. I'm happy to transfer it back to Callahan."

"A little late for that, don't you think?"

Ian stiffened. "What does that mean?"

"Well, that might have been a possibility before you transferred the money out of your bank account to who knows where."

"I don't know what you're talking about."

Aaron chortled. "Dude, Sean's not an idiot. That banker gave him a way to keep an eye on the account. No access, but a portal to watch money going in and out. Sean knew the minute you took the money out of your bank account last night. And your car's been lowjacked since he hired you. You think he'd put nine million into your hands and not keep an eye on you? We found the car in northeast Minneapolis parked outside some apartment building, then backtracked the signal here. You should've run farther and faster, my man."

"I didn't know—*I don't know*—that the money's gone," Ian declared. "And I wasn't running away. I'm here because some guys, who I think are working for Rory, attacked me in Minneapolis last night. There was even a shooting. I came up here to get away for the night and decide what to do next."

Aaron leaned back, his incredulity a neon sign. "To recap, then, Counselor: the trust money disappears, you end up in a strange house half an hour away from home, and your best excuse is you were attacked last night in Minneapolis. Well, you've sure got me convinced. Now you can try it out on Sean. Get up. We've gotta go."

The image of Callahan's tanned and timeworn face came back to Ian, him seated in his shadowy living room with the gaudy chairs—looking at Ian the way his assistant was now as he interrogated Ian in his Irish accent. It was the last place Ian wanted to go, especially if the money really was gone.

"If I was running," Ian said, not moving, "why would I stop half an hour from home? Wouldn't I be in Canada by now? Or Mexico? And where's my bag? Did my plan fail to include a toothbrush?"

The Marine shrugged. "Maybe you travel light."

"No, really, think about this," Ian said firmly. "If I'm the lawyer with a plan, you think *this* is the best explanation I could come up with? I mean—" he stopped himself—"wait. There's somebody who can prove what I'm telling you is true."

"Educate me."

"She's . . . she's with the U.S. Attorney's Office. The shooting last night, I think one of the shooters got hit. My friend could confirm it. It would be a stomach wound. She'll confirm a gunshot victim last night."

Aaron smirked again. "Not very likely we're calling her."

"No," Ian pressed, still eyeing the gun. "Put the pieces together. What I'm telling you is true. You need to know what Rory's doing here, and she can confirm it. We can make the call on your cell. Put it on speaker. You'll have your gun pointed at me. I won't say a word about you and this."

The Marine stared at him before glancing at his watch. "Stay put."

Aaron stepped inside the house, out of earshot but with the barrel never deviating from Ian. He made a single call. After a few moments, he returned to the porch.

"Alright. Sean says one call—and I'm to do your kneecap if you say a word out of order. So tell me the number."

Ian recited Brook's cell number from memory. Aaron set the phone down onto a table between them, on speaker. After two rings, Brook's voice answered.

"Yes?"

Ian leaned closer to the phone. "Brook, it's me."

"*Ian. Where are you?* And what are you doing calling me? Whose phone is this? You know better than this. I thought you'd come to my apartment last night. We should only talk in person. But we've got to talk."

"Slow down, Brook," Ian said, surprised at how calm his voice came out. "It's okay. I've only got a minute now. We can talk more soon. But I need you to confirm something for me. Can you check to see if there was a reported shooting last night? In northeast Minneapolis. After midnight."

"What are you talking about?"

"A shooting. Rory Doyle was supposed to meet me at a bar. A couple of guys came instead. They slit my tire, beat me up, then followed me onto the street. Before they caught me, Willy Dryer shot one of them."

"Willy Dryer? Your client? *Shot somebody?* I don't know what you're talking about. Are you okay?"

Ian took a deep breath. "Brook, please. I'm okay. But I need you to check Minneapolis police reports for any shootings last night, plus any gunshot victims reporting to a hospital. Probably HCMC. A shot in the abdomen."

The line went silent. Ian looked up at the smirk that had returned to Aaron's face.

"There were no shooting reports in that area last night," Brook's voice returned. "No shooting victims at the hospitals that I can see. Ian, what's going on?"

Aaron leaned his gun across the table, signaling for Ian to end the call.

His hope plummeted. "I've gotta go, Brook," he said. "We'll talk later."

"*Wait*," she came back. "There was a call to our office. Somebody said you'd ignored my instructions from the interrogation and left town. An anonymous tip. You were just a witness before, but with this news you're becoming a target. Eldon's running with this thing, and a clerk on steroids is elbowing in between him and me, so it's possible more has happened and I haven't been told. If so, they could be watching for your car."

Ian noticed Aaron's expression had grown stone-cold. He

turned back to the phone. "Thanks, Brook." He took a quick glance at Aaron, then rushed on. "Believe me, I didn't do anything wrong. I need your help to figure this out. And you've got to get Mom to someplace safe, away from the house. I think she's in danger. Call Katie—"

Aaron grabbed the phone and killed the call. "Which kneecap are you less fond of?" he said, aiming the gun.

Through the windows facing the front lawn came a faint flash of headlights. They grew gradually brighter, accompanied by red-and-blue colors rolling across the walls of the room.

Aaron peered out at the lights, then back at Ian. He pointed the gun toward the stairs leading from the porch to the ground below. "Move it," the Marine commanded. "*Now.*"

10:17 P.M.
MARTHA WELLS RESIDENCE
LYNNHURST NEIGHBORHOOD, MINNEAPOLIS

Katie pulled her car into the driveway of Martha's house, disappointed to find Ian's car not there. Where had he gone? She had to get to her boss before this strange client found out about the missing money, and without drawing the U.S. Attorney's Office down on them.

She cut the lights, plunging the neighborhood into blackness. Only a streetlight half a block away and the waning moon just above the horizon illuminated the house. Getting out of the car, she walked to the garage door and peered through the glass at eye level. Ian's car wasn't inside.

She looked to the house. Martha must be asleep at this hour. She didn't want to wake her or the neighborhood, but she'd vowed this time to camp out here until Ian came or called.

Was there any chance Ian could be here, even without his car? Stranger things were happening, and it wouldn't be hard to check the kitchen or knock on the window of his old room.

Skirting the garage, she passed by the vegetable garden on her way to the back deck, feeling the dewy grass on her ankles. She walked quietly up the stairs. No lights came from the kitchen or living room. If she remembered correctly, Ian's window was located at the far end of the deck.

Something crunched beneath her feet. Katie stopped and looked down. Nothing was visible in the faint light. She looked up at the patio door. A thin seam bisected the glass near the bottom. She moved closer. Deep gouges marked where the patio door had been pried, cracking the glass. She traced the door's edge with her hand. It was still ajar.

Somebody had broken in. And if Ian *wasn't* home, that left Martha in there alone.

Katie patted her pockets, then let out a low, frustrated hiss. She'd left her phone in the car. If she went to retrieve it now and the intruder was still here, she could get caught between them and the street. Not where she wanted to be.

She considered sliding open the patio door and entering the dark house that looked like a bear's den . . . except she couldn't get her feet to move another step closer.

I will not leave Martha alone in there with a burglar, Katie commanded herself silently. She wouldn't. With Ian gone somewhere, nobody was around to watch out for Martha.

Katie walked backward down the steps without turning her face from the door. On the grass again, her fear eased enough to let her pivot and race across the lawn to behind the hedge at the rear of the vegetable garden. She turned to face the house again.

She cleared her throat and tried to imagine herself surrounded by her choir. She began to sing. "'Amazing grace, how sweet the sound . . .'" It was the first song that came to her, and one of the few she could remember all the words for in the grip of her distress.

Her voice came out thin and weak, like hands were tight around her throat. Slowly, the fingers relented and her voice rose in volume: "'. . . was lost, but now am found.'"

She felt the fear lifting as she sang. Boldness took its place.

Lights came on in a neighbor's house. Katie raised the song to another key, keeping her eyes locked on Martha's back patio door.

The door was moving, sliding slowly open . . .

Katie stopped singing. *"I've got a gun!"* she called out. "You just go right out the front door and I'll let you be."

The figure didn't move for a long moment. Then it took a step toward her, crunching glass underfoot.

Nausea filled Katie's stomach. Her mind said *run*.

She pictured Martha inside the house. She stayed.

A buzzing sound began. The figure hesitated before pulling a phone from a pocket and putting it to an ear. After another minute, the figure stepped back into the dark interior of the house.

Katie heard the distant slam of a door. It took several deep breaths before she began crossing the backyard toward the house again.

The figure reappeared at the patio door and stepped out, freezing her.

Stunned, Katie blurted out, "I told you, I've got a gun."

"It's me," a voice answered softly.

Katie's breath came out of her. "Martha, honey, is that you? My Lord, protect me. I thought you had a burglar."

Martha stood on the deck like a statue, a breeze rippling her cotton bathrobe. "I don't know," she said at last. "I really don't know."

34

Ian led the way in the dark down the slope toward the lake through brush and trees several yards to the right of the staircase. Twisting around the larger bushes he could make out, he fought to maintain his footing on the uneven, descending ground.

The heavier footfalls of the Marine behind him signaled his nearness. With each of the big man's steps, Ian could imagine the handgun pointed directly at his back.

The wood-chip path grew visible below, washed white in the pale moonlight. Ian lifted his foot for another step when he heard a grunt followed by a muffled *"Uumph."*

He looked over his shoulder. High above, multiple room lights were coming on in the house. Only ten feet up the slope, the Marine lay splayed on his back. The gun was no longer in his hand.

Ian spun around and plunged the remaining distance down to the path, twisted left, and began to run. He passed the staircase and the dock. Slowing, he began scanning the woods to his left for the rotted log.

A crash of brush up the trail told him the Marine was up and onto the path. Ian could feel the gun's sight on his back. He gasped out a prayer that the Marine wouldn't take a chance firing with houses so close.

There was the log, straight ahead. Sweat stinging his eyes, Ian vaulted over the log. He crouched down and felt for the hollow gap. His fingers brushed the cold steel of the barrel. He pulled it out, got his fist around the handle. Staying low, he raised the weapon toward the path with both hands.

The Marine came into view. He was moving more slowly now, scanning the woods. Leaves and dirt covered his shirt. The gun was back and raised in his right hand.

"Lower the gun," Ian commanded, crouching even lower.

The Marine stopped abruptly and squinted into the darkness, in the direction of the tree line and Ian's voice.

Ian swallowed his fear. "I *will* shoot you, Aaron. I'd rather face the police than your boss."

The Marine slowly lowered his gun.

"Now drop it to the ground."

The gun fell.

Ian looked around, calculating how to keep the man from following him. Past the outline of Aaron's still form, a loon flapped its wings on the surface of the lake.

"Drop your phone to the ground too," Ian said. "Then turn around and walk into the lake."

"What the . . ." the Marine protested. He started to bend toward his gun.

"Which lung are you less fond of?" Ian said.

Aaron stopped and straightened, shaking his head. With a

curse, he pulled his phone from his pocket and tossed it to the ground. He turned and walked to the water's edge, then started taking off his shirt.

"Clothes stay on."

Cursing again, the Marine stepped gingerly into the water up to his ankles.

"Keep going. Keep going until I tell you to stop."

Aaron waded slowly out into the lake, his arms in the air. Thirty feet out, the water was up to his waist. Another ten feet and it reached his chest.

"Good enough," Ian called out.

Picking up the Marine's weapon and phone, Ian headed back up the path at a run, away from the house where he'd spent the night.

———

11:45 P.M.
MARTHA WELLS RESIDENCE
LYNNHURST NEIGHBORHOOD, MINNEAPOLIS

They sat with teacups on their laps as though it were a summer afternoon of catching up, Martha on the couch and Katie in a chair. Except Katie's eyes were scanning the clutter of boxes that were now blanketed with torn chair cushions, emptied drawers, and the broken frames of every large picture that once hung on the walls of the house.

Martha sat calmly amid the destruction, sipping her tea. Thank goodness for small favors, Katie thought. The woman didn't seem to notice that the room looked like it had been bombed.

Katie knew she should already have called the police. But she couldn't do it. The police coming would mean news of the burglary could get back to Brook. She'd then tie it back to the retainer money of stolen cash Brook claimed they'd deposited. Which would mean discovery of the trust money in the new firm account—and the fact that the money *was now missing*. Then the *client* would learn the money was gone. At which time that poor woman sitting on her living room couch sipping tea would be dragged somewhere and bombarded with questions she wouldn't even comprehend.

It was a horror show with the volume turned up. She may not be right about it all, but Katie knew she couldn't call the police—not without first reaching Ian.

"Hon," Katie piped up using her best carefree voice, "you're sure you didn't see anybody tonight? Hear anything?"

Martha shook her head. "Why, no, Katie. Do you know when Connor will be home?"

"No, dear," Katie said, gratified, at least, that Martha continued to recall who she was. "I'm sure it will be soon, though."

Martha frowned. "Maybe I should tidy up a bit before he does."

"You know what, Martha? I think you ought to get some rest now. Let me do the tidying for you."

"Thank you . . ." The older woman paused and took another sip of her tea. Then she smiled. "They'll never find it, you know."

"Find what?" Katie asked.

"I don't even understand how they know about it. But they'll never find it," she repeated.

Martha was looking straight through her now. Katie rose, took Martha's cup from her hand, set it on the coffee table, and then led her to the bedroom.

Minutes later, Katie surveyed the mess in the living room.

She steeled herself. This was her forte, bringing order from chaos. If she could do it for three lawyers over her career, she sure could do the same for a few rooms.

Within an hour, she'd made a stack in one corner of the room of the prints, paintings, and photographs that had been torn from their frames. The boxes that once occupied the living room she'd moved to another corner. The trash of broken frames and destroyed cushions she piled in the middle. With a sigh she picked up the first armful of trash to take out to the garbage cans.

The lid to the largest trash can in the garage was ajar. Katie dropped her load, set the trash lid on the floor, and leaned down to pick up her load again.

On top of trash already in the can was a yellowed newspaper lying atop a closed box marked with an X of red tape. The newspaper was clearly very old. Curious, Katie picked it up.

It was a copy of the *Star Tribune*, dated January 15, 1983. The oversized print of the front-page headline read, *Rockwell Paintings Stolen in Daring St. Louis Park Art Theft*.

Katie stared at the headline. She read the first few paragraphs of the article.

"What in the world is this doing here?" she called out.

Her voice echoed in the quiet garage. Shaking her head, Katie walked back inside the house. She went to Martha's bedroom door and opened it a crack.

Martha lay asleep. After a moment's thought, Katie backed away and closed the door again.

She looked again at the newspaper in her hands. Why had Connor or Martha kept this newspaper? And why was it thrown away now, so many years later?

She heard her cellphone ringing from her purse in the living room. Katie returned there and lifted the phone into the light.

"Katie," a familiar voice said when she answered it.

"*Ian.* Ian, is that you?"

"Yeah, Katie. Sorry I've been out of touch. Listen, I'm worried about Mom. I haven't been back there since yesterday afternoon. It's a long story, but—"

"Don't worry about Martha," Katie interrupted. "I mean, there are things we've got to talk about, but she's fine right now. I'm with her at her house."

She heard a sigh of relief. "I owe you so much, Katie. Thanks. But I need you to get her out of there. I need you to take her someplace safe."

"Yeah, I was thinking the same thing."

"Why? What's going on?"

Katie exhaled, trying to think how best to explain things. "Hon, do you know about the cash in that new account at the office?"

"I do. It's the trust money. I'll explain about it later."

"Okay. But you ought to know the money's gone."

"I heard that."

"You did? How?"

"Very long story. One I can't go into right now. What else?"

"Your mom's house got broken into tonight."

"Is Mom okay?" Ian asked breathlessly.

"Yeah, hon. She's fine. But the place was trashed. They even tore down all the frames and pictures, every one of 'em. And your mom said something about 'they'll never find it.' You know what she's talking about?"

Ian's voice rose in alarm. "You've *got* to get her out of there. You can't take her to your home either. That's too obvious—and risky for your family."

"Yeah. I've got a cousin who's out of town. I've got the keys to her house. I'll take your mom there."

"It's asking a lot, Katie, but can you stay with her? She'll be disoriented in a different place."

"Of course."

"Thanks. One more thing. Your notes said Brook implied the trust money may be stolen cash. I think she's right. The retainer and the rest of it."

Katie realized she was no longer surprised at the notion. She explained her full encounter with Brook at the office. "Ian, can I trust Brook? Can I talk to her?"

"Yes. She called me in for an interrogation on the stolen money, but managed to tell me more about the investigation than she got out of me. There's more I need to tell you, Katie. A lot more. But . . . wait. A pickup's slowing down." The line went silent. In the background, Katie could hear Ian talking. *"Minneapolis . . . or actually, St. Paul,"* he was saying. *"That'd be great."*

His voice returned fully to the call. "I'm hitching a ride now. Can't talk anymore. Please, move Martha as soon as possible."

The phone went dead. Katie put it back in her purse. She folded the yellowed newspaper and slid it into her purse as well.

Suddenly she felt as though not alone, as though the house were alive and watching her every movement. As though if she walked out the front door, the police or the crazy St. Paul client would be standing there ready to pounce.

A tremble went through her. She recalled the fear that had frozen her on the back deck and how she'd gotten past it.

"Enough of this," Katie said out loud. She'd let Martha get

her sleep, and use the couch for herself. Then, in the morning, she'd get her moved.

Ian and this family had been at her side her whole life. She wasn't going to let them down now.

Humming "Amazing Grace," she launched herself into the task of carrying the rest of the trash outside.

35

Ian looked out the window of the pickup as they passed through Minneapolis neighborhoods that melded seamlessly into St. Paul. Thick, puffy clouds were closing in, obscuring the stars. Maybe rain, he thought.

The truck took the Snelling ramp off Highway 94, pulling to the top of the exit and stopping in the far right lane.

"This work for you?" the driver said in a slow drawl. Ian hadn't noticed the license plate, but took a guess at Kentucky.

"It does," Ian replied. "I really appreciate it." He pulled out his wallet and extended a twenty.

The driver held up his hands. "That's not how it works in this rig. Don't you worry about it."

Ian thanked him, opened the door, and started to step down to the pavement.

"Hey, son?"

He looked back up at the driver. "Yeah?"

"Next time you hitch a ride somewhere, figure out a better

place to stash those hog's legs instead of under your shirt in your back belt. Those two pieces must've hurt like a son of a gun the whole ride. Besides, you're liable to shoot the truck or yourself."

"That obvious, huh?" Ian said, embarrassed. "Why'd you pick me up then?"

"Boy, something's clearly on your mind that's got you carryin' those pieces—my four-year-old daughter could've told you that. But I've never seen a gangster in a suit needs cleaning, hitchhiking in the middle of the night."

As the truck rolled off, Ian looked around and got his bearings, then started walking.

Reaching Callahan's house twenty minutes later, Ian stood on the sidewalk and stared at the front door bracketed by tall windows. Shaking his head, he walked around the back. There were no windows for anyone to see who was knocking. He pulled one of the handguns from his belt and banged repeatedly on the back door.

Footsteps finally approached, and the door pulled open a crack. Ian thrust the barrel of the gun through.

Dressed in a robe and slippers, Sean Callahan stepped back and made room for Ian to enter. "Living room," Ian said, kicking the door shut behind him. He followed Callahan down a shadowy corridor to the familiar room.

"Didn't expect all this after you missed our appointment yesterday," Callahan said, taking a seat in his usual spot. Ian took the orange chair. "Though I was wonderin' why Aaron hadn't arrived or called back again."

"I'm sure he would have," Ian said, "if I hadn't taken his phone before he went into the lake."

Callahan's eyebrows rose, but he didn't ask for more explanation. "So why'd you come back to me?" he said, resting his hands on his thighs.

"Aaron must've relayed my story when he called. I came to tell you it was all true. I don't know anything about the money being gone. I was planning to transfer it back to you this morning. I want to be done with the trust."

"Um-hm." Callahan's accent fully returned when he opened his mouth again. "That story you're talkin' about—ya mean about Rory trying to have ya beat up or killed? And ya goin' out to Medicine Lake to 'think it through'? I definitely want all the details. In fact, I'm plannin' to write it down to share with some of my friends at the pub."

"What do I have to do to prove I'm not lying?"

"Returnin' my money would make for a fresh start."

"First," Ian said, "I thought it was the trust's money. Second, I'm telling you that's what I want to do. I just don't have a clue who took it or where it's gone. Not yet."

Callahan raised his eyes to the ceiling. "Mr. Wells, do ya know why I've got that single, dreadful-lookin' orange chair you're sittin' in, and why I seated you in it the very first time you were here?"

"No."

"'Cause that chair, done up in Ulster orange amidst all this lovely Irish green, helps me remember who in the room I can trust."

"I didn't steal your money."

"Then who did?"

"If it wasn't you, I'm thinking it was Rory. Or the banker."

Callahan shook his head. "The banker gets shaky at his own shadow. He'd not touch a penny of the trust. And Rory? He's not as stupid as he looks, but I doubt he's got a way with computers and hackin' electronic bank transfers—which is the only way he'd have gotten the cash out of your account without your say-so, wouldn't you agree?"

Ian waved the gun in the air. "Then I don't know. But I've got to have time to find it. For all I know, you took it."

"Aye. That's why I sent Aaron chasin' after ya. That makes a lot of sense."

Ian was growing concerned staying so long in Callahan's house. He'd planned to confront the man and get out.

"I've had some time to think about Aaron showing up on my way here," Ian said. "You could have taken the money, but wanted it to look like I took it before you put me into the hands of the police. Or you could have taken the money and then planned to make me disappear so the police would go chasing the wrong way."

Callahan smiled. "Why in the world would I want the police anywhere near the trust money?"

"I don't know that either. But somebody does. Somebody's been circulating bills from an art heist—and the prosecutor's office knows it."

It was the first time Ian had seen Callahan look genuinely surprised. Surprised and worried. "What're ya saying?" he asked softly.

Ian leaned forward. "The U.S. Attorney's Office dragged me in for questioning yesterday. No, actually, the day before. They said they'd recovered stolen money from an old art theft. Some of the bills surfaced the day I deposited your cash retainer. In our conversation, the attorney brought your name up. Along with Rory's and Ed McMartin's."

Callahan's face grew ashen. "While I don't admit to knowin' what you're talkin' about, ya insult me if ya think I'm stupid enough to ever give a lawyer cash that could be traced to a theft."

Which, Ian realized, made sense. He shook his head. "I don't know then. I don't understand any of this. But I've got to have some time to figure it out."

The Irishman wiped his palms on his pants. "How much time?"

"Two weeks."

Callahan shook his head again. "With prosecutors involved? Sounds like time has become somethin' of a scarcity."

"That's your fault. Or the fault of whoever started circulating hot money."

"I suggest ya look around at your other clients for that kinda behavior, Counselor," Callahan hissed. "I hear ya represent a lot of criminal types." Before Ian could answer, Callahan said, "Let's stop bandyin' this about. I'll give ya three days—countin' this one. That's the same time ya had to complete your investigation for the trust. After Tuesday I'll want the money *and* your report. You do a good job, ya still can have the big fee I promised."

Ian didn't believe the last statement in the least. He wanted to argue for more time, but discomfort was beating like a hot light on his skin. "Alright," Ian said. "I also need some information."

"Such as?"

"I have to know my father's and mother's role in this art theft. Other than Dad preparing the trust."

The Irishman leaned forward. "I'm not sayin' I know anythin' about any theft, Counselor, but I'll tell ya this. So far as I knew, your da did most of the things he did because he was married to your ma. Seemed to have a protective instinct about the woman. Kinda like his son. So she can tell ya what ya need to know."

"My mother has Alzheimer's," Ian shot back. "She can't tell me what I need to know."

"I heard somethin' about that," Callahan replied. "Well, that's all I have to say about the affair."

Ian's chest ached, filled with tension between wanting to press for more information and wanting to get out. "Then promise me that whatever happens, my mother will be safe. You'll leave her out of it."

Callahan paused. "That's not an assurance I'm willin' to give ya."

"Why not?"

"Mostly I'd like ya to have an incentive to return the money. But also, because your mother and da have some responsibility here."

"She's got Alzheimer's," Ian repeated. "She can't harm you."

When Callahan didn't budge—didn't even blink—Ian raised the barrel of the gun. The next words came out as firmly as a statement in court. "If you harm *her*, if you even try to, I'll kill you."

Callahan grinned. "Still protecting her, little Master?"

A picture surfaced. Of staring into the face of a powerful man leaning down at a graveside, squeezing Ian's shoulder until it hurt—and calling him that name.

His birthday dream. And something more.

Ian's face flushed with rage. His finger strayed from the trigger guard to the trigger.

There was a click of metal. Ian turned his head.

The Marine was standing in the hallway leading to the front door, his clothes dark with dampness. In his hand was a new gun.

Ian exhaled. He moved the finger away from the trigger and lowered his weapon.

"Ease off, Aaron," he heard the Irishman say once Ian's gun barrel pointed to the floor. "Our guest was just leavin'. We've come to an understandin'."

Callahan followed Ian to the front door, where Ian slid the gun under his shirt and belt before stepping out onto the stoop. Once there, he stopped. An impression took shape in his memory. Another image from his dreams. He turned back to Callahan. "Tell me, are you going to keep your promise to Jimmy Doyle not to harm Rory if I prove it was him who took the money?"

Callahan's eyes widened into a stare—looking every bit as though he were staring at Jimmy Doyle's ghost and the specter was looking back, straight into his heart.

"You've quite a memory, boyo," the Irishman murmured. "You weren't more than nine or ten at the time. But I'd suggest ya be forgettin' that conversation and concentratin' your questions on findin' that money instead. Because if ya fail at that, there'll be nobody ya care about who'll be safe."

36

As her call on her cell was answered, Brook nearly jumped in surprise. "Katie?" she said anxiously. "Katie, is that you?"

"Yes, Brook. It's me."

"Katie, I know you don't trust me," Brook said quickly, "but I'm trying to help Ian as much as I can. My office is trying to find him because they think he has access to stolen money from an old case—that he had some role in handling or laundering the cash. I don't think they're right. I'm putting my career on the line here, Katie."

"It's alright, hon. Slow down. Ian said I should trust you. It's okay."

Brook let out a sigh. "That's great. Do you know where Ian is? I spoke to him last night. He was using somebody else's phone."

Katie gave a shaky whistle. "That's the million-dollar question. I talked to him too—real short. It sounded like he was

249

hitchhiking somewhere. Girl, this is getting out of hand. I don't understand why Ian would disappear for so long with his mom in such rough shape. It's not like him. And Martha's place got broken into last night."

"A break-in?"

Katie described the burglary at the house. "First thing this morning, I got her out to a cousin's place who's on vacation. I'm staying with her now."

"Did you report it?"

"What do you think?"

Brook hesitated. "Katie, I think we can do a lot more good if we work together. I've got to know more about what's going on."

"I agree. I'm scared. Really scared. I'm afraid to even go to the office. I don't know when to answer calls on my cell. Could my phone be bugged?"

Brook hesitated. Was she really about to cross that line? From making a few calls and subtle hints in an interrogation to full-blown obstruction?

"You're not being bugged—at least not yet," Brook answered. "They won't have gone that deep with Ian still mostly a suspected material witness. Staying away from the office? Not sure. It may be a good idea right now, though I don't know if they're watching it or not. Martha's house as well."

She'd done it. Crossed the line. *Ian, you'd better be the man I think you are.*

Brook's phone vibrated with an incoming message. She held the phone out to read it: *11:00 lunch, where we met this week.*

The number was one she didn't recognize. But this week she'd only met one person for lunch outside the office.

"Katie," she said excitedly, "Ian's trying to reach me. I'll call you this afternoon. Don't answer any calls except from me or your family." She paused. "Any numbers you don't recognize—or even a call from me—don't answer until the third try."

"Okay." Katie hung up.

Brook looked at the time, grabbed her briefcase, and headed to her closed office door.

She was turning down the hall toward the elevators when she saw Chloe at the far end of the hall. The clerk glanced in Brook's direction.

Minutes later, Brook left the federal courthouse. She was nearly to the corner when a careful glimpse over her shoulder revealed what she'd suspected from her glance into the law clerk's eyes.

Chloe was leaving the courthouse fifty yards behind, following in her direction.

▌11:12 A.M.

Standing in the foyer of Kieran's Irish Pub, Ian shifted back to his left foot, juggling in his right hand the phone he'd just bought to text Brook. The shirt and suit pants he'd worn the past three days felt stiff and uncomfortable. The single gun he'd kept in his possession was a hard, cold lump against his back.

He was about to check the time again when something tugged on his elbow.

"Ian," Brook whispered. "Come with me."

She looked so fresh and pretty and safe, even trailing a hint of her perfume, that Ian felt the urge to kiss her. She didn't give him the chance. He followed as she walked rapidly through the restaurant.

They came to the kitchen door, and Brook pushed through with Ian following. Startled staff looked up; one or two protested. They passed out a back door and into the street.

Ian kept following until they'd crossed Hennepin Avenue, where Brook ducked into the foyer of an old office building before finally stopping.

"Are things worse than I thought?" Ian asked as she turned to face him.

Brook shrugged. "Maybe. Nothing new in the investigation so far as I know, but I have a law clerk on steroids watching me. I don't know yet what she's figured out. I think she followed me when I left the courthouse."

Ian's shoulders slumped. "I can't take you further into this."

"Too late, cowboy. I just advised your legal assistant how to avoid detection by the police. I even gave her a code to avoid phone calls. So we're past noble gestures. Just repeat what you said on the phone again. You know, the innocence thing?"

"I swear, Brook, I haven't done anything wrong. Not intentionally anyway." He hesitated. "Not sure I can say the same thing about Connor and Martha Wells."

Brook watched his eyes carefully as he spoke. When he finished, she took his hand and led him through a side door to the fire escape staircase. They sat together on one of the concrete steps.

"Alright," she said with finality. "All of it."

It took nearly an hour to bring her up to speed. The only part he hedged was telling her more about the shooting in Northeast Minneapolis. He held that back, halting the story with the fight at the bar. That and his mother's words the previous night about exchanging information with Ahmetti. For some reason, that seemed too fresh and personal to share just now.

He ended with the impressions, images, and words he could recall from his recent dreams.

"Those are no dreams, Ian," she said. "Or at least you're dreaming from something you actually experienced."

"Yeah," he acknowledged. "I figured that part out. I have to have been with my mom at the '98 Doyle funeral in Florida and afterward. Getting involved with Callahan and Rory Doyle has brought those memories to the surface. I can't say how much, but I saw and heard at least some of what I'm dreaming. And the old man has to have been Jimmy Doyle."

"You mentioned dreaming something about a painting and a date," Brook said. "You should know one of the Rockwells stolen was *The Spirit of 1776.*"

Ian stared at Brook. "I wish I could remember more."

"You remember enough. If you're right about even half of it, your dad was up to his eyeballs in this." She thought a moment. "That part about your mom telling Jimmy Doyle they didn't want the money? Whether they ultimately took it or not, it would have to mean your dad was *entitled* to a share of the money. Which means he must have participated at a high level in whatever they did. So your dad must have known everything. Including about the killing."

Ian felt the blood go out of him. "What killing? You've never mentioned a killing."

Brook's eyes filled with worry. "Sorry. Don't know why, but I just assumed you knew."

"I've got to hear it all now. All of it."

Brook leaned back on her elbows and told him about the crime. She related it like an opening statement at trial. Ian listened with pained but grudging admiration. So detailed. Almost personal. Through the shock at what she related, he recalled that he hadn't seen Brook in trial in years—and that she must be very good. Hearing her skilled portrayal of the crime made his father's role in it that much more sorrowful.

By the time Brook finished with the shooting of the security guard, Ian felt sick. He recalled his mother's comments, telling "Connor" they had to be done with this once and for all.

"Look, I'd rather you wouldn't pass on the crime details to Katie just yet," he said. "I don't want to draw her too far into this." Brook nodded her agreement.

Ian leaned forward and pulled the gun from behind his back.

"That's what you threatened Callahan with?" Brook asked. "Is that your dad's gun?"

Ian nodded as he ejected the magazine. "Yeah. I stashed another one in Loring Park." He went silent as he counted. "There are two bullets missing," he said softly.

"You haven't fired it?"

"Nope." He pushed the clip back into the grip.

"You know how to use it, though?"

"Well enough. I took a class in college."

Brook shook her head. "Ballistics could prove if that gun was used in the art theft thirty-five years ago."

Ian felt worn and jagged. "A week ago, my dad was a quiet guy who took care of his family and didn't overcharge his clients. Not wealthy like your folks, but content to make an honest dollar. Now ballistics can prove he was a murderer at a multimillion-dollar art theft whose only saving grace was that he may have turned down his share of the money after killing a security guard."

Brook looked away. "Sorry. Telling you that way, I must have sounded clinical. This has got to be terrible for you."

In the distance Ian heard people entering the foyer, followed by elevators rising. A few muffled voices passed through as well. No one entered the stairwell.

"The only thing worse than my dad's involvement is my mom knowing about the crime and just carrying on. Living her life with Dad—raising her kids—like nothing happened. It changes everything I know about her too."

"Ian," Brook said, taking his arm, "you don't know what she knew or when she learned about any of it or how she felt about it. You told me your parents didn't even get married until 1987. That was four years after the art theft. Look, this is really, really hard, but we've got to set some of this aside for now and try to figure out what's going on. Size up who took the money, for starters. Before it's too late."

He looked at her and nodded. "Yeah. Sorry. You're right."

"Good. Now, let's start with motive to steal the money from your account."

"Okay." Ian thought for a moment. "Either Rory or Sean had plenty of motive to take the money. Sean could have wanted *all* of the trust cash and not just his share. He hadn't the opportunity under the trust terms until the banker moved it the other night, because the trust said until then only the banker was to have the account information on where the money was being stored. On the other hand, Rory had motive because it's looking like he didn't qualify for his share at all."

"Yes," Brook said, "but we've got to assume that whoever stole the cash from your account is likely the same one who's been passing hot money the past couple of weeks. Who had a motive to do that?"

"Nobody," Ian said. "Throwing around hot money would get the FBI to sniff around and maybe reopen the case—just at the moment they'd planned on taking the cash for themselves."

"There's one possibility," Brook began. "The thief might have wanted to spread the hot cash to set you up for the blame. They could have assumed that once the money disappeared from your account, you'd likely go to the police yourself and the case would get reopened anyway. So the thief might have been trying to set things up in advance to look like you were the one who stole the trust money. Then you *couldn't* go to the police. Plus there'd be the added benefit that the other trust beneficiaries would also think you were the thief."

"I said something along those lines to Callahan last night," Ian said. "I suppose that when my dad was still the lawyer set to handle the trust distribution, there wasn't any risk he'd turn to the authorities, since it looks like he was involved with the art theft. But once he died, things changed. Come to think of it, that's why I was the natural to replace him as the attorney for the trust."

Brook looked perplexed. "Why?"

"Think about it. That decision was Callahan's to make. If Callahan *never intended* to take the trust money for himself— you know, was content to allow it to be distributed and just get his share—his choice of me to replace Dad would make sense, because if I learned about the art heist, there was at least a chance I wouldn't go to the police since it would implicate my own parents. Especially my living mother. But if, on the other hand, Callahan *was always planning* on stealing the trust money, I was a good choice because I could be set up as the trust thief in advance, just like you described. The FBI and the U.S. Attorney's Office would buy it, thinking I'd 'inherited' Dad's right to part of the theft proceeds. So either way, choosing me made more sense than grabbing a lawyer off the street."

Brook nodded. "And I assume part of the banker's job was to keep the transfer from being traceable back to the Caribbean banks holding the money—and ultimately to the Doyles or Callahan or that McMartin. That's probably why he did the transfer in the middle of the night the way he did."

"Makes sense."

"There's one glitch with our reasoning, though," Brook went on. "Regardless of who the trust thief was, they had to know there was *some* risk you'd go to the police. It wasn't a sure thing you'd stay quiet to protect Martha. How did they plan for that possibility?"

"That's easy," Ian said grimly. "If it came to that, kill me and make my body disappear."

The words sounded alien coming out of his lips. It grew more real when he saw the horrified expression on Brook's face.

"What are you talking about?"

"Well, if the thief gets the spotlight trained on me, and I disappear at the same time the money disappears, the FBI would think I ran with the cash. With me dead and hidden, they'd keep chasing that dead man while the real thief slipped away."

"No. I get that. I mean why are you so convinced they'd go that far and actually *kill* you?"

"Apart from the fact that they already murdered somebody in the art theft?"

"Nothing else?" she pushed sternly. "Like we haven't gotten to the shooting you told me about last night."

Ian grew defensive. "Yeah. I was getting to that."

"Please do."

"Well, the guy Willy Dryer shot was one of the same ones who attacked me in the bar. They'd followed me out onto the street. One of them had a gun, the other a knife. I think they were planning on silencing me. Especially given that we now know the trust thief took the money out of my account around the same time those guys were closing in on me."

Brook swung a fist hard into his chest. *"What else haven't you told me?"*

"Whoa, cage fighter," he said. When that failed to lighten her up, he grew serious. "That's all. Really. I didn't want to worry you."

"Then you're an idiot," she said. "Ian, we're done. We're going to my office now."

"*NO*," Ian said. The sound of his voice echoed in the stairwell. Brook stared at him, silent but undeterred.

"No," he said again more softly. "Not now. With the evidence as it is, I could be taken into custody—and I can't protect my mom while in jail. Callahan thinks I took the money, so he *will* punish my mother if he can't reach me. I know he would, and you'd believe it too if you met him. I've got to trace down this money and get it back to Callahan. After that, we can figure out what we're going to do, and how."

They grew silent together once more. "Okay," Brook finally said. "So both Callahan and Rory had motive. Then who took the money?"

"It had to be Rory," Ian said flatly. "It's either him or somebody we don't know. Callahan or Rory could have set me up to go to Larry's Bar on Friday, I suppose, and used that opportunity to break into Mom's house. But if the bigger point of that exercise was to make me disappear, his Marine could have shot me out at Medicine Lake or where I sat in his living room. And Callahan's performance at his house was *too real* last night. He genuinely thought I took the money. So it's got to be Rory. Or somebody we still don't know. McMartin maybe."

"Alright. So what do we do?"

"Well, I've got to find Rory. Face him and see if I can confirm he's the one who took the cash, then figure out how to get it back. And if he's not the one, we're back to the starting line on who else might have taken it."

Brook grew silent. Ian looked at her, and the notion of kissing her returned. Instead he reached out and pulled her close for a long hug.

"You're going way out there for a guy you recently told to shove off at Kieran's Pub," he said. "I haven't had much time to think about what you said, or how to answer your questions about us, but—"

"Stop right there. I'm sorry I got so worked up. It was nothing but misplaced anger. Forget it."

"Don't think that's likely."

"Yeah, well we can work on it later. Bond with a game of truth or dare."

Truth or dare. It reminded Ian of his mother's words from the hallway the night before that he hadn't shared with Brook—about her telling Ahmetti something as payback for information the Albanian had shared before.

If his mom knew where the Rockwell painting was, could that be what she told Ahmetti to 'get even'? What else would have interested a man who prided himself on knowing everything fenced in the Twin Cities?

The door to the stairwell opened. A stooped man with a tattered sleeping bag, straw hat, and several shopping bags stuffed with clothes stepped in.

"*You're in my house!*" he shouted. "*Get outta my house.*"

Ian and Brook stood and brushed quickly by him, back into the building's foyer.

Alone again, Ian said, "I've got an idea. There's a guy who I think could fill in some big gaps for us. Maybe help me find Rory too. I want to go see him now while the idea's fresh. If that doesn't pan out, I may have to go to Florida."

"Who's in Florida?"

"Ed McMartin. The only beneficiary I haven't tracked down."

She nodded supportively. "Okay. I'll see if maybe I can slow things down a bit at the U.S. Attorney's Office."

"That's not a good idea. Don't take any more chances with your career."

"My career, my choice," she said. "But don't you take any more chances yourself. No more walks at night. And I recommend against more conferences in Callahan's living room too."

Ian nodded. "Time's running short. Even if Callahan keeps his word, my mom's a target for him in three days."

They parted on Hennepin Avenue, Brook heading back to the courthouse, and Ian walking just up the street toward Doggy's Bar. The last time he saw her, Brook had stopped on the other side of the avenue. She was looking his way too.

37

The white-haired man appeared at the door of Doggy's right on time, just as the bartender promised. Right behind him came the mountain.

Ian was sitting at Ahmetti's table. He saw Ahmetti motion for Prima to stay at the door before he shuffled slowly toward the back to join him.

"Didn't expect to see you again so soon," Ahmetti greeted him.

"Me neither," Ian said as the man sat down.

"Don't tell me you've already gotten my grandnephew off."

"No. But I'll get there. I need some more information now."

Ahmetti waved at the bartender, who waved back. "I'm not Wikipedia, you know."

"I need information to protect my family."

The bartender brought a glass of something clear on ice. "I'm not a sentimentalist either," Ahmetti said. "Knowledge is money."

261

"I know. Tell me, did you say that same thing to my mother when the two of you met for the first time?"

Ahmetti looked at Ian out of the corner of his eye. "Don't know what we're talking about."

"Martha Wells came to you years ago. You told her something she wanted to know. Maybe she was Martha Brennan back then. Since she wasn't exactly somebody you'd run across here at Doggy's, she must have sought you out that first time you met."

"Still don't get it."

"Then the *last* time you spoke with her she came to tell you something you would want to know as payback. That's true, isn't it?"

The Albanian took a sip of his drink.

"Tell me what my mom told you," Ian said.

Ahmetti looked straight ahead.

"Alright. Let's try this. She told you she had a painting taken in the 1983 art heist on Excelsior Boulevard in St. Louis Park. *The Spirit of 1776* by Norman Rockwell."

The Albanian shook his head. "Not true, Counselor."

Ian was surprised to sense truth in Ahmetti's denial. "Then if that's so," he picked up, "there's only one other bit of knowledge I can think of that would have had value to you. Martha told you who the crew was on the art job. It was something you wanted to know because you'd made it your business to find out since they didn't come to you to fence the paintings. That didn't sit right with the guy who knew every stone, stereo, and sports car that got sold in your town. And who got a cut for every one of them."

The Albanian took another sip. Ian leaned closer.

"And when she told you who did that job, you learned that Jimmy Doyle led the crew. Which was news to you because

262

he wasn't an art thief. Or even a thief at all—not in the usual sense of the word. Doyle had done it because, like you told me the other night, he was out of money with Cann's rackets closing down."

"Sheldon," Ahmetti called out to the bartender, "there's too much ice in this. Bring me another." The bartender nodded.

"That crew," Ian said, "was made up of Jimmy Doyle, Sean Callahan, Rory Doyle, and Ed McMartin."

The bartender arrived. Ahmetti took a sip, then thanked him. "That's better."

"And," Ian added after the bartender went away, "my father, Connor Wells. He was the fifth member of that crew, wasn't he?"

The Albanian looked over Ian's shoulder toward the front door and raised his chin. Prima appeared at the table.

"Yeah, boss?"

"Tell our friend here—Mr. Wells—the year *Connor* Wells first got involved with Jimmy Doyle's family. You know what I mean. Really connected with them."

Prima looked at the ceiling. "Sure, boss. It was . . . 1987. Yeah, 1987. That year Jeff Fenech was Super bantamweight champion of the world. You want me to tell you about the bout where he won it?"

"Not now," Ahmetti said. "Leave us alone."

When the big man had retreated, the Albanian looked at Ian again. "I didn't lie to you last time on that score. You asked if I knew of Connor Wells being mixed up in the Cann rackets. That was all you asked."

Ian didn't care. 1987. Four years after the St. Louis Park art heist. He'd grown so sure his father was there at the art heist. Ahmetti's news tore him between relief and utter confusion.

Then how did his father earn his share?

Ian turned back to Ahmetti. "So now tell me what it was you told my mother that put her in your debt in the first place."

Still looking another direction, Ahmetti shook his head. "Some information's exclusive."

"What's that mean?"

"Just what I said. Some information is for resale, some's not. So are we done? You just come here today to talk to yourself?"

"No. Then if my mom didn't tell you she had the Rockwell painting, I need to know if Jimmy Doyle ever sold it."

"Which painting?"

"*The Spirit of 1776.*"

"How would I know if that was sold?"

"I didn't say you know. I'm saying you could find out."

"You know you're already running up quite a tab today. My grandnephew doesn't even begin to cover it."

With a knot in his stomach, Ian nodded his agreement. "Find out about the painting and let me know. Add it to my tab. Plus I need to know where I can find Rory Doyle."

"What do you plan to do if I tell you?"

"I just need to talk to him. But I need to talk to him now."

Ahmetti took a napkin and pulled a pen from his pocket. "You're a lucky man," he said as he wrote on the napkin. "Rory Doyle and I aren't particularly close, and he doesn't run his schedule by me. But I had a similar inquiry in the last twenty-four hours and can help you on that last business right away. So here. You'll find him at this location around seven-thirty tonight."

"Who else is looking for him?" Ian asked. "Is it Sean Callahan?"

"You may find out," Ahmetti said. "You may cross paths. But you'll not learn it from me. Now, I don't want to hear about something nasty happening tonight. I couldn't care less about

264

the Doyles or Callahan. But I won't let it get out that information I distributed led to something bloody. Very poor for business. Especially when I'm on parole."

Ian shook his head, processing the new information. "Don't worry," he said distractedly, already thinking ahead to the night. "I'm a lawyer. If it comes to that, I'll talk Rory to death."

5:14 P.M.
U.S. ATTORNEY'S OFFICE, FEDERAL COURTHOUSE
DOWNTOWN MINNEAPOLIS

Seated in her office, Brook stared at the closed door. How was she going to accomplish this? How in the world was she going to slow the investigation down without giving herself away?

She'd returned from meeting Ian only to find the gunners and people facing high-priority deadlines still at the office on a nice Sunday afternoon. Eldon and Chloe were among them. She'd barely acknowledged the clerk as they passed each other in the hall. For a moment, she thought she caught a smirk on Chloe's lips. Hope you had a disappointing lunch, Brook thought.

An email popped onto her computer screen, her personal account. It was from Sophie, another prosecutor from her law school class working with Eldon. The subject line read, *Burn after reading*.

Brook opened it.

Chloe's been asking questions about you and Ian Wells. I've blown her off. I remember you and Ian were friends in law school, especially third year, but I figure it's none of my business and I'm not saying a word to her. You may want to watch out for that mountain lion.

265

You probably know they're talking about expanding Ian's status from witness to target. Getting out a warrant for his firm's bank accounts too. Crazy stuff. Hard to believe he might be mixed up in this. I didn't know him well at law school, but he seemed like a good guy. Kind of quiet. Isn't that what they always say about serial killers on the news? Anyway, hope you're having a good weekend and I'll see you Monday.

Sophie

Brook's heart sank as she deleted Sophie's email. Things were moving even faster than she'd thought. And Chloe was probably fanning the flames, capitalizing on her big chance to shine on Eldon's career-making case.

Another email caught her attention in a string of junk. It was addressed from Zach at his Paisley, Bowman, Battle & Rhodes work address.

She opened it cautiously.

Brook, I miss you so much. Can't we talk this through? I know we've been drifting further apart the last year. But you know I've been getting close to partnership and that means longer hours, especially at this place. I thought we always accepted this part of the profession. We can figure it out. Maybe you could get a job here. They've got no rules about that kind of thing at Paisley. We must get a dozen "confidential" résumés every year from your prosecutor's office alone. If you were here, we could coordinate things better. Make a plan that would be easier . . .

Near the end of the message, Ian's name surfaced.

I've always thought you still had feelings for Ian Wells. I know you've denied it. I hope I'm wrong, because he can't be what you're looking for, Brook. Please. You can't be settling for that guy.

Brook looked away. Settling for that guy? Zach had no idea. A suicide pact might be a better description. He'd probably be reading about both of them in the paper before long.

She sighed and shook her head. If Zach wanted an explanation, it would be that in law school, Ian always made her feel like the person she wanted to be. Zach always made her feel like somebody else. Successful. Destined for a house on Lake of the Isles and a condo at Lutsen. But always somebody else.

Her thoughts returned to Sophie's message and how she could possibly slow things down.

Zach's email came back to her. The mention of résumés from the prosecutor's office. *Confidential* résumés. She rose and headed down the hall to Chloe's office.

The diminutive clerk looked up and brushed a length of hair from one eye as Brook appeared. "Brook!" she said. "Putting in a long day, huh?"

Like Chloe had invented long hours. "Yep. We need to talk."

"Sure," she said, pointing to her client chair. "What about?"

Brook didn't sit. "I heard Eldon might be authorizing a warrant to search the bank records of Wells & Hoy Law Office."

"Yes, I heard that too."

"Then why didn't you tell me? What happened to 'you'll know whatever I know'?"

"Oh, wow, I'm really sorry. I've been so busy. Eldon's got me scrambling the last few days."

Brook nodded. "Uh-huh. Well, I also heard you've been asking people how well I knew Ian Wells in law school. So now that we're face-to-face, you want to ask *me*?"

Chloe took in Brook's stare for a moment. The smile faded. The bubbly quality in her voice disappeared.

"Okay, Brook. Tell me, why haven't you mentioned to Eldon that you were good friends with Ian Wells in law school? Very good friends, I've heard. That maybe you're still good friends. In fact, I'm wondering if those ICRs you got weren't a favor for him. Where'd you go to lunch today, and with who?"

Brook stepped into the office and closed the door behind her. She smiled indulgently. "Chloe, you think you've got this place figured out. Who to please, who to take down, who to step over. Well, add this to your database. I've been here five years to your four months. You're standing in a minefield with blinders on—you just don't know it. You have no idea how many favors I've done for some of the people you've been asking about me, or how many count me as a friend. You don't know how many projects I've handled shoulder to shoulder with those lawyers. You don't really know, truth be told, even how Eldon thinks. And you know *nothing* about my personal life."

She waited a moment for her words to sink in. They seemed to have had no impact so far.

"But I know something about you," Brook continued. "I know you've got a résumé out to Paisley, Bowman, Battle, and Rhodes."

The law clerk's expression went blank.

"Right," Brook said, hiding her joy at the successful bluff. "So here's another educational tip. Eldon is *really big on loyalty*. Like paranoid big. Résumé floating? No humor about that. None at all. I doubt he'd wait to see if you got that job before he relieved you of this one."

Chloe cleared her throat. "What do you want?"

"I want to be friends, Chloe. And a good start would be for you to stop snooping around in my private life—stop making insinuations about me. And as a show of *my* friendship, I'm willing to forget about your little shout-out to private practice. What do you say to that?"

The clerk's face had turned red. "Alright."

"Great. Oh, and as a friend, I'd like back the copies of those ICR and FBI reports I know you kept. All of them."

Chloe reached into her drawer and pulled out a thick Redrope expandable file. "You know Eldon already knows about these," she said. "I mentioned them in my memorandum. What if he asks to see them?"

"If he asks, send him to me," Brook said sweetly. "That's all of them?"

"Yes."

"Good. And lastly, I really have to ask that you keep me in the loop about this Ian Wells matter. Like the 'first call' kind of friend. Think you can do that?"

Chloe nodded.

Brook left the office and walked down the hall to the locked receptacle for storing documents for shredding. With a quick glance around, she pushed all the files Chloe had handed her into its wide mouth.

As she turned away, Brook thought she'd feel a sense of victory. She didn't. In fact, she felt sick. As much as she loathed Chloe and her no-holds-barred ambition, the truth was Brook had become involved in a betrayal. Of her job. Her profession. Her oath. Even her colleagues. Chloe wasn't wrong. She was right for the wrong reasons.

Brook shook her head hard. Fine. So Chloe's conduct wasn't exactly wrong. But in this case—in this one case—the system *was wrong.* About Ian Wells. She'd bet her career on it. Actually, she already had.

Brook strode down the hall toward her office to collect her things and leave. This didn't slow the process down, not yet. But it probably ensured she'd know what was coming before it happened. Like the issuing of the warrants.

Because once Eldon got a warrant and reviewed Ian's bank records—and saw the trust money transfers—it would all blow up. She hadn't derailed this train. Maybe she'd slowed it down a bit.

She turned off the light in her office as she left, feeling scared and lousy all at once. Scared for Ian. Lousy about herself.

Still, taking Chloe down had been a little bit satisfying, hadn't it?

Yeah. It had. A lot, actually.

38

Through the beginning of a light rain, Ian approached the entrance to Victor's 1959 Café. He was tugging the hood of his sweatshirt over his head at the same moment someone else left the restaurant door just ahead, wearing a blue windbreaker and a hood already drawn up. The person turned away just as Ian slipped past.

Every inch of the small restaurant's yellow-painted interior was covered, wall to ceiling, with graffiti. The place was crowded, although given its size, Ian wondered if it was ever otherwise. He weaved across the uneven floor through tightly packed benches of patrons until he saw Rory sitting by himself in the back.

Rory's eyes flashed recognition as Ian approached. "What are you doing here?" he snarled over empty dishes on his table.

Ian slid onto the bench opposite him, pushing a plate aside to rest his arms on the table. "We need to talk."

"I gave you all my information last time."

271

"You stood me up at Larry's."

Rory squinted. "I don't know what you're talking about."

"Our meeting you set up Friday night?"

"Don't know who you talked to. If it was Larry at the bar, we had a falling-out. Seems like too many people were learning my business. But you know what? It doesn't matter. I don't need to meet with you anyway. I've decided I don't want the trust money."

Ian leaned back in the bench, his questions forgotten. "Why not?"

"First off, you've been talking to Ahmetti and listening to his lies. The old scab told you I fenced things after my mother died, didn't he? Except I didn't. I sold him some things when I got separated from Lisa, but they were mine. I told him they weren't stolen, but he and his yeti of a sidekick didn't believe me. Just like you're not believing me now."

"Then that would mean you qualify for the trust. What if I believed you . . . still don't want the money?"

"Nope."

"Why?"

Rory shrugged as he started to spin the ring. "My business."

Ian shook his head. "The money's gone, Rory. You don't want it because you've already got it."

The thin man's head snapped up. "Whaddya mean, gone?"

"Somebody hacked it out of my account two nights ago—the night you were supposed to meet me."

"That's bull." His attention drifted, and he looked over Ian's shoulder.

"It's not. And it was your guys who attacked me at the bar too. Planning to make me disappear."

Rory was looking straight through Ian now. He shook his head, pulled some cash out of a pocket, and dropped it on the table.

"Wait a second," Ian said as Rory stood. "I've got more questions."

"Not for me, you don't."

Ian stood as well, leaning over the table and grabbing the gaunt man's arm. He pulled him close and whispered, "I know the trust money was from the art theft. I know somebody died in the robbery. Ahmetti told me my dad wasn't connected to your family at the time. So how'd he get involved and how'd he earn a piece of the trust?"

Rory's expression was a mix of angst and anger. "Connor and I grew up in the same neighborhood. I knew him then."

The first sliver of truth. "Friends?"

"No. I just knew him."

"Then how'd he connect to your family?"

"He fell for my sister," he replied, growing more agitated. Then he pulled his arm free and walked away from the booth.

Rory had no sister. It would have shown up in his search of Jimmy Doyle's genealogy. Infuriated, Ian called to Rory, "Callahan thinks one of us has that money."

"Then I suggest you give it back to him," Rory shot back, then headed toward the restaurant exit.

Ian moved to follow, but a waiter stepped in his way, bringing him to a halt and leaving him several paces behind as Rory was going out the door.

Seconds later, the air outside was misty and cool as Ian emerged from the restaurant. He searched every direction before seeing Rory thirty feet away on the corner, looking both ways before crossing the street.

A black car pulled across the empty intersection against the red light. It stopped as the rear passenger door came abreast of Rory. The door opened.

The wiry man leaned forward, looking into the car. He slid inside.

Ian hadn't even thought to start moving again before the car was pulling away from the curb, splashing water as it disappeared up the wet street.

Martha stared out across the parking lot that lay below her chair on the patio of the third-floor condominium. Somewhere in the apartment through the screen door behind her she heard Katie greet her son, who'd just arrived. Martha could just make out the voices of Katie and Ian and Brook in the apartment, speaking low enough that she couldn't understand them over the freeway traffic in sight a block away.

The low conversation faded, then stopped.

"Have you tried Wet Willy again?" she heard Katie ask a minute later, calling from the kitchen.

"Yep. I got him on the fourth try," Ian answered, nearer at hand. "I told him he could keep the car till I get back from Florida."

Martha sighed. A swallow swooped down from a telephone pole, darting back and forth like the tip of a conductor's baton.

She ached in a way she hadn't in a long time. If only Connor were here. He could always bring her back from these moods, convince her they'd really done the right thing all these years. Where was he now when she needed him so?

She tried thinking of other things. Katie—dear Katie—was humming a familiar song in the kitchen. She loved when Katie sang or hummed. Deep-throated, carefree. It softened the edges of the void within her.

"Mom. I'll bet you miss your gardens."

Ian had appeared on the deck and taken a seat beside her. She felt him take her hand.

Her gardens? She *did* miss her gardens. Why had they taken her away from them? Why couldn't she go there now?

"I'm flying to Florida in the morning, Mom," Ian was saying gently. "Brook's driving me to the airport. I'm going there to talk to Ed McMartin."

Florida. She remembered going there as a child with her mother. The hot sand underfoot, the shells of Captiva piled deep like a snow sculpture on the beach. Warm rain drifting in from the Gulf to pound the roof of the house they'd rented.

"I wish you could tell me what happened." Ian was speaking again. "Like what you meant when you told Katie they wouldn't 'find it.' You meant the painting, didn't you? Where is it, Mom? And how Dad earned his share. Anything to help me recover the trust money before Tuesday. I need to know so I can protect you. And me. Everyone. I don't care what Dad did, but I wish you'd speak to me and save me this trip."

The pain gathered again around her heart. Oh, Connor, where are you?

"Hon, supper's about ready," Katie called.

"Great," Ian called back. He let go of her hand. "Five minutes till we eat, Mom."

Martha's mind flowed back to Florida and the man arriving in the rain, ringing the doorbell of their house that lay within sight of the Gulf's waters. Leaning down and tickling her chin when she answered the door. Her mother in a green dress, coming out of her bedroom and greeting him, kissing him. The man taking off his wet coat and crouching down to give her a brightly colored plastic turtle.

The swallow had been joined by others on the telephone wire. Martha watched them gathering for a moment, then glanced over her shoulder. In the apartment, Ian was filling glasses with ice, Brook setting dishes on the table. Katie stood at the stove.

She turned back to the parking lot.

Why didn't Mother ever explain? You never should assume what a child knows or believes. Never. Though she understood that sometimes it seemed too painful. Too painful to lay bare what you were doing or what you'd done or, hardest of all, why you'd done it—even to a child who had a right to know. Martha understood that now. Still, her mother should have at least tried to explain.

The man had left them in the morning. The rain hadn't stopped, but he'd gone out into the shower with only his hat and coat and no umbrella, walking slowly to the black car, pelted by drops as big as pebbles, to drive away.

Martha sighed.

"Hon, it's time to come in and eat." It was Katie, standing at her shoulder with a wide smile on her face.

Martha shook her head. "Tell Ian to bring an umbrella," she said quietly. "It rains a lot in Florida."

Then she began to cry.

39

Ian had flown into Fort Lauderdale instead of West Palm Beach. No flights were available into the airport nearer to his destination. He'd rented a car for the extra hour drive to Port St. Lucie.

Brook had driven him to the Minneapolis-St. Paul Airport the night before. She'd offered to lend him money, but he'd turned her down. *"You're already in way over your head,"* he'd said with thanks. Accepting money from her made it all the worse.

He'd promised to be careful. *"If somebody was trying to harm you before,"* Brook told him, *"they almost certainly still are."* And this time he wouldn't have the gun he'd left behind with Katie.

They'd hugged before parting. In the midst of the hug, he'd remembered the name of the perfume she always wore in law school and was wearing again last night: Chantel Spring.

Ian saw the exit for Port St. Lucie ahead. Feeling blind without GPS, armed with only a cheap cellphone he'd bought yesterday, he left the freeway and began watching the street signs carefully, recalling from memory the map he'd reviewed.

Within minutes he entered a neighborhood of winding streets and tropical-colored ramblers with tall palms rustling overhead. Each house looked a little different from the other. It was a rare one that didn't have a pool behind it.

Then he saw it.

It was as though a snapshot buried in his mind had come to life. The long sidewalk curving from the street to the front door. The coral walls and green shutters. A single palm centered in the front yard. By the time he parked, he knew that confirming the address was unnecessary.

This was Ed McMartin's home. Ian had been here before.

He got out of the car into air like that of a sauna. As his feet hit the pavement, he had the strange sensation he was a child again, missing the grip of his mother's hand. He took the sidewalk in rapid strides and rapped on the door.

A large woman answered.

"Mr. McMartin?" he asked.

She shook her head. "Mr. McMartin isn't living here at present," she said in a Jamaican accent. "I'm the cleaning lady. Mr. McMartin's current residence is the Shannon Transitional Care Home."

"Could you tell me where that is?"

She disappeared, returning moments later holding a Post-it note with the address and directions written on it.

The drive to the medical facility took less than ten minutes. The man behind the front desk acknowledged Edward McMartin was a resident patient and led Ian into a dining hall with brightly colored tablecloths decorated to look like an ice cream parlor. "Over there," he said, and pointed toward a corner.

The figure there was hunched in a powered wheelchair with an oxygen canister attached to its back.

Ian approached. "Ed McMartin?" he asked.

The man looked up. With wisps of stray white hair and tubes running to his nostrils, the man resembled a shrunken version of someone familiar. Ian tried to picture him as the man at the pool from his dreams, but the gap of age and wear was too great.

Yet the opposite apparently wasn't true. The withered man looked at Ian with such ferocity that he half expected a renewal of the poolside demand to know who had brought him there.

"Do you remember me?" Ian asked unnecessarily.

"Yeah, I know you." Ed raised a bent hand holding a cloth and wiped at the edge of his mouth. "You're Martha's brat, the one she brought with her to Christina's funeral. Still look like you're ten years old. Come back to bury me, now, did you?"

Ian shook his head. "I'm here because I need to know some things about the art robbery and the money."

Ed coughed into the cloth in his hand, glancing around uncomfortably. "Don't know what you're talking about. And I don't want to talk now—I'm tired."

Ian shrugged. "Well, I've got all day. I can start with a few questions to jog your memory, and you can join in when you feel like answering." He looked around. "Anybody in this place *not* hard of hearing?"

Ed glowered. His hand went to the joystick on the arm of his wheelchair. "My room," he said.

The one-bedroom apartment was barely furnished and held little that was personal, hinting at either a recent arrival or no plans for a long stay. Given the man's frailty, Ian wondered if the sparse décor was wishful thinking. Ed drove his wheelchair to a corner window that looked out over a green lawn. He spun the chair around to face Ian.

"You want to know about the money, eh?" He shook his head.

"What good's that gonna do you? What good's the trust money going to do anybody after all these years?"

"Then tell me about the robbery," Ian said, trying to stay calm. "I need to know my parents' role in it."

Ed coughed, louder and harsher this time. Ian realized he felt no concern for the man, only a powerful worry that he might collapse before he could tell Ian what he needed to know. That and a mild curiosity to learn whether McMartin really was as ill as he looked. Because if so, it was impossible he could have had a hand in launching the events up in Minneapolis the past week.

"Sean was right," McMartin said. "You don't look like a lawyer."

"I've been hearing that a lot lately."

"Yeah. Not jaded enough yet. You don't give me the urge to hide my wallet. Give it time, I suppose."

"If you've been talking to Callahan, you know I represent the trust."

Ed nodded. "Yeah. He called me last week."

"Good. So tell me my dad's role in the robbery."

Ed waved him off with a gesture of his hand. "What's that matter to passing out the trust money?"

Ian's voice hardened. "Because you need me to make decisions to distribute the cash and I want to know my dad's role."

Ed shrugged. "Your dad wrote the trust. Jimmy wanted it that way."

"That's not what I meant. I want to hear how my dad earned his share from the art gallery job itself."

The old man's nostrils shrank as he drew a gulp of oxygen through his nose. "Not sure what you think you know."

Ian looked up at the ceiling. "It happened on January 14,

1983, at the Elaine Art Gallery on Excelsior Boulevard in St. Louis Park. There were a dozen paintings taken. Also around fifteen thousand in cash."

"You could've read that in the paper."

Ian closed his eyes, pulling together the dream impressions. "You found me beside the pool the day of the funeral—your sister's funeral. You asked me who'd brought me. I followed you into a bedroom, where Jimmy and Rory and Sean Callahan and my mother were. Jimmy Doyle told you there wouldn't be a distribution, but the money would go into a trust."

"*Who told you all that?*" Ed's voice was suddenly stronger.

"Some I remember. Some Rory and Sean told me," Ian lied.

The old man shook his head as much as the tubes would allow. "I've still got nothin' to say."

Ian felt his patience give way. "Listen, Ed, I've been told my dad wasn't involved with the Doyle family until years after the art theft happened. All I want is a confirmation if that's true. Just tell me—was my dad there the night of the art theft?"

Ed squinted at Ian, as though to read his face. "That's it?" he asked quietly.

"Yes."

Another pause. "Okay. If there *was* any kind of art job, and I'm not saying there was, your dad wasn't there that night."

Even hearing it a second time, Ian still couldn't believe it. "That's the truth? He wasn't there?"

Ed nodded. "That's right."

"Then why was my dad entitled to a share of the money if he wasn't there?"

The old man's chin came up. "You want to know why he was entitled to his share of the money?" McMartin let out a loud laugh, followed by a groan of pain and a low hacking cough.

"If you really don't know, I suggest you ask your mother," he gasped out.

"Ed," Ian said, his voice softening, "in case you haven't heard, my mom—Martha—has Alzheimer's. She can't tell me. And what's it matter at this point anyway? No matter what you tell me, the trust is supposed to get distributed in two days. I only get my fee if I meet that deadline. What's the harm in letting me know a few facts about my own parents? Who'd be hurt by that?"

The old man shook his head. "Me, if Callahan ever found out. The Keeper of Family Secrets." Ed closed his eyes. "All that money you're gonna hand out—it's no use to me. When Doreen was alive, well . . ." His voice drifted off.

Ian was wondering if he'd gone to sleep when Ed opened his eyes again. "Okay," he said in resignation. "Fine. Forget about Callahan. What can he do to me now? And it looks like I won't be rid of you until I say something. So I'll tell you a little family history. The rest you can figure out from there."

Ed looked at Ian again, his eyes hinting at guilty pleasure, like he was about to say something he'd been wanting to say for a long time.

"The man you're *really* working for here? The guy who decided what shares got handed out and who got 'em? Well, the joke's on you, kid. 'Cause that man, Jimmy Doyle, was Martha's father. Which makes him your grandfather. Grandpa Jimmy, the lowlife scum who had the guts to let his illegitimate daughter and her punk kid come to his own wife's funeral."

40

MONDAY, JUNE 11
11:20 P.M.
PORT ST. LUCIE, FLORIDA

Ed McMartin's house, like the neighborhood around it, was drenched in a damp darkness. Covered with perspiration, Ian stared through his open car window, hearing McMartin's words resonate in his ears.

Ian Wells. Martha Wells. Connor Wells. None of them were the same people they'd been that morning. In the space of a few sentences, Ed McMartin had shredded Ian's identity and his memories of his parents forever, leaving him to try to reinterpret his life in a matter of hours.

At first, he'd tried to tell himself it was all a lie. Harry Christensen once said that if you were listening honestly, the truth was always on key; even good lies were a little off pitch. Ed McMartin might have spent a lifetime lying—even lying up to the minute he told Ian the news—but he'd delivered the note about Jimmy Doyle and his mother perfectly.

If it wasn't a lie, then it was the truth—which sounded

283

obvious, but carried so much more weight. He truly was Jimmy Doyle's grandson. The grandson of a murderer and a thief.

Ian stared numbly into the dark. So why had he come back here? Even if it was true, what was he looking for?

He pulled out his new cellphone and played the voicemail again. *"Ian,"* Brook said in her recent message to him, *"I got a call from Chloe. Apparently she's taking our new friendship seriously. She said Eldon's got her preparing the new warrants today. They'll go to the judge in the morning. They could be executing them by tomorrow afternoon. Call me when you get a chance so we can talk this over."*

Ian didn't need to talk anything over; he knew what it meant. By the end of the day tomorrow, the prosecutor's office would see bank records showing nine million dollars coming in and out of his client account in less than a week. Which meant they'd be coming to arrest him by nightfall. And his mother, the loose end, would be all alone and unprotected when Sean Callahan came to silence her. And then there was Katie who was involved now too.

It ought to have been devastating to contemplate. It would be when he got past this place. But he needed to do something here before he could even begin to grapple with it.

He couldn't take his eyes off the house.

Ian got out of the car and walked to the front door. It was locked, just as he'd expected. A few houses along the street had their lights on, revealing front lawns. Not McMartin's house. The housecleaner obviously didn't live there. The place was dark, as silent as a tomb.

He walked around the house. A pool extended into a backyard topped by a mesh roof and enclosed by adobe-like walls with windows chest-high. He saw no wires that would indicate a security system, and no security warning stickers on the windows or lawn.

Ian picked up a fist-sized stone bordering some bushes. Shedding his shirt, he wrapped the stone and then tapped hard on the nearest window glass. There was a cracking sound. He pulled the broken glass apart carefully, dropping the pieces to the grass at his feet. Shaking out his shirt, he put it back on and cleared the last shards from the window edges before climbing through.

The pool glimmered turquoise in the starlight coming through the mesh roof. A sliding glass door separated the pool from the interior of the house, where he could see a black grand piano. Ian circled the water, the faint chlorine smell tickling his nostrils, and went in the door.

A switch was on one side of the door. He reached for it—then stopped. That would be foolish. Instead he crossed the living room in the dark.

On the far end was a short hallway. He took it to a single door. There he paused for a moment before reaching for the knob.

The bedroom inside was lit by a night-light plugged into the far wall. He wanted it to seem familiar, to tap into his dream memories. Except the room was too generic for that. A bed extended into its middle. A chair bordered the wall to his left. There was a window in the far corner. All resonated vaguely. But it could have been one of a thousand bedrooms in a thousand homes.

Ian backed into the hall, then returned to the living room. If his dreams were correct, there should be another hall and room. He walked across the living room and found a second hallway that led to another solitary door.

He opened it and entered. No night-light here. Windows on one side of the room were covered in a closed sash. He chanced turning on a lamp on a desk.

Ian started as the room came alive in light.

The walls were covered in children's wallpaper, festooned with whales and dolphins from floor to ceiling. Bamboo furniture rested on thick shag carpet: a desk, two dressers, a chair. His sense of familiarity gained strength.

On the far side of the room was a wide closet. Ian went to the closet and pulled its double doors apart. The pungent odor of mothballs hit him squarely in the face. Inside, suits and dresses hung neatly from a single rod. Beneath were stacks of shoe boxes.

Ian separated the suits, revealing a white wall above the shoe boxes. Reaching out a hand, he ran his fingers along the dark wood of the closet wall about the height of his waist.

His fingertip grazed a small gap.

And he knew. He knew why he was here. He'd come back after Ed's announcement to see his grandfather again. Through this spy hole. Like he'd seen him the last and only other time in his life, apart from the funeral. Standing here, in the dark.

Ian crossed to the desk and turned out the lamp, making it like it had been that night. Returning to the closet, he felt for the crack again, then knelt and pressed his eye against it.

He could see the dimly lit bedroom beyond once more. For a moment it was the same nondescript place but seen from a different angle. Spare and empty.

Except images began to trickle back to him. Fuller images than his dreams. Rory Doyle sitting on the single bed, his head bowed. His mother talking with Jimmy Doyle about Connor creating the trust. Discussion of a single painting that remained to be sold—and the old man demanding that, as a price for their refusal of a full share, Martha and Connor keep it for him until it was sold, insisting that no one else would know. The scene, moments later, when his mother was gone and it was Callahan standing beside the old man and promising not to hurt Rory. Then Callahan smiling as Jimmy Doyle elicited no similar promises about Martha and Connor Wells.

Ian focused on the impressions of the old man with the outdated hat. A man who'd led a crew into an art gallery thirty-five years before in a job that killed a security guard. Led *his own son*, young Rory, on that job. What kind of monster did something like that to his own child?

The kind of monster who then coolly and patiently sold the paintings over decades to maximize their value. Stringing everybody along to suit his timetable and keep law enforcement in the dark. Holding on to the money into his grave and then, with the trust that Connor created, even beyond.

He refused to believe he was related to that man; he just happened to share his genes.

Ian allowed his gaze to drift down the bedspread in the nightlight's glow just as he had in his dream. It reached the line where the bedspread touched the floor.

And the dark room was gone.

He wasn't looking into the room of his memories anymore. He was there. He could feel the beating of his young heart like an accelerating metronome in his chest, could feel the thin wall cold against his eye socket. His breath was racing from his nose so loud they should have been able to hear it in the adjacent room. The girl who'd brought him here was still standing somewhere just behind him in the study, watching.

He saw again what he'd seen then, but could not recall in his dream. It was sticking out from under the bedspread, splayed on the carpet invisible to Callahan and Jimmy Doyle, who stood a few feet away on the far side of the bed.

Four small fingers. The fingers of a child's hand.

Ian was pulling back from the spy hole again as he had that day, looking for the girl who could explain who was under the bed and had been all the time. Then he was tripping once more over the boxes at his feet and falling noisily to the closet floor. Trying desperately to rise amid the cardboard and disgorged shoes as the room lights came on.

Staring at shiny black wingtips, silk socks, and under-cuffed pant legs.

A powerful hand was wrenching him into the air and dropping him hard onto his own trembling legs.

"What a curious, tenacious little rat ya are," Callahan was saying in a harsh Irish brogue, bent over and speaking only inches from Ian's face. Spittle pooled at the corners of the man's twisted mouth, his face red with anger. "Listening to things we shouldn't be hearing again, are we?"

Ian couldn't speak, any more than if the Irishman's hand was crushing his throat instead of his shoulder.

"I don't know how long ya were standing there, boy," Callahan said, "or if ya understood a word of it, but let me be very clear. If ya ever breathe a word of what ya heard today, I will slit your mother's throat from ear to ear in front of ya. And there's not a single thing in the universe ya could do to stop me. Do we understand, little Master? Do ya believe me?"

Ian was nodding his quivering head.

"You will forget it all. Every syllable. Every gesture. Every word."

Ian kept nodding.

Sean Callahan's expression transformed to disgust. "Your family's been a curse on Jimmy Doyle and always will be. The mistake that won't go away. Ed was right. Ya shouldn't be here at all, stainin' Christina's memory with your presence. And don't think that pathetic man your mother married can protect ya— 'cause he can't. Nobody can save ya or that unholy mistake of your mother if this gets out."

Callahan released him and stomped from the room. Alone once more, Ian looked down at the dark staining the carpet beneath his feet. No tears would gather in his eyes. No sound would come from his throat. Only a shudder that took the whole of his body—and the certainty that, as commanded, *he would forget*.

The images fled. Ian was kneeling in the darkened closet again, looking through a small hole into an empty bedroom lit only by a night-light. The shame, terror, and confusion of the memories left him weak and drained, as if he were waking from an overpowering nightmare. All he wanted was to return to his car and begin the journey home. Get back to Brook. Back to a mother he would, now more than ever, protect from Sean Callahan and the whole world if necessary.

Ian began to lean back when a figure stepped into the doorway of the bedroom opposite the spy hole. It appeared so suddenly—then disappeared so quickly—that he barely had time to register what he'd seen. Dark clothes. A hoodie. A face too indistinct to make out. And the glint of the night-light's faint beam off something metallic in the figure's left hand.

He stood. Sounds of movement traced a path in the living room, approaching.

He scanned the study. The only door was the one he'd entered through. The only windows were above the desk, covered by the sash.

The footsteps neared the study door. Ian stepped backward within the closet, away from its open doors. He slid several suits and dresses around his shoulder and into the gap he'd made in front of the spy hole.

The footsteps were in the room. They walked to the middle and stopped.

Ian held his breath and counted the seconds. *Nine. Ten.*

The steps retreated toward the study door, stopped and turned again.

This time they came fully up to the closet. The mass of clothing Ian had pushed around him was shoved hard, back into his chest. He could hear heavy breathing as the figure crouched.

Whoever it was, the person was looking through the spy hole.

Ian focused on remaining still. *Twenty-seven. Twenty-eight.* His lungs began to ache. He imagined himself crashing through the clothing, down on the person . . .

Twenty-nine. Thirty.

The figure stood. Slowly retreated from the closet. Left the room.

Ian took a careful gulp of air. Then it struck him: the person knew he was here somewhere, had seen his car, and wouldn't be leaving until Ian was found.

He slid aside the clothing and left the closet. The study door was still open. Ian walked softly to it, leaned down, and examined it. The door had a pressure lock.

He gently closed the door, pressing the lock into place. Stepping to the windows, he pulled on the nearest sash cord as though it held a bell he didn't want to ring. He watched the sash rise slowly toward the ceiling.

It reached the top. Ian pulled the cord to the side to secure it. He let it go.

The sash came tumbling down.

A grunt of recognition came from the direction of the pool.

The sound of footsteps began approaching rapidly, into the living room toward him again.

Ian tore the sash aside, feeling for the lock atop the window. He caught it and flipped it open. With both hands he threw the window up and then leaped through the light screen separating him from the outside air.

The screen popped free and he was falling. His shoulder hit the grassy ground. He rolled—at the same moment he heard a thud on the study door he'd just locked.

Scrambling to his feet, Ian sprinted toward his car, fumbling for the keys in his pocket. Two more heavy thuds followed, and then he heard the study door smashing open.

He was nearly at the car door when he could make out sounds of someone fighting the sash. He was dropping into the driver's seat when the first silenced shot registered with a different kind of thud against the bumper. A second slammed into the front quarter panel.

Ian started the engine and threw the car into reverse. He pushed the accelerator to the floor. The car roared backward in an uncontrolled weave, up the street and away from the house. Another bullet careened off the pavement where the car had been parked seconds before. A fourth hit the bumper again.

He twirled the wheel around and felt the rear tires leap the curb onto a darkened lawn. He quickly shifted into drive and stomped on the gas.

The car raced back over the curb onto the street again. He didn't ease his foot from the accelerator until he was half a mile away.

41

"And so, Your Honor," Brook listened to herself saying, "we believe the evidence is clearly admissible, given that—"

"Inadmissible," the judge interrupted.

"Your Honor?"

"Inadmissible. You said the evidence is 'clearly admissible,' but you meant the opposite. You are arguing on behalf of the United States, aren't you? As opposed to the accused?"

She looked down at her papers a thousand yards away. "Of course, Your Honor. *In*admissible."

The remainder of the argument passed in the same blur. The absence of questions from the usually voluble Judge Fitzsimmons was the clearest sign he viewed her as impaired this afternoon and was inclined to cut her some slack.

She packed up her papers as the courtroom emptied, her mind already reverting to Ian. He hadn't called since arriving in Florida. She was supposed to pick him up in an hour at the airport, and she didn't have a clue whether the trip had yielded any information that could help recover the money.

"Brook?"

She turned. Chloe was standing behind the bar, uncharacteristically subdued.

"Yeah, Chloe."

"I . . . your secretary said you had this motion. I wanted you to know right away that the search warrant on the Wells & Hoy bank accounts turned up some serious things."

"Like what?" she asked over her plummeting stomach—though she knew what she was about to hear.

"Nine million dollars-plus went through the Wells & Hoy firm's client account in a matter of days. In and out. Eldon thinks it could be proceeds from the art theft, especially since Ian Wells seems to have disappeared. The guy's partner, Dennis Hoy, says he hasn't seen him for days. Eldon's going to broaden the search to include the law office and Ian Wells's home. They're drawing up warrants now."

It was expected but still filled her with dismay. Even that Chloe was cooperating didn't assuage it.

"Thanks, Chloe. Thanks for the update."

Chloe smiled wanly and walked away.

Brook stepped to a corner of the now-vacant courtroom and took out her cell. Once more she punched in the number for Ian's temporary phone and waited.

He still wasn't answering.

Even if Ian was successful, he was running out of time. If they completed those searches of his home and office yet today or tonight, an arrest warrant would be issued before midnight. How could she possibly help?

Minutes later, Brook was stepping off the elevator and making her way down the hallway toward her office. The deposit list was still on her desk when she arrived. It was a sign how quickly the investigation was focusing on Ian that nobody had asked her how the search for depositors of the stolen money was coming. For all they knew, she'd completed it already.

Brook stopped . . . thought for a moment. She spun on her heel and hurried toward Eldon's office.

Her boss was standing behind his desk when she came to the door.

"Eldon," she said.

He looked up. "Yeah, Brook?"

"I'm pretty much done with the deposit review you gave me last week. Chloe mentioned you were going to be preparing new warrants to search the home and office of Ian Wells. I thought I'd volunteer to handle that."

Eldon nodded. "Didn't think you were available. I just assigned Sophie. She was pretty swamped, but I told her it's a priority."

Brook smiled. "Okay. Just thought I'd check."

She headed down the hall to Sophie's office. She found her friend at her desk, facing her computer screen with a pile of file folders at her side.

"Hello, Sophie," Brook said. "I'm glad I caught you. Hey, I just spoke with Eldon. He mentioned you're swamped. So I volunteered to handle the search warrants for Ian Wells's office and home."

Sophie's face relaxed with relief. "Really? Because that would be great. I've got three omnibus hearings to prepare for. That would be *so great*."

Brook was still smiling when she left Sophie's office with the paperwork and information she needed for the warrants.

4:05 P.M.
MINNEAPOLIS-ST. PAUL INTERNATIONAL AIRPORT

"Tell me what happened," Brook demanded worriedly as they picked up speed on the drive away from the airport terminal. "You didn't answer my calls. Plus you look terrible."

Ian sat in the passenger seat, staring out at a rain that had only intensified since the previous Sunday. "I know who stole the money," he said remotely. "Or at least I think I do."

"*Who?*"

Ian's mind felt broken into pieces too small to reassemble. "Do you know your father?" he asked. "Really know him? What he does when you're not around. How he's done it. What he's *capable of* . . ."

"I think so," Brook answered, her eyes showing fear at Ian's vacant tone.

"What if you don't? And what about his father, and his father before him? What about the genes they passed on to you?"

"I've got a mother who contributed a few genes too," Brook said, glancing in his direction. "And we're not preprogrammed machines. We make choices." Her voice grew kinder. "Come on, Ian. What really happened down there in Florida?"

"It doesn't matter." He closed his eyes to focus his thinking. "I need you to do something for me, if you're willing."

"Have I ever denied you? What is it you need?"

Ian reached into a pants pocket and pulled out a crumpled sheet of paper. "Could you research these names? Find out everything you can about them. Where they've lived. What jobs they held. Whatever your resources can dredge up in the next twenty-four hours."

She took the paper. "Sure. Now, tell me who stole the money."

He pointed to the piece of paper. "Them," he said. "One or both."

She read the names. "Oh, wow. Really?"

"Really."

"And you think they spread the hot money from the art thefts?"

"They probably had access to some of it. After I realized Callahan was obviously right when he said he had no incentive to spread hot bills from the robbery through his retainer, I remembered we got another retainer the same day as Callahan's. It was a referral through Harry Christensen. One of my suspects could have gone to Harry, given him cash, then told him they needed representation on days they'd figured out he wasn't available. It wouldn't have been tough to do—Harry talks about his vacations on his radio show. Then Harry referred them on to me, as they also knew he would from the show, and I end up being the one depositing the cash retainer with the hot money."

"Okay. Assume you're right. Assume it's them. What can you do about it? Can you make them give the money back?"

"Maybe. If I can work a trade before I run out of time."

"With what?"

Ian pulled out his cellphone, tapped the screen, and held it up for Brook to see.

The screen had a highlighted message containing a single word: *No.*

Brook scrunched her face. "What's that supposed to mean?"

"It's Anthony Ahmetti answering a question I asked him on Sunday. I gave him the number so he could text me. He's telling me Jimmy Doyle never fenced the final Norman Rockwell they stole in 1983. *The Spirit of 1776.* One I think Doyle told my parents he wanted them to hold. By now, if fenced right, it would be worth more than all the other paintings combined."

"And you think your parents—your mom—still has it?"

"Yeah. I think the trust money thieves believe she does too—hence the burglary. And I have a theory about where it is."

"How much time do you need?" Brook asked.

"Another twenty-four hours. Freedom of movement for another day." He looked at Brook with concern. "Will I have it?"

Brook nodded. "Yes. I think I can safely say the warrants needed to search your office and make an arrest have been unavoidably delayed."

42

Ian entered his darkened office suite, a rolled-up poster under his arm. Without turning on the lights, he strode the familiar hallway into his own silent office.

His absence had been only a few days, but with all that had transpired he felt like a stranger in the place. He stopped and scrutinized his desk. Nothing had been moved or disturbed.

He turned to the broad wall above the safe.

The enlarged photograph of his parents' wedding day loomed over the room with a new significance. He gauged its height and width, the depth of the wood frame. He'd never appreciated before that there wasn't another picture of its size anywhere else in the office.

Could he really find his target on his first try? It seemed so unlikely—but for the fact that the burglar at his mom's house had already eliminated every other contender for a framed painting that he could imagine.

He lifted the frame off the wall and gently set it facedown on the desktop. Simple clips held a thin slice of wood to the back of the frame. Dislodging them, Ian lifted the wood out and set it aside.

The reverse side of the photograph was white, blank. It was obvious at a glance that there was nothing else in the frame but the photo.

Ian dropped into his chair, stinging with disappointment. No canvas. No *Spirit of 1776*. He'd convinced himself the location made sense, that his parents would have placed it here because it was close to his father every day and well disguised.

But logical or not, it wasn't here. And now he had nothing to trade and no way to convince the thieves to return the trust money to Callahan.

Ian looked despondently around the office. The black mood that descended on him in Florida had lifted at the prospect that he'd find the painting. Now, with nothing to trade, he had no way forward. Tomorrow Callahan would be coming after them, with the prosecutors just behind.

Ian stood to replace the wooden backing onto the picture frame when something caught his eye: a thin strand curled upward from the frame's edge like a stray hair. He pulled it free and held it up to get a better look.

It was thick and sturdy. Canvas.

The painting *had* been here once. His heart started racing. That meant his parents had moved it. Or his mom had moved it after his dad died and before her Alzheimer's began. She might have wanted to be sure it was under her watch since Connor wasn't in the office anymore.

The painting was likely still around.

He pulled out his phone and punched in Brook's number.

When she answered, he said, "No luck. I didn't find the painting. But I think I found proof it used to be at the office. I just have no idea where to look for it now. I would've said at Mom's house, except the burglar already ransacked the place."

He could hear Brook's sigh of distress. "Then what are you going to do, Ian?"

"I'm going to meet with the thief anyway. Maybe I'll bluff. I don't know."

"If your mom moved it from the office," Brook said, "she'd put it someplace she was confident would be safe and under her watch, right?"

"Right, which should be at home. But from Katie's description, the burglar already looked everywhere I'd look."

"Maybe. Except you know that house much better than them. Tell me," she went on, "where around her home would your mother feel the safest or most secure?"

This seemed like a waste of the little time he had left. "Well," he said, "pretty much anywhere in the house."

"That doesn't help. Think, Ian."

"Okay. Bedroom, living room, kitchen . . ."

"Broader."

"Garage. Local park, I suppose. Her gardens."

Brook cleared her throat for emphasis. "So, did Katie tell you the burglar picked any flowers or vegetables while they were there?"

Ian's pulse picked up again. "*You're right.* Brook, are you at home or with Katie in St. Paul?"

"St. Paul. I'm trying to stay out of reach of the office just now."

"Can you get over to Mom's place? Get a spade out of the garage and start checking the garden?"

"Checking? What's that mean?"

"Digging. The front flower garden she can see through her picture window—focus on where she has the begonias. She plants in the same order every year. If that doesn't work, try the marigolds. And you may have to go four feet down, beneath the frost line. It would likely be in something metal, and something insulated. Three to four feet in length. Like a poster roll."

"On my way."

Ian rushed toward the door, not bothering to return the photo to the wall.

43

Ian parked the Camry around the block from Lisa Ramsdale's house. The living room was lit behind drawn shades as he walked up the sidewalk bisecting the neat yard.

A woman in her fifties opened the door a crack at Ian's knock. "What do you want this time of night?" she demanded nervously.

"I need to see your daughter. Maureen."

"Go away." The woman's voice turned harsh. "Or I'll call the police."

"Ask your daughter if she wants you to call the police," Ian said more loudly.

"It's okay, Mom." Maureen appeared at her shoulder. "I've got this."

Maureen brushed back hair from her face as she stepped out onto the stoop. Ian saw that the mother had left the door slightly ajar. "Walk with me," he said.

A few minutes later, the two reached a corner where Ian stopped.

302

"What's my philosopher lawyer want now?" Maureen asked.

"You were brilliant," he replied. "And so *patient*."

Maureen's expression darkened. "I don't understand."

"It was you. You took the trust money," he said, watching her reaction.

"Crazy talk, philosopher lawyer. You should stop while you're ahead."

"You were there that day at the funeral," Ian continued, speaking deliberately and with conviction. "You were at the gravesite the day they buried Christina Doyle. Afterward, you were there at Ed McMartin's house, where you led me to the spy hole in the study."

Maureen shook her head. "What funeral?"

Ian ignored her reply. "You must have been to 'Uncle Ed's' place on other occasions. That's how you learned about that spy hole in the closet wall. What were you doing that day? Playing hide-and-seek, I suppose. You were looking through the hole and saw me in the room with all those men—and then you watched Callahan lead me out. That's when you came to get me."

The girl with the red hair studied him. "Sounds like family rumors. I told you, I don't do family rumors."

"You might as well admit it," Ian said. "And I know your brother Liam was there that day too. He was hiding under the bed when all of them were talking about the trust. He was still there later when Jimmy Doyle told my mother about the last painting. I saw his hand."

Maureen fell silent.

"Did you know then that I was your cousin?" he asked.

Silence. Ian looked up at the stars.

"C'mon, Maureen. I know you took the money. Liam told you what he learned in the bedroom that day of the funeral—

whatever you hadn't already heard yourself. Then you two planned and waited all these years for the day when the trust money was to be transferred into an account at my firm. You got the exact day by paying the owner at Larry's Bar to tell you what he heard from Rory on the phone, or from my meeting at the bar. Or maybe it was even easier than that; maybe your dad told you himself. Just like he gave you his cash from the heist—out of guilt. When the time neared, you spread the hot cash around, linking it to me, then hacked in and stole the trust money from my account. You tried to take the painting too. At my mother's place."

Maureen took a nervous step back toward the house. "It's getting cold." She turned to go.

"Leaving now would be a mistake. Because I've got the painting."

The redhead stopped, though she didn't turn around. Ian watched her in the moonlight, heard her soft breathing.

"It's worth much more than the cash you got, Maureen. But you know that. I did some research on Norman Rockwell's *Spirit of 1776* and found it could be worth twice the cash you're holding. And I'll bet you already figured out exactly where and how to sell it, planning for the day you took it from my parents. It wouldn't be through Anthony Ahmetti. He's no art guy and too close to the family. But you've had years to figure that part out. Yep, that Rockwell is worth so much more to you than the cash. I know you'd planned on having both the money and the painting, but given a choice, you'd take the painting, wouldn't you? Plus there's an added benefit if you give the cash back. You don't have to worry about Sean Callahan chasing you the rest of your days. Well, I'm ready to make a trade."

Maureen rotated slowly back to face Ian. "Why would I ever trust a word you say?"

"Check me if you want. I'm not wearing a wire. And why would I turn you in? If I did, I'd send my own mother to jail for holding the painting all these years. No, I have no interest in the money or the painting. I'm only interested in getting the cash back to Sean Callahan before he kills me and my mother for losing it in the first place."

She stared at him through the darkness, a smile slowly forming. "I asked my mother at the gravesite who you were," Maureen said playfully. "You must have been ten or eleven, standing over there behind Sean Callahan and Grandpa. I thought it so strange, you standing next to the two men who terrified me more than anyone else in the world."

"Who did your mother say I was?"

"She whispered to me. She said, '*It's a family secret. You mustn't tell anybody else. But he's your cousin.*' I didn't even know I had any cousins. We were big on family secrets in those days. It was only later that I got the full story about your mother being the child of Grandpa's mistress. Like everyone else, I kept the secret."

"What about your brother?"

Maureen nodded. "Liam knew the secret too. Did you know I was trying to help you that day—later, at the house? That's why I came to get you. You looked so terrified after they threw you out of the room and separated you from your mom. I was amazed you didn't cry."

"I knew you were trying to help me."

Her smile faded. "So tell me what you want to do."

"First I want to know whether Liam told you what he learned about the money and the painting that day in the bedroom, and if after that you acted alone. Or whether I'm right in betting that Liam told you about the money and painting and then you worked *together* all these years."

Maureen began shifting from foot to foot. It seemed talking about Liam made her nervous. "More family rumors, Ian Wells," she whispered.

"Alright. Keep that one to yourself. It doesn't matter really. But here's the deal: an exchange of the painting for the cash. We meet in a public place where you transfer the money electronically to an account in a way I can confirm on the spot. Then I hand you the painting, and we both walk away."

She didn't say anything for a moment, then finally, "Where?"

"Guthrie Theater. Out on the patio overlooking the river and the Stone Arch Bridge, nine-forty-five tomorrow night. That's after intermission when the theatergoers are back inside watching the play. I'll give you the account number once you're there."

"That location's kind of dramatic, don't you think?"

"Mostly, it's very public."

Maureen nodded. "Actions and consequences and some credit for good intentions. That's your deal, isn't it?"

"That's my deal."

She paused, then gave him a smile. "I seem to have lost your card. Give me your number and I'll let you know."

Ian left her on the sidewalk leading to her front door, walking back to the Camry and feeling satisfaction roll through him like thunder. He had more questions, of course. Accusatory questions about the attacks in Northeast Minneapolis and in Florida. For now, they could wait. He didn't want to risk scaring her off just yet.

But he'd gotten the confirmation he was looking for. About Maureen's involvement, and probably Liam's too.

The moment's satisfaction began bleeding away. Of course, the exchange was a bluff. He didn't have the painting. That would be obvious within minutes of their meeting. How likely was it he could accomplish what he needed to without it?

He was pressing the button to unlock the Camry door when he felt the buzz of his phone. He pulled it from his pants pocket and read the text from Brook.

1776, the text read. *I got it.*

44

Nearing the Twin Cities on 35W, Ian heard Callahan answer his phone, his voice deep and throaty coming through the Camry's speakers.

"Yeah," Callahan said.

"I can retrieve the money tomorrow. I need you there."

A pause. "Why do you need me there?"

"Because as soon as I retrieve the money, I want to distribute it to the trust's beneficiaries. Immediately. I want this to be over with—and you can keep my fee."

Ian could almost hear the Irishman thinking. At last he said, "Where?"

Ian described the time and the setting.

"You're kidding. No way. That's way too public."

"It's there or nothing. The people with the money insisted. And I've got no way to reach them again before the meeting. Don't think there'll be another chance either."

His lie was followed by more silence.

308

"Anything else?" Callahan asked.

"I need your help to locate Rory. They want him there too."

"He's not entitled to any of the money," Sean growled.

"It doesn't matter. They want him there and I don't have time to locate him."

Callahan snorted. "That part won't be a problem. Rory's been stayin' with me the last few days till we saw if you had any luck retrievin' the cash before the deadline."

"Did he tell you anything?" Ian asked, worried.

"No. I've a feelin' he knows who took the money, but if he does he's kept it to himself so far. On that topic, since it obviously wasn't Rory, who *did* take the money?"

"You'll find out tomorrow. That was another condition of the exchange."

The pause that followed was pregnant with distrust. "Alright, boyo," Callahan said, his suspicion belied by the grin in his voice. "We'll do it their way."

The line went dead.

45

Harry Christensen was in top Talk Show form, seated across from Eldon Carroll and two other prosecutors—including the smallish woman at the end of the table they'd introduced as Chloe. Despite being outnumbered, Harry was nudging the bobber of their negotiations as if he were sensing a fat walleye.

Ian sat silent, something he was unaccustomed to in conferences like this. Being a client was a first for him, and he didn't like it. He'd quickly come to realize that trying to keep a calm demeanor was a lot harder when all the talk was about him.

"So, do we have a deal?" Harry repeated.

Eldon Carroll wanted this deal. He wanted it with every fiber of his ambitious being. The chance to crack the biggest art theft in Minnesota history? After decades as a cold case? The burning desire was apparent in the U.S. Attorney's straight-backed posture as he sat there gripping his pen too tightly in one hand, his eyes wide and brimming with energy.

"No," Eldon said. "We'll accept the rest of it. But your client has to lose his bar license at least."

"For being a good Samaritan?" Harry laughed. "I don't think so."

"For handling nine million dollars in stolen funds and not coming to us or the FBI. He's a lawyer. He has a higher standard to live up to."

"He held the cash for *one week* while he figured out where it came from and how to protect his family."

"Then we get his mother. You can't have both."

Harry smiled. "We can't, huh? That comes as a disappointment since I was counting on that. Oh well. So sorry we couldn't do business today." He began stacking and putting his papers away.

"Hold on," Eldon said. "Just hold on." He thought it over for a moment—as though any hesitation could hide his hunger for the deal. "Okay," the U.S. Attorney finally said, relenting. "We'll arrange for an exam. If the mother really does have Alzheimer's, we won't prosecute her either."

A smile wreathed Harry's face. "That's wonderful. So glad we could make this happen. Write it up."

"So when do we move?" Eldon demanded, all restraint gone.

Harry looked at Ian. "Your show."

"Tonight," Ian replied. "Have the FBI ready to move from here no later than nine. I'll send a text saying when it's time, and telling them where to go."

"Wait a second," Eldon sputtered. "You're not going to tell us which building you'll be in? That's too vague. We need to be at the site and set up ahead of time."

Ian shook his head. "I'll have them all there, but the people with control over the cash spent years planning how to get the money. They are *meticulous*. They'll have eyes on the site all day. You make a single move in that direction and they'll be gone, and the rest with them. And once they're all gone, that money and any possibility of prosecution are gone forever. This is the only way it could work."

"Without setup, it's impossible," Eldon pleaded. "We've got to have *some* kind of eyes and ears on this thing."

"Alright," Ian said, "but I won't wear a wire. It's too likely they'll check me. Set up your people on the Stone Arch Bridge, near the middle. Erect a utility tent or something to hide yourselves. The team will be within scope and binoculars sight of the meeting. As soon as I text you and they know where to look, they'll be able to see what's going on."

Eldon looked shaken with frustration at the meager information he was getting. "What if it all goes south? How will we know if people are in danger?"

Ian thought for a moment. "Have somebody from your office with the team on the bridge, somebody who can call it if they see my signal. I'll wipe my forehead with my hand if I need you to step in early. Have your person ready to confirm the signal and give the word to send in the FBI."

Brook, he thought—an instant before he said aloud, "I want the prosecutor who interviewed me. Brook something. I want her to be your person on the bridge."

Eldon cocked his head in a way that reminded him of the prosecutor's disbelief at Ian's flat-tire story the past week. "She's on mandatory leave," he said cautiously. "She missed a critical deadline in a big case."

That was news Brook hadn't shared. "Take her *off* leave," Ian said firmly. "She's who I want."

Eldon's grip on his pen tightened again. "You're setting us

up for failure. The only thing worse than a failed investigation is a failed operation."

"It's all I'll agree to," Ian said.

Eldon turned to Harry, then back to Ian. "Alright. You're calling the shots. But listen—and hear me clearly. If we aren't successful tonight, the deal's off. At that point, all I'll have is you and your mother, and believe me when I say I'll prosecute the both of you."

46

The highway noise was fading with rush hour passing. Seated on the patio, Martha pulled her sweater closer as she looked out into the clear evening air.

"That's all your research found about him?" she heard Ian saying from inside the apartment.

"Yes. Just a few addresses on Liam Doyle in Los Angeles over the years. Big gaps in time. The jobs I could locate, I've listed. There's nothing more I could find in this short of time. Maureen's stayed in the Midwest, with odd jobs and work in the Twin Cities—before she started the nursing program two years ago."

"Okay." Ian's voice again. "Thanks for checking. We need to go now."

"You should take your dad's gun," Brook said worriedly.

"I can't. Callahan or his Marine will check for weapons on the patio."

314

The concern Martha heard in each of their voices was wrenching. It reminded her of Connor and herself when they were young. When talks like this one were commonplace, and guilt always near at hand.

"You're going to be careful," Brook said. It wasn't a question.

"Of course. Now, we should get going. I want you to drop me a few blocks from the Guthrie."

Ian emerged onto the patio and knelt at Martha's side. "It's all going to be fine, Mom. After tonight it'll all be behind you—behind us. Maybe not the way you and Dad planned, but done all the same."

He waited expectantly. Martha didn't look in his direction. She felt a longing to speak, but couldn't. Not now. Not knowing what she had to do.

"You'll be alone for a little while now, Mom. But Katie will be back from her house very shortly to stay with you. And I'll come get you tomorrow. We'll all be safe then."

He kissed her forehead and returned inside. There was a jangling of keys in the kitchen and the closing of a cupboard door. Then the apartment door opened and shut and all grew silent.

Martha waited, listening to the evening birds chirping in the dusk. Waited ten minutes, or as near to it as she could guess.

She rose and went inside.

Standing in the kitchen, Martha inventoried the upper cabinets with her eyes. She pulled a chair close, using it as a stool to reach them, opening each in turn.

She found the hiding spot in the third one she checked. The keys she slid into her pocket. The gun she weighed in her hand after stepping carefully back to the floor. With a single motion, she ejected and checked the magazine. Two bullets were missing. She pushed the magazine hard back into place, the effort hurting her hand, unaccustomed to the force.

Then she dropped the weapon into her purse and headed out the door.

47

Ian's hand, slick with sweat, pressed the steel bar to enter through the tall glass doors of the Guthrie Theater. With great effort he slid the insulated metal tube under his arm and casually approached the box office will-call desk.

"Ian Wells," he said with a smile. "For *Richard III.*"

The attendant returned the smile as she slipped the ticket to him across the counter. "Sorry, it's already past intermission. There's only an hour left."

Ian grimaced and shook his head. "I know. My business meeting went long. No worries—I read the CliffsNotes."

A long escalator carried him to the upper level, where *Richard III* was in progress. He walked past the hall that led to the theater, toward a ramp that sloped upward to an outside patio overlooking the river.

Aaron, the Marine, was standing before a bar that fronted the patio. Twin entrances on either side led outdoors. His hands

317

were in his pockets. No bartender was in sight—either paid off or gone for the evening with intermission finished. On both patio doors were signs with the word *Closed* printed in large letters.

"Dried out yet?" Ian asked.

Aaron's face grew hot. "Hold your arms up," he growled. Reaching behind the bar, he grabbed a wand, similar to the one Prima had used at Doggy's. He ran it over Ian's torso, arms, and legs.

"You got a phone in there?" Aaron asked, pointing to a pocket.

"Yeah." Ian pulled it out for Aaron to see. "Satisfied?"

Aaron pointed to the metal tube. "What's that?"

Ian unscrewed the tube's end and allowed the Marine to peek inside. "It's for the meeting."

He grunted at what was obviously no weapon. He looked away as Ian went on through one of the doors. As it swung shut, Ian heard the Marine stiffly announce to someone else approaching, "Sorry, ma'am. Got a wedding shoot on the patio tonight."

The open-air patio thrust out from the Guthrie's main building like an outdoor stage, towering over the lawn several stories below. From the door Ian had passed through, steps descended along a series of concrete terraces running the patio's width. The small space was illuminated only at foot level, though at the patio's lowest point signs pointed to emergency walkways left and right.

Ian saw all of this, yet his eyes were mostly drawn straight ahead, beyond the prow of the patio toward the dark ribbon of the Mississippi and the Stone Arch Bridge, its curving structure lit with a string of bulbs from end to end.

Sean Callahan was standing at the lowest point of the patio next to a waist-high balustrade. His back was to the river, his hands behind him. He said nothing as he looked up and eyed the cylinder in Ian's hands. Rory was seated just a few feet from Callahan on a concrete terrace, facing away from Ian's approach. Maureen Doyle stood beside her father.

"Seems to be a family reunion," Sean said to Ian in his Irish brogue. "Everyone ya expected here?"

Ian was momentarily shaken at the realization that Callahan's sarcasm was more than just that. Rory Doyle really was his uncle. Maureen really was a cousin. "I don't know," Ian said uncomfortably. He looked at Maureen. "Anyone else attending?"

Footsteps approached from behind. Ian turned—and took an unsettled step backward.

Wet Willy was striding down the steps. His hair was uncharacteristically combed and pulled back into a bun. He wore pressed slacks and a collared shirt, also strange for the man. Under his arm was a laptop computer.

Ian had difficulty speaking. *"What are you doing here?"* he finally got out.

Willy just smiled, halting two levels up from the others.

Ian glanced down at Maureen, then back to Willy. "What's going on?" he demanded.

Willy took a seat on the concrete level where he'd stopped. Ian saw that Maureen's gaunt father was staring at Willy as though he were seeing a ghost.

"Hello, son," Rory said quietly and with unmistakable disappointment. "It's been a very long time."

"Hello, Dad," Willy replied calmly. "Yes, it surely has."

Rory's expression was one of tenderness and pain. Maureen watched them both without reaction.

The earth opened up and swallowed Ian. "You can't be Liam Doyle," he muttered, disembodied. "You're William Dryer. You've been my client for five years. I've defended you in two trials."

"Three trials, counting the one we'll have to miss," Willy said as he began typing on the computer. "You're a fine lawyer, Ian, getting me off each time. But then Willy always came to you with an alibi, didn't he?"

In the near darkness, Ian couldn't see Rory's eyes clearly, but he felt the wave of intense grief when the man spoke next.

"You shouldn't have done this," Rory said, stricken. He looked back and forth from Liam to Maureen. "This is a terrible mistake. Sweetheart, Maureen, you told me you and Liam didn't want the money. At Victor's you told me to drop my claim to the trust. I was so glad you did. Now what are you doing? Tell your brother all this is a mistake. Just leave now and be done with it."

"You were going to lose it all," Liam answered as he worked the keyboard. "You let Jimmy Doyle hold back your money for *thirty-five years*, and then you *still* figured out a way to lose it. You were a waste of a dad and you were going to waste Grandpa's trust money too."

Ian looked to Maureen, still reeling. "You're smart," he said, adding his voice to Rory's. "How'd you get talked into all this?"

She shrugged. "Like we discussed at Mom's place—money's not bad, just depends what you do with it."

"Ready for the account number, Counselor," Liam declared.

Ian struggled to formulate his thoughts. "How long have you two been planning for today's meeting?" he asked Maureen.

"How old were we at the funeral?" Maureen turned the question to Liam.

"Twelve."

"Since we were twelve," Maureen said to Ian. "Sometimes in California where Liam lived. Sometimes here."

"Can I have the account number, Ian?" Liam repeated impatiently. "Please?"

Through his daze, Ian pulled a slip of paper from his pocket and handed it to Liam.

Ian turned back to Maureen. "If you're really a part of this, you must know your brother tried to kill me, right? Was that always part of the plan?"

"That bit on the street by the alley was just theater," Liam jumped in without looking up from the computer. "Those guys I brought in from California were never going to *seriously* hurt you. Just scare you a little. Keep you off track. It was you who went and ruined Sam's knee. Maureen knows all about it."

"You weren't in any real danger," Maureen agreed, smiling reassuringly.

Ian's hand brushed the phone in his pocket. He held his breath. In his shock at Willy's arrival, he hadn't sent the text to Eldon Carroll and the SWAT team. Everyone was here; the money was about to be transferred. But the FBI's team at the courthouse hadn't even left the building yet.

"I'm not talking about that business," Ian said, stalling for time. He slid his hand deeper into his pocket and felt for the button to send the text message he'd preprogrammed. "Just to be clear, Maureen, your brother's lying about that too. What happened by the alley was supposed to get me murdered—if not on the spot, by making it look like I was running with the money so that Callahan would kill me." He pressed the button and prayed he'd gotten it right. "But that's not what I'm talking about. I'm talking about what Willy—what *Liam*—did when Callahan and Aaron didn't oblige. Your brother followed me to Florida and tried to kill me there himself."

Maureen looked confused. "What's he talking about, Liam?"

"What, now you're listening to the lawyer?" Liam said, his attention still locked on the computer screen.

"It was either Liam or you who tried to shoot me," Ian said more forcefully to Maureen. "Because whoever followed me down to Florida, they knew about the spy hole in the closet wall. That narrows the field."

Rory had begun spinning the gold band on his finger frantically. "*Don't do this*," he pleaded to Maureen. "Don't get mixed up in murder. Walk away, sweetheart. You always followed Liam too much. Don't follow your brother now. Not with this."

Callahan raised his hands. "As much as I appreciate the touching poignancy of the moment, given the public locale chosen for this transaction, let's get on with it. Even *Richard III* won't last forever."

Maureen turned deliberately away from her father and Liam, gazing out toward the river.

"Agreed," Liam answered the Irishman. "Not feeling much like conversation just now anyway. Let's do our business before the play ends." He looked at Ian. "You got the painting?"

Ian picked up the metal tube from the terrace, where he'd placed it beside him. Removing the end cap, he slid the canvas free and unfurled it in the dim light.

"Take a close look," Liam ordered Maureen.

Moving more uncertainly now, Maureen approached Ian. Using a flashlight app on her phone, she leaned in close to get a good look at the painting. "Yes. It's genuine. It has the damage on the edges from the original theft."

Ian rolled up the painting and slid it back into the cylinder, replacing the end cap.

Callahan's eyes were steeped in disbelief. "*That's what this is?* You're tellin' me Jimmy never sold the last painting?"

"So it would seem," Liam said. He stopped working the computer and looked with concern at the Irishman. "Your lawyer here assured my sister that you were ready to exchange the painting for return of the trust money. Was he lying?"

Even in the low light, Ian could see Callahan's jaw clenching and his hands fisted in his pockets.

"I need to know now," Liam said, his fingers moving toward the keyboard's Delete button. "If you want my opinion—and I've thought about this a lot—I'd say you should take the cash. I've already got a buyer lined up for the Rockwell painting, one you'd never find. That painting's worth a whole lot more to me than it ever will be to you."

Callahan's swagger was gone, replaced by frigid fury. "Aye," he muttered. "Transfer the money."

"Good," Liam said with relief. "Now, Counselor, pull up the account number you just gave me on your phone. You'll be able to see the transfer take place."

Ian brought up his phone. If he'd pressed the button to alert the SWAT team, it would appear brighter on the screen.

He looked at that corner of the screen first. The button was dim. He hadn't actually pushed it yet.

His stomach dropping, Ian pushed it now. Then he fumbled as slowly as he could to locate the bank transaction page.

"*C'mon*," Callahan growled. "We haven't got all night."

The transfer appeared on the screen. Nine million-plus dollars. He waited a few seconds longer. "I've got it," Ian said at last.

Maureen took the cylinder with the painting from under Ian's arm.

Ian glanced around. Rory looked deflated and lost. Maureen, holding the painting, appeared unsure and nervous. Only Liam seemed calm as he closed his laptop.

Callahan's cheeks were crimson.

The Irishman straightened his back and nodded toward the

patio door. Instantly, Aaron the Marine stepped through onto the upper terrace.

"You should know," Liam said, looking up at Aaron's sudden entrance, "that this transaction can be reversed for twenty minutes."

Aaron had begun a slow descent of the steps as Callahan's face grew stony. "What're ya meanin'?" he asked.

"Just what I said." Liam stood, still calm and under control. "If Maureen and I don't reach a friend of ours in the next ten minutes, a guy who can authenticate the painting and confirm we're okay, he'll undo the transaction. It's the only way we could be sure you'd let us go after the money was sent."

"Don't worry. You'll get your money," Maureen said, her effort at reassurance sounding unconvincing as she watched Aaron descend the steps. "Like Ian said when we met, we don't want to be looking over our shoulders forever."

"So I'm to believe," Callahan growled, "that you're gonna traipse away from here with the paintin', then refrain from undoin' the money transfer? Is that it? Is that the other lie your brother told ya about how all this was workin', Maureen, darlin'?"

Still spinning the ring on his finger, Rory rose and stepped protectively between his daughter and Callahan.

"You'd never let us leave if it wasn't set up this way," Liam said, his voice tightening. "You're making that obvious right now."

A gun appeared in the Marine's hand, its barrel pointed at the ground. He moved to Callahan's side.

"I might've done this accordin' to Jimmy's wishes," Callahan added. "Truly. But you all had to foul it up with your schemin'. Rory lyin' about his past to get a share he doesn't deserve. The lawyer doin' a disappearin' act till Aaron runs him down. Now the paintin' reappearing. I might've done it according to Jimmy's plan. But we'll certainly do it my way now."

"Sean," Rory said, "you can't shoot everybody. Not here."

"I'll do as I please, *where* I please," Callahan snapped, pulling a small handgun from his jacket pocket. Callahan held it low and pointed to the emergency exit to his right. "This way."

"The transaction will reverse in less than six minutes," Liam said, the alarm creeping deeper in his voice.

"What can be reversed can be reversed again," Callahan replied in a murderous tone.

It was all falling apart, Ian thought. And the FBI's team still had to be minutes away. Growing desperate, he began raising a hand to his forehead.

The patio door opened once more. A thin woman stepped through and began walking ethereally down the steps.

It took Ian a moment for it to register that the woman was Martha. And that in her hand his mother held the gun she'd given him to destroy just nine days before.

"*What are you doing here?*" Ian cried out. "*Drop the gun.*"

"Aye, drop it," Callahan said soothingly. "Ya don't need to get into this now, Martha. It's all under control."

"She doesn't know what she's doing," Ian pleaded, turning to the Irishman. "It's her Alzheimer's. Let me talk to her."

"Rory," Martha said, ignoring both Ian and Callahan and looking to the wraithlike figure standing beside Maureen. "It's been so long."

Some strange quality in her words brought silence to the patio. Martha stopped her slow descent of the steps and glanced around.

"No, wait," she went on. "It hasn't been so long, has it, Rory? You came by the house the other day. When I was in my garden."

Rory shook his head. "No, Martha, I didn't."

"Of course you did. Though you looked so young." Her gaze drifted again, stopping on Liam. "Why, no. It was you who came by and spoke to me in the garden. Twice."

Liam stood still and quiet.

Aaron's gun barrel began to rise slowly. Martha's head turned, and she gripped him in a stare.

"Do you think I'd miss at this distance, young man?" she asked firmly. "My Connor taught me better than that. We practiced often after we married, when we still worried about what Father or Sean might do."

Aaron's gun stopped its upward arc.

She returned her scrutiny to Rory. "You look so worn. It has been a weight, hasn't it? It's weighed terribly on me too. Just like it did on my Connor."

"What's that, Martha?" Rory said quietly, though his eyes seemed to understand.

"The security guard we killed that night. We all carry the guilt for that young man's death. And Father making you burn the body . . . a terrible thing to force a seventeen-year-old boy to do. Although he bears the real guilt, don't you see? It was Father who brought us to that gallery, who searched out the children he'd left confused and haunted and alone through the years, and brought us together for that dreadful night. And we all came. We came to prove something to the great Jimmy Doyle, didn't we? To our father."

"I suppose," Rory said in agony.

Ian felt his world collapsing. It was one more disclosure—added to the words of Ed McMartin, the revelation at McMartin's house, and the shock of Liam's identity.

One revelation too many to bear.

"*Mom!*" he cried out. "It couldn't have been you at the art robbery."

Martha looked at Ian with intense sadness. "Oh, sweet Ian, my darling boy. I wish I could have told you and Adrianne. Connor and I both wanted to. But we couldn't. Not until we could make things right."

Rory was shaking his head again. "Martha, you're right. Dad brought us there that night and I've hated him for it. But I pulled the trigger."

"You pulled the trigger," Martha said, "but you didn't shoot anybody. I wish we'd spoken of it. If we'd seen each other alone, even once, in all these years. It hasn't been an easy thing for me to carry either."

"Ya need to back out of this, Martha," Callahan insisted with narrowed eyes. "Do it now and I'll see to it your boy gets his fee from the trust."

Rory stiffened, looking at Callahan, then back to Martha. "You're wrong," the gaunt man said to Martha. "I shot the guard twice."

"No." She shook her head. "Our father never taught you how to shoot; you told me so yourself. He kept you out of his business until the robbery. You told me that too. And I could see it when you fired that night at the gallery, because I was behind you. Your shots were high. I shot high too—deliberately. There was only one marksman at the gallery. Don't you remember how he bragged that night how he'd handled a gun since he was a young boy in Belfast?"

Rory turned to Callahan. "You told me I killed him. You told Dad too."

Breaking through a fog, Ian recalled Eldon's SWAT team on the bridge, felt their eyes on them like ants on his skin. They'd be watching, he realized. Ever since he sent the text, they'd have been alerted and watching the patio. Ready to act if people were in danger.

And there stood his mom, a gun in her hand.

Callahan's voice was ragged with fury when he broke the silence that had fallen over the patio again. "This chat is over," he muttered.

Aaron's weapon rose again. To Ian's horror, Martha's gun came up too.

"It's time, isn't it, Sean?" she said calmly as her gun reached shoulder height. "It's time we set things right."

"Don't!" Ian screamed. He put his hands on the concrete terrace at his knees and vaulted toward Martha.

9:59 P.M.
STONE ARCH BRIDGE, MINNEAPOLIS

In the small utility tent set up on the bridge, Brook held a pair of binoculars tightly to her eyes, her attention focused on the Guthrie Theater patio. The FBI SWAT chief at her elbow was watching the scene at the theater through night-vision goggles. Both Brook and the chief wore earbuds, linked to the SWAT team coming from the courthouse. Brook could hear the breathing of the two snipers seated directly in front of them.

Since the team at the courthouse had radioed that they'd received Ian's signal, the snipers' scoped weapons had extended through narrow embrasures aimed at the Guthrie patio, keeping an eye on the same scene Brook was seeing unfold through her own gap in the tent's side. At the moment, all eyes were trained on a large man—the Marine, she guessed—coming down the steps on the far side of the patio area.

Then a gun emerged from the man's belt.

The SWAT team from the police station could still be minutes away, Brook realized, her alarm growing.

The action on the patio froze. Ian's hand, which had been rising toward his forehead, halted in midair. Aaron stopped beside Callahan and turned, his gun still pointed at the ground.

What had changed? Brook raised her binoculars to the upper section of the patio.

Another figure came out of the theater building. Brook adjusted the binoculars to focus on the face of the woman walking down the steps.

It was Martha. And in her hand was a gun.

"Chief, we've got another target," the nearest sniper at her feet said evenly.

"I see her," the chief answered. "Female. With a weapon."

"Yes, sir. Do you want me to leave the tall one at the end of the patio and switch to her?"

"No, wait!" Brook said. "She's *not* a target."

"She's armed so she's a target," the chief confirmed. He nudged the man with his knee. "Yes. Switch to the new target. Sniper two, you've still got the other armed man?"

"Yes, sir," the second sniper replied.

This couldn't be happening. "That woman, she's got Alzheimer's," Brook pleaded. "She probably doesn't know what she's doing."

"She's got a gun, Counselor. She's a *target*."

Another long minute or two slipped by. Brook felt paralyzed, helpless.

"We've got a weapon rising," the first sniper announced. His voice intensified in pitch. "Now we've got two with weapons rising. Repeat, both armed targets are raising their weapons."

"Follow orders," the chief told him. "Fire if they go parallel."

Brook watched with mounting horror as the Marine's arm straightened. She shifted the view. Martha's gun hand was nearly at shoulder height.

"*No!*" she shouted, letting the binoculars fall as she lunged toward the sniper's back.

A rifle cracked in the narrow tent, the shot echoing out over the river.

Then the second sniper's weapon roared and kicked—the same instant Brook's hands reached the hard surface of his bulletproof vest.

48

Ian gritted his teeth as he trudged along the hospital corridor. Even walking gingerly, each movement sent fresh agony through his left shoulder, held tight to his chest with a bound sling.

He reached his mother's room and took a deep breath to dispel the pain before entering.

Flowers lining tables and along the floor were brightened by sunlight streaming through the windows. He recognized Brook's large bouquet and another from Brook's parents. Dennis Hoy's. A large bunch of flowers from Talk Show. A larger one still from an unnamed benefactor Harry insisted was Anthony Ahmetti.

There was a smaller bouquet of lilies set apart on the windowsill that hadn't been there the day before.

His mother lay propped on the bed, gazing at the flowers as though staring through her living room window at her own flower garden. Ian took a seat on the edge of the bed and reached out for her hand.

331

"Mom," he said, using the same words that began each of his visits, "you're going to be fine. The bullet that went through me went through you too. You were very lucky. We both were."

A chilling scene swept through his mind: of the cold cement terrace beneath his chest; the Marine like a crumpled doll at Sean Callahan's feet; the SWAT team roaring through the patio door; his mother lying pale and still at his side. "You're going to be fine," he repeated as if to confirm this for himself.

He waited. As with each day before, she didn't respond.

"I spoke with Greg," Ian went on, naming their neighbor across the backyard. "He said to give you his best. He said he'd take care of the yard and gardens until you get back."

His mother still didn't stir. Her hand lay limp in his own.

"You know, Adrianne's going to be here on Monday. She's gotten a few weeks off from her clinic and will be with you. She said a trauma like you suffered can be a setback, but it doesn't have to be the end, Mom. You have a lot of good days ahead."

Still nothing.

Ian sighed and looked away. "You know, I thought all my life that Dad was a quiet, calm man. Steady but no sparks. Did his work well but never took chances. I had no idea how wrong I was. He knew, didn't he? He knew all about you and the robbery. Prima was right when he tagged Dad's connection to Doyle the year you married—because when you married Dad, he married everything you were carrying. The connection to Jimmy Doyle, the guilt from that night in the art gallery, the shame of it all. He did it with eyes wide open. Rory told me Dad had 'fallen for his sister.' I thought he was being sarcastic since I thought he didn't have one. But he was talking about you. Dad fell for you and spent his life protecting you and everybody else around him. Including Katie. He loved you that much."

A nurse came in with medications. Ian stood while she gently cajoled his passive mother to take the pills. She settled Martha back on the pillow and left the room.

There was a knock on the door the moment the nurse left. Brook stepped into the room with a scolding look. "You're not supposed to be walking so far."

It was so good to see her. "Apparently I come from a long line of overachievers."

"No response yet?"

He shook his head. "But I think she notices the flowers."

"That's good."

"They're letting me out the middle of this week."

"That's also good," Brook said. "Hey, I got a text from Sophie that Rory's going to testify against Callahan and McMartin—including on the murder charge. He's doing it for a reduced charge for his daughter. Not for Liam. Just Maureen."

"Yeah, I heard something about that too," Ian said. "I'm the one who got Harry to represent him."

"Doesn't surprise me. Didn't see it coming, but it doesn't surprise me."

"Yeah. I'm going to owe Harry for this. Seems like I've gone into debt to a lot of people lately."

Brook smiled. "I resigned," she said flatly. "Left the U.S. Attorney's Office."

That came as a blow. "I'm sorry, Brook. This is my fault. They didn't ask you to leave, did they?"

"No. Other than Chloe—who's almost begging to wash my car—only Eldon really suspects I was helping you. Don't feel bad. I'm glad I did what I did, but I couldn't stay on after the decisions I had to make. Doesn't mean I'd make different ones, though."

"I'm sorry. I know you loved that job."

She shook her head. "I *really, really liked* the job. It's the people I worked with I loved. Finding a replacement for that won't be easy. Have you decided what you're going to do with your practice?"

"I'm done with the old office. I'm not renewing the lease when Dennis moves out in a couple of weeks. Besides, it's time I refocused. I'm done with estate plans and trusts."

"So, what's next?"

"I have a thought about that. We can talk about it later."

They grew quiet once more. Brook glanced at the side table, where a deck of cards lay. She picked them up. "How about a game of gin?"

For the briefest moment, from the corner of his eye, Ian thought he saw his mother's eyelids flutter. If so, she'd stopped when he looked fully at her face.

Smiling, he sat back down on the end of the bed. "Deal. If you've got the courage."

49

Katie sat across from Ian at a table near the back of the coffee shop. Ian was pleased she'd agreed to see him today, after taking the last few weeks off to "think things over."

The mug in front of her was still full, though no longer steaming. Ian wondered how long they would keep the silence.

"So, the family's okay?" Ian finally asked. "Nicole? Richard?"

"They're fine," she said quietly. "How about Martha?"

"Still healing, but still unresponsive. Adrianne's with her now. She's optimistic we can draw her out."

"Um-hm. That's good. Martha will love having Adrianne around."

"Thanks for the flowers," Ian added. "I noticed the lilies."

Katie looked up, surprised. "You're welcome."

Another long silence passed. Katie's eyes began to rim with tears. "Your mother was *there*, Ian," she burst out. "She was there when they killed my dad."

It was out at last. "I know," Ian replied.

"How could they keep that from me all these years? I thought they cared about me. Now I know they were just easing their own consciences."

Every notion about how he'd handle this conversation, all his practice as an advocate, fled from Ian's mind. "You know I wasn't aware of any of it when I started at the law firm, don't you? Even when I saw the old newspaper about the art robbery they'd packed with the crew's tools, it didn't occur to me the security guard could be your father. I only started figuring it out when I got back from Florida, but there wasn't a time or place to talk with you about it."

"I don't blame you, Ian. But I had a right to know."

"Me too," Ian said softly. "They were wrong not to tell either of us. But for what it's worth, I'm convinced they genuinely thought they could do more by supporting you and your family and keeping the secret than by turning Mom in. At least until the time was right."

Katie looked thoughtful for a long while. "I never thought about how this affected you." She picked up her lukewarm coffee. "I don't remember enough about my dad," she said. "I've got memories that he was kind. He was hardworking—doing his job, then taking on other work like the kind that got him killed. But I didn't get to finish growing up with him. At least you had that."

Ian felt he was the wrong one to make the next point. "It's not much consolation, Katie, but I think Dad and Mom were trying to make that part up to you too. They loved you. They really did. Mom still does."

Katie ran a hand across her eyes. Ian handed her a paper napkin.

"I can remember your dad interviewing me. I was all of eighteen and so nervous. He was asking me questions that had nothing to do with my typing speed or what I knew about a law office—which was slow and nothing. Had I traveled? What made me happy? Did I think I had a promising future ahead? Was I happy?—again. How was my mother making ends meet? All I'm thinking is, *What am I doing here?* If the high school counselor hadn't dragged me to the interview, saying your dad was looking for people without experience, I never would've thought about a career as a legal assistant."

"He wasn't looking for people," Ian said. "He had only one person in mind."

Ian reached into his pocket and pulled out a slip of paper. He slid it across the table.

"What's this?" she asked.

"The amount of the check Lloyds will be issuing you."

"The insurance company? Why? Why would Lloyds send me money?"

"Lloyds insured the stolen paintings. After paying off the art owners thirty-four years ago, they had a 'no questions asked' reward for the return of any of the Norman Rockwells. It was never rescinded. Part of our deal with the U.S. Attorney's Office was that we got the credit for the last painting's return."

"I don't want more money, Ian. You keep it."

"I couldn't keep it. And my parents wouldn't have wanted me to. If you don't want it, give it away. Or give the money to your daughter. But take it. Besides the job support through the years, I think getting you a final payout is the only other reason my parents didn't turn themselves in sooner. I'm not talking about this reward for the painting. But I think they'd decided to give you the two-hundred-thousand-dollar fee for the trust work when it was distributed. After that, I'm betting they would have turned themselves in and taken the rest of the crew with them."

Katie stared at the slip of paper. "It's a lot of money."

"Yeah. But if you're still looking for work, I've been doing some research. I may have an option."

"If I take this, you have to let me use some of it for Martha's care. I want to settle that stupid malpractice case as well."

"Don't worry about the lawsuit. Harry told me he'd represent me on the malpractice case at a cut rate. As for Martha, we can talk about that later."

Ian rose to his feet. Katie stood too and gave him a long, tight hug. "I love you, Ian Wells."

"Love you too," he said.

She pulled away and wiped her mascara-blackened eyes one more time. "As slow as you can be, hon, I hope you're smart enough to have figured out I'm not the only one feeling that way."

Epilogue

Ian looked past the end of the conference room table, taking in the rest of the small law office visible through the glass. The place wasn't ostentatious. Not the kind of office designed to wow clients with thousands of dollars of art. But it was functional, focused, a place where things got done. He liked the solid sense of that.

He glanced at Brook at his elbow. In her eyes he could read a similar positive reaction.

"What do you think about our suggestion?" Brook asked.

Seated across from them, Jared Neaton looked up from their proposal in his hand. Like the office itself, the attorney struck Ian as the pragmatic type. A few years older than him, Ian had been hearing for some time about the lawyer's growing reputation for civil litigation.

"Well, like we've been telling you all week," Neaton observed, "we weren't in the market to grow the firm. But a criminal law practice would complement our civil work. You two have very impressive credentials. And the deal's fair."

"When I was looking around," Ian said, "I thought of you and how you handled the Paisley, Bowman, Battle and Rhodes firm a few years back."

Jared smiled. "Not a fan of big firms?"

"Not my first choice for a career anymore," Ian answered truthfully.

"What do you think, Jessie?" Jared asked, turning to the slender, pretty woman at his side. She smiled with discerning eyes.

Jared's wife and legal assistant, Jessie had been in on every meeting and conversation they'd had about this merger over the whole of the past week. It had taken a few days of talks before Ian realized Jared wouldn't even consider the merger without her complete comfort, advice, and assent.

Though she'd been amiable all week, today Jessie was all business. She set her copy of the proposal on the table and leaned forward, aiming her response at Brook. "Seems like it could work out well. So tell me, are there any ghosts in the closet likely to come back to haunt us?"

Ian felt a chill at the nature of the question. Apart from the irony, it wasn't an area he was prepared to elaborate on. While sitting next to his sleeping mother in the hospital, he'd sworn that the trust and his parents' role in it would not be going public. In fact, his anonymity with the press had been a critical element in the settlement Harry finalized with Eldon Carroll's office. If he was forced to testify, his role would become public record. Short of that, it stayed in the background—for his mother and father's reputations even more than his own.

Still, Jessie's question hung in the air, spreading serious discomfort. *"Actions have consequences."* The words drifted silently back to him, spoken in Martha's convicting tone. What would he do when the tab came due from Anthony Ahmetti? What other consequences awaited from his family's past?

Ian saw Brook's chin drop briefly at Jessie's question, a subtle sign she felt the struggle as well. But she recovered instantly.

"We're good," he heard her say. "Right, Ian?"

"Yep," Ian responded immediately, knowing he'd make it true.

Brook turned the question back on their hosts. "How about you two?"

Jared smiled slowly, following with an equally slow shake of his head. "Nothing to share from our end either," he said.

Jessie stood and extended a hand across the table. Jared followed suit.

"Sounds like we've got a deal," she said. "Partners."

And they shook on it.

Acknowledgments

Thanks again to my fabulous wife, Catherine, for her support of a two-career husband and for her critical editorial eye. Thanks to Libby for patiently listening to her father's chapters as they unfold, and to Ian—the namesake for this book—who does the same whenever his own writing permits. Thanks also to Elizabeth Carlson and Stephanie Mullaney for helping me navigate the shoals of social media.

My appreciation as well to Luke Hinrichs for his excellent editorial reviews and suggestions.

And once again, a special thanks to the readers who keep the art of book-writing alive.

Todd M. Johnson, author of *Critical Reaction* and *The Deposit Slip*, has practiced as an attorney for over thirty years, specializing as a trial lawyer. A graduate of Princeton University and the University of Minnesota Law School, he also taught for two years as adjunct professor of International Law and served as a U.S. diplomat in Hong Kong. He lives near Minneapolis with his wife, his son, Ian, and his daughter, Libby. Learn more at authortoddmjohnson.com.

More Suspense from Bethany House

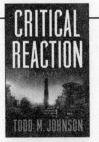
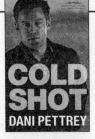

♦ BETHANYHOUSE

You May Also Like . . .

With the public eye fixed on the governor's Missing Persons Task Force, Detective Evie Blackwell and her new partner, David, are under pressure to produce results. While they investigate two missing-persons cases in Chicago, their conviction that justice is possible for all will be tested to the limit.

Threads of Suspicion by Dee Henderson
AN EVIE BLACKWELL COLD CASE
deehenderson.com

When U.S. Marshal Mercy Brennan is assigned to a joint task force with the St. Louis PD, she's forced back into contact with her father and into the sights of a notorious gang. Mercy's boss assigns her colleague— and ex-boyfriend—to get her safely out of town. But when an ice storm hits and the enemy closes in, can backup reach them in time?

Fatal Frost by Nancy Mehl
DEFENDERS OF JUSTICE #1
nancymehl.com

◊BETHANYHOUSE